THE REVENGE WE SEEK

MEG JOLLY

Published in 2021 by
Eldarkin Publishing Limited
United Kingdom
© 2021 Meg Jolly
www.megcowley.com

ISBN 9798502641845

Cover design © Meg Jolly 2021

BOOKS BY MEG JOLLY

The DI Daniel Ward Yorkshire Crime Thriller Series:

The Truth We Can't Hide

The Past We Run From

The Revenge We Seek

The Mistakes We Deny

For B.

CHAPTER ONE

H e had watched Amelia Hughes for quite a while now—in more ways than even she realised.

Now, he sat at his checkout at the Sainsbury's Local in Bingley town centre, covertly eyeing her as she flitted past the ends of the aisles at the other end of the mini-supermarket. She studiously avoided eye contact, but he had grown to expect that now. It was one of the few things that irked him about her.

He adjusted his name badge, an unconscious habit. It said 'Harry', but that wasn't his real name.

She'd started shopping there six months back, just after he'd begun his contract as a checkout operator, and frankly, general dogsbody. It was the emerald green wool coat that caught his eye at first—she was a bright jewel amongst the sea of grey and black in the morning and evening commutes.

Amelia Hughes was what he would consider breath-takingly beautiful. Mid-twenties just like him, sleek, shiny, brunette hair tumbling down her back in a river, piercing green eyes that he wished would stare at him with anything but indifference, smooth olive skin, and a slender figure that cut an elegant path through the plebs surrounding her. She was every inch a lady, with Duchess of Cambridge vibes of class rolling from her.

Harry considered himself more of a Jesse Eisenberg. *Perhaps,* Harry Styles on a good day, when his curly tangle of brown hair played ball and when he was clean-shaven, and certainly not when he wore the burgundy and orange Sainsbury's uniform. But mostly Jesse. Slightly socially awkward and abrasive, he struggled to make friends, especially at the store of misfits he worked in, and he knew it—but he was still handsome. *Handsome enough to win Amelia*, Harry reasoned. He unconsciously smoothed back his hair.

'Hey. Service.'

Harry's attention snapped to the man standing before him. A middle-aged, greying, balding man with a faded stain on his white shirt. A decidedly less pleasant sight. He stared at the man blankly—insolently, even—before taking his items, a lunch deal presumably for the next day, and scanning them.

'One Euromillions for Friday, one Lotto for Saturday, and Five Thunderball for Saturday. Twenty Marlboro Lights and a lighter.'

Harry was fairly used to not receiving manners from half his customers. It was why he rarely offered them. He wordlessly printed the lottery tickets off the noisy, ageing, blue machine, and swiped the requested cigarettes from behind the shuttered display.

'Nineteen eighty-three,' Harry said blandly.

The man tapped his card against the Contactless hub, folded his tickets into his wallet, grabbed his meal deal, and left with nary a thanks or goodbye.

Harry's lip curled in disdain as he watched the man go.

Rose, vanilla, notes of amber. A waft of familiar perfume turned his attention from the closing automatic door to his next customer, and unbidden, he relaxed, a smile coming to his face. His frustration at the man ebbed, even as his heart stuttered a little, his ease giving way to anxiety and excitement at her proximity. He'd ask her out tonight. For sure. Definitely.

'Hey, Amelia, isn't it?' he said, feigning that he knew no more about her. Of course, the first time she'd come in to buy wine, he'd asked for her ID. She hadn't looked sixteen, but the store had a *'Think 25!'* policy, though he'd stretched that a little...besides, he'd been captivated by the young woman. She was gorgeous and charismatic, a far cry from the troglodytes he worked with. No one there liked him, which suited him just fine. He thought they were all arseholes and idiots anyway.

Amelia, chatting brightly on her phone that first time he'd seen her, had seemed like a breath of fresh air. Every time she came—every Tuesday and Thursday or Friday, usually, in the evening, to provision with a luxury ready-meal and bottle of wine—she lifted his mood.

So, naturally, he'd ID'd her. She'd given her driving licence up willingly from her scarlet, leopard-print, leather purse, a little giggle and a blush making her even more charming as he flattered her with the thought that she was young enough to be questioned on her age. He'd memorised every detail on that driving licence: it was the blessing of his otherwise entirely wasted eidetic memory.

'Oh, yes,' she said, with a faint smile, her eyes averted, as though she'd rather not chat. She was playing hard to get alright.

'Looks like a nice Friday night in,' he said, grinning widely for a moment. He scanned through her luxury ready-meal—a Beef Wellington, dauphinoise potatoes, a Belgian chocolate sundae, and a bottle of wine—her usual weekly treat, and packed it into her ready and waiting jute bag.

'Er, yeah.'

'Well, you enjoy that,' Harry said, more warmly than he ever spoke to anyone else. He infused a twinkle in his eye, a friendly spark that she would see and she would recognise when she met it.

'Thanks.' And then, the smile she flashed him did seem genuine, her eyes warming as her gaze grazed his. The smile lasted a second before she picked up her bag of shopping and left, taking that alluring waft of perfume with her.

And leaving behind only stale body odour and dying dreams in her wake.

'Damn it,' Harry mumbled to himself. He'd bottled it again. Next time, he promised. Next time, he'd bloody well ask her.

———

Amelia Hughes was shy, perhaps, and she might be hard to get, but Harry was convinced that he wasn't mistaken, the way her gaze had lingered on him for a moment there. He had replayed the moment dozens of times already. It was like she *saw* him, as a fellow human being and a man, not just a robot sat behind a till to serve. Harry needed to show her how much more he was. How good he could be for her. How much he deserved a chance.

Harry had already started following her. Just a little, and at a distance, always unseen. Jeez, he wasn't a creep and he didn't want to spook her. He was just learning about her, which was harmless enough. Finding out where she worked, who she visited, who came to see her at the address he'd memorised from the driving licence—a small but pricey new-build terrace down by the canal.

He knew where she worked—a high-end estate agent, *Smythe & Winter*, on the high street. No wonder she could afford such a nice house if that was where she worked. They only sold the most luxurious properties in the district. He bet that her commission from one house sale beat his yearly bonus.

Harry knew she worked there Monday to Wednesday, Friday, and Saturday. On those days, she went to the cute independent coffee shop on the high street en-route from her home to work for a latte with a croissant or Danish pastry. Mostly the Danish pastries, when he tallied it up.

Harry also knew that she was a keen jogger—and where she went for her morning jog in the dawn of each day. Sometimes she went with her workmate, a slightly older lady with ghastly self-fitted bleached-blonde extensions that only made her look all the more aged. But on a Thursday? Amelia *always* ran alone. On her day off, with nowhere to rush to, she took a much longer route across the Leeds-Liverpool Canal and the Bingley Bypass on the road bridge, through town, through Myrtle Park, across the River Aire on a small footbridge, and in a great loop through the secluded fields, back across the waterways, through town, and back home down the canal towpath at the bottom of the Five Rise Locks.

Harry had never been much of a runner, but he'd taken it up to figure out her route. It was starting to drop cold in the mornings now, as September brought with it a chill to the air, so he'd invested in some red running trainers, and a black hoodie to keep him warm. Amelia never realised. With her earphones in, Amelia Hughes was oblivious to the shadow yawning over her life, closer with each step she took.

Harry had been devastated—and furious—when he'd realised she'd had a boyfriend. A beefed-up sted-head who spent most of his time in the gym. In every way Harry's opposite. In every way, better than Harry, damn it. It tortured Harry to imagine that brute touching her, being with her, screwing her, the way Harry wanted to. Harry hadn't seen a way forward then, hooked on Amelia like a fix, with the impossibility of satisfying that crush a constant anguish.

And then, the sted-head had disappeared. The Amelia who'd visited him at the shop that following week was subdued, her eyes red-rimmed. She hadn't given in to his gentle prodding, but he'd watched her that weekend, and sted-head hadn't shown for their usual Saturday night date. They'd broken up. Harry's heart had soared at the prospect. Finally, he could move. Except, he was too scared. How laughable. But that look had changed everything. Amelia, it seemed, was maybe ready to move on, and Harry was waiting, filled with the bounty of information he'd gathered, to make sure that he could woo her. He only had room for one result: success.

Harry even knew the bar where she met her friends on a Friday night in town. He'd found her on Matchmaker, a dating app for Yorkshire, but she'd never replied to his 'heart' with a matching tap of her 'heart' to agree to chat. He wondered if she'd be active on there, now that sted-head was out of the picture. Perhaps it was an old account. Still, the insecurity of that niggled at him. What if she had rejected him, and he didn't even realise?

He knew now that she watched a film by herself every Saturday night, because she left the curtains open, and he'd watched a few times, wondering what it would feel like to be next to her on the light grey sofa, her warm body in the crook of his arm as they tangled together.

When Amelia came the following Tuesday for her usual, Harry was eagerly waiting. He'd hyped himself up all weekend for it. This time, he wasn't going to chicken out. The store was empty, except for Jamal doing stock in the back—and nicking a cheeky pack of cigarettes or two whilst he was at it, no doubt—so Harry swallowed, took a deep breath to still his jittering nerves, and slid out from behind the checkout.

It had been a month since the boyfriend had left the picture. Harry had gathered his courage. Surely, she'd be ready to move on now.

'Hey, Amelia, how's it going?' he approached her casually, stopping a good distance away, giving her her personal space—she liked that, he'd noticed, even in the bars with her friends. He appreciatively breathed in her perfume. God, it was alluring. He wanted *more*.

'Oh, uh, good thanks. You?' she replied, automatically.

'Oh, you know. Same shit, different day.' Harry chuckled. 'Listen. I don't want to be forward...'

She looked up from the food on the shelf that she'd been choosing between. Her gaze snagged on him as he bit his lip, a coy smile teasing his lips.

'I really like you. I wondered, if you're not seeing anyone, whether you'd like to go for a drink together—or a movie? Are you free Saturday night?' Of course, he knew she was. She *never* went out on a Saturday.

'You're asking me out?' she said, straightening slowly —ever so slightly taller than him with her heeled boots.

'Yeah,' Harry said, more confidently than he felt. 'How about it? Dinner and drinks on me—we can go to The Library Tap, I know you'd like it there,' he said casually, knowing she very much did, since it was the bar she stayed in longest with her friends on a girl's night out.

He didn't figure that a suppressed smile would crease her lips. A half-concealed laugh would snort out. 'Ha! Um, no. I don't think so.' She looked him up and down, disdain and amusement clear in her eyes.

Harry's heart sank with his fading smile. He recognised that look. The '*as if I would go out with a checkout boy*' kind of look. The '*you're not good enough for me*' kind of look. Anger rumbled in the depths of him, rising fast, a spike ready to lash out. His fists clenched.

'Right. Ok,' he said tightly through gritted teeth.

Harry turned and strode away so Amelia wouldn't see his building fury at the embarrassment of her rejection.

Into the stock room he stormed. Jamal jumped as he opened the door with a crash. Packets of cigarettes jumped from his hands to the floor. He relaxed when he saw Harry.

'Oh good, it's just you, Hazza. Thought it was someone important then.' Jamal gave a nervous laugh, scratched the patchy beard his young face was trying to grow, and turned to gather the cigarettes up from the floor, angling so the security camera in the corner couldn't see him slip one into his trouser pockets as he recounted them loudly into the stockpile.

'Can you do tills, please? I need a break.'

Jamal looked at him, and his smile faded as he recognised the mood Harry was in. 'You alright, Haz?'

'Fine,' said Harry. His clenched jaw twitched. He grabbed his coat from the hook and strode through the back fire door without another word. As it banged shut behind him, he turned and kicked the wall beside it, with a growl of frustration that barely took the edge off his suppressed feelings.

How could she have rejected him? After everything he'd done, she hadn't even given him a chance.

He wasn't about to let her end things there.

CHAPTER TWO

That evening, Harry swiped Matchmaker until he came upon Amelia. He tapped the 'heart' icon on her again. Only, it wasn't as Harry. It was as another alias, James Denton. A catfish made up from Harry's middle name and his mother's maiden name.

The picture wasn't him, nor the description. James Denton was just shy of thirty, working in marketing in Leeds city centre, and the stock picture Harry had used depicted a casual handsome man no woman could resist, from his chiselled jaw grazed with stubble, to the cheeky half-smile and the inviting spark in his brown eyes.

The ping came barely an hour later.

A frisson of excitement fluttered through Harry as he opened the app to see that Amelia had swiped the Matchmaker heart on him too. Or rather, on James Denton. Still, that was something.

He started the chat.

They chatted in the app until late, and Harry had entirely lost track of the time before she excused herself to sleep, much to his regret. As he'd suspected, they'd hit it off. When she wasn't blinded by the supermarket uniform, they were perfectly compatible after all. He'd just have to make sure that she realised that too.

Best of all, she'd agreed to meet. Exactly as he'd asked her as Harry, she'd even suggested at The Library Tap on Saturday night.

That soothed his frustrations for now. She had said yes. But anger still seethed deep within, that she would say yes to an alias that wore a different skin, but not to him, the self-same person. The shallowness of the dating market infuriated him. He'd gone over and above to earn her with how much work he had put into understanding her as a person, who she was, where she worked, what she liked and disliked.

Harry even knew what that alluring perfume was that she wore—a vintage Chanel—and it had taken him an age at the shopping mall in Leeds to work that out with the help of an assistant whose patience had worn thin after the first hour. But it was all worth it, for Amelia.

———

Harry was a bag of nerves by Saturday night. He'd spent the best part of a hundred quid on a new outfit, and he'd never felt as sharp. Brogues, polished and shining on his feet. New jeans from Burtons. Topped with a polo and blazer, and a squirt of *One Million* aftershave that had cost the rest of his savings.

He swung by his own shop for a bunch of flowers on the way into town. Jamal whistled at the sight of him. 'You scrub up well, Hazza.' Harry barely spoke to him as he paid for the bunch of flowers—pink roses, white chrysanthemums, and baby's breath with some fraying greenery to add a dark contrast. A bouquet as fragrant and elegant as Amelia herself.

Harry lifted his chin as he walked into The Library Tap—and his pulse thundered up another notch as he saw Amelia waiting by the bar. Standing tall, she was the picture of a model, dressed in a little black dress with matching strappy black stilettos. Her legs went on for miles, it seemed. Her hair fell in luxurious waves over one shoulder, pinned back on the other side by a jewelled clip, leaving one shoulder bare, and pulling Harry's gaze across an elegant collarbone and to her slim neck.

As Amelia turned, her eyes sweeping the corner, still oblivious to him, her sultry makeup, nude and natural but for a darkening around her eyes and a striking red lipstick. Arousal surged in him. Gods, she was *hot*. He hoped he might be taking that little black dress off her later.

Before his nerve could desert him, he quickly strode over to the bar and greeted her.

Her eyes snagged on the flowers held out before him, and her face already lighting up in a smile before she clocked him, and that smile faltered.

'Hey, Amelia—it's me. Harry.'

Confusion. Her brows lowered into a frown.

'From the shop. Sainsburys Local. Harry,' he said, just in case. Like she could forget him, he hoped.

'Hi,' she said slowly. Her gaze swept over the bar again. 'Listen, nice to see you—but I'm on a date.'

'I know. What can I get you to drink?'

Her eyes flicked to him, widening slightly. 'Look, I don't know what your deal is—'

Harry laughed, holding up a hand to stall her. 'Amelia, it's *me*. James Denton. It's my online alias. You do have a date—with me.' He grinned, and held out the flowers. 'These are for you. You look gorgeous. What can I get you?' Harry gestured to the bar.

But Amelia's confusion fell away to horror. 'Wait... you catfished me?'

'No, don't be daft,' Harry started to say, but it was the wrong thing.

Amelia drew back, stumbling into someone else, who angrily exclaimed at her and pushed her back towards Harry.

Amelia fell into his arms and he caught her—gods, he never wanted to let her go. That fabric sliding sheer under his hands, her warm, firm figure beneath his palms. But she wrenched away.

'You sick fuck! What kind of loser catfishes onto a date?'

'Whoa, no need to be like that.' Harry, leaving the flowers on the bar between them, held up both his hands. 'You wouldn't give me a chance as Harry the checkout boy, but James the marketing man is better? We're the *same person*, Amelia. You like James... that means you like me. Right?'

'No.' Amelia's lip curled in disgust as she moved out of his reach, one hand clutching the edge of the bar. 'I can't believe you tricked me. What are you, some kind of creepy stalker?'

'No! It's nothing like that, I promise—I just want to get to know you. I have a massive crush on you, alright? You're gorgeous, clever, funny, I know we'll hit it off, I just want a chance.'

Amelia was pale with fury, her lips thin. 'You don't know *anything* about me. I don't want anything to do with you. Don't contact me again!'

With that, she stormed past him, dodging out of his way as he moved to intercept her, as if she couldn't even stand to touch him. She was gone.

Harry remained in stunned silence for a long moment, surrounded by the noise of the bar as bodies heaved around him, hearing none of it.

She hadn't even given him a shout.

What had he done wrong?

He couldn't give up. He wouldn't.

Harry left the flowers on the bar and ran outside—but Amelia had already disappeared.

CHAPTER THREE

Amelia's hands shook as she picked up the small, cellophane-wrapped box on her doorstep. It was a bottle of her favourite perfume. And with it, a note written in a messy hand.

Her breath caught in her chest with panic as she clutched that box and re-read the note. As if to prove to herself she'd imagined it. Wishing she had. Knowing that it was quite real.

Amelia, I'm really sorry we got off on the wrong foot. Let me make it up to you? We can chat over dinner. I really like you and I don't want to screw this up. Give me a chance? Harry x

She looked around the darkening street. The street lights had just come on, though it was still half-light. It was light enough to see that the street was deserted. But there had been a knock on the door... he must be hiding, or he must have legged it. Either way, Amelia backed inside, locked the door, and bolted it.

Part of her, paranoid infinitely in that moment, felt

the sentient malice of the box of perfume watching her, *taunting* her. She slammed the box down on the side table in the hallway as if the innocuous item had stung her. On an afterthought, Amelia grabbed it, raced to the kitchen, and threw it in the bin, unopened. Then, she ran around the house, turned on all her lights and closed all the curtains.

How the hell did he know where she lived? A whimper escaped her. She'd thought he was weird enough at the shop, but this was next-level creepy. The way he always stared at her, made a point to call her by name, tried to engage her in conversation every time, even when there were other customers waiting. It was so *awkward*. She hated it. It made her cringe.

That he'd found her on Matchmaker was perhaps an unlucky coincidence, something he'd jumped on with his fake profile. She groaned. James Denton had been too good to be true, quite literally. She could kick herself for falling for that. A rebound from Darren, she'd figured, one she'd enjoy, and if it became anything more serious, well, bonus. Perhaps she'd lowered her guard too far.

But this? This was next-level. He'd found out where she lived, and that was *disturbing*. Until that moment, she wondered if maybe she'd been too hard on the guy. It wasn't his fault; she just wasn't attracted to him. OK, that was his fault. He wasn't as good looking as she liked, and he was weird. First impressions counted for a lot and he wasn't someone she'd ever considered romantically— perhaps that had been harsh, but it was the truth. It hadn't been anything personal though, it was what it was.

Now? Now she was glad she'd stayed away. Now, she

wouldn't touch the sick fuck with a bargepole. Amelia stormed to the front door again to check it was locked—and then to the back. All secure. But her racing nerves would not steady.

There was a phone number on the bottom of the note.

Amelia retrieved her phone from the sofa arm and typed it into WhatsApp with shaking hands.

STAY THE FUCK AWAY FROM ME. I don't want anything to do with you. If you contact me again, I'll report you to the police.

She hit send, and then blocked the number. On a second thought, because the note seemed to be stinging her very fingers, she thrust it into the vanilla and sandalwood candle burning on the coffee table as though it was poisonous—watching it blacken and crumble to nothing.

The next message she fired was on WhatsApp to her best friend, Sacha. Sacha had been so keen to know how the date went... well, she wouldn't believe the latest development.

You're not gonna believe this, S! AAAAHHHHH I am so FREAKED OUT!!! Amelia started typing.

CHAPTER FOUR

Amelia did not come to the shop on Tuesday.

That only made Harry's mood worse.

He'd been fuming after her text. No matter how many times he replied, she didn't respond. When he called, it wouldn't connect. He realised she'd blocked him pretty quickly. And spiralled from there.

How dare she? The thought taunted him.

Now, he realised that he'd had it wrong all along. He'd been trying to desperately prove he was worthy of her. He'd put so much time, care, and attention into knowing and understanding her, so he could show her that. Yet, it was painfully clear. It had nothing to do with whether or not he deserved her. Amelia Hughes had never deserved *him*—and he would punish her for it.

It festered away, nagging at his every waking moment. He couldn't cope anymore. The embarrassment, shame, anger, rejection, humiliation, and hurt all gnawed at him until there was nothing left.

He'd gone to watch her as usual around his shifts, and

he'd had to back off. She looked over her shoulder wherever she went now, far less blasé about it—clearly with him on her mind. It both pleased and annoyed him that she feared him, that she thought of him, but that he couldn't study her so freely and closely as usual.

At home, he couldn't see in anymore from over the canal—her curtains were permanently closed, even in the daytime. He wondered if she knew or suspected he was watching, or was just running scared. That feeling of power pleased him too, feeding the malevolence within him.

The bitch.

There was only one way he could end this. End the torment of seeing her every day, knowing she would never be his.

She'd never turn him down again.

Harry would make sure of it.

———

It was Thursday morning. The weather was dry for a brief respite, but chilling, a coldness that had no place in early September. The hair had risen all over Harry's body in response to it as he waited in stillness and silence. Fog wreathed the dip he stood in, a welcome accomplice to the crime he was about to commit.

He'd scouted the most deserted spot, out of sight and sound of any houses. A place where he knew no one would come across them, because he'd gone on the route enough times now to know that this was a shade too late for the dog walkers or anyone else to be out and make it to work on time. A place he knew no one would be, because who on earth would come past Harden Beck? Amelia ran solo, and she had planned her routes to avoid as many people as possible. That would be her downfall.

Harry smiled, satisfied he'd planned this well. He savoured each moment, the rustle of the trees with each sweep of the cold wind that braced against him, the gentle babble of the nearby brook hidden amongst a tangle of foliage that gave him cover. In the large central pocket of his hoodie, he fingered the kitchen knife—gently, of course.

He had prepared. No one would see him. No one would catch him. He would kill her and then he would disappear—just another runner on a morning jog, merging into those who ran a shorter route around Myrtle Park of a morning.

At last, Harry saw the tell-tale ponytail bouncing along on the deserted track ahead of him. He'd gone ahead—getting up painfully early to do so—for the sky was growing lighter, but the last dregs of night still clung to the dull valley. All he had to do was wait.

She crossed the bridge over the beck, her head down, earphones in as usual, unaware.

And then, she saw the bright red trainers waiting for her.

Amelia faltered. Looking up. Stopped.

Harry revelled in the flash of abject fear that flashed across her.

'What are you doing here?' Amelia said, her voice shrill, ringing out in the silent woods, where it seemed not even animals or birds stirred.

'Oh, just running,' Harry said casually. 'Want to run with me?'

Amelia backed away a step. 'No.' He saw her calculating, as she glanced around.

They were in a deeply wooded area. No help would be coming if she screamed.

'What do you want?'

He crossed to her swiftly and grabbed her arm, pushing her to the side of the track, and against a tree. 'I want an apology, Amelia.'

Disgust broke through her fear. 'Or what?' she spat at him. This close, her breath rolled over him—fresh toothpaste. 'Get away from me. I'll call the police, I've warned you!'

Harry moved closer, his body pinning her up against the tree—and, unknown to her, the knife laying flat between them against his belly in the pocket of his hoodie. He felt her resist him, and he had to force her step, but he was bigger. Stronger. Able to dominate her. And damn it, he still wanted her even after she'd wronged him. He shoved the thought aside.

Harry laughed in her face. 'You're a stuck up bitch and not half as good as you think you are, Amelia Hughes.' He backed up a step, and pulled out the knife.

Her attention snapped to it, captured by the flash as it reflected light in its arc of movement. 'W-Wait! What are you doing? N-no!' She struggled, her arms free, lifting them before her, as if she could protect herself from him. 'You don't have to do this. Please don't hurt me. We can go on a date, okay? Any time you like.'

She spoke quickly, breathlessly, her eyes never

leaving the stainless-steel blade—the largest he'd taken from the block at his house. It cut through meat like butter. He'd carve her up good with it. His hand tightened about the handle as she spoke. He saw through every word for the lie it was, and it only made his disdain and anger grow.

A mist descended as that anger took hold. She wouldn't shut up, her pleading, every word like a drill into his damn brain. One of his hands found her mouth, silencing her. Her hands batted him away, her nails scratching him as she fought, but she faltered as the knife plunged in. Easy as slicing through water. He groaned with pleasure at it. Again and again he went, until he could no longer hear her voice vibrating against his palm, no longer feel her hands scrabbling at him.

Harry Denton stepped back, and freed from his grasp, the lifeless body of Amelia Hughes, gazing at him in horror, slid away and crumpled to the ground. Time halted.

She would never refuse him again. Power thrummed through him, charging every fibre of his being with purpose and enormity. He drank in that feeling—godlike, he could only describe it as. No longer was she beyond his power.

For a moment, he bathed in the sight of her. Her lilac top was stained violently red, pooling blood around the jagged, severed edges of the fabric. The iron tang of her blood fused with the scent of her, unwashed and sweet, with yesterday's perfume stale on her neck, no doubt waiting until after her run to shower.

A dog barked in the distance, jarring Harry from his

daze. He blinked through the mist, and gulped in a deep breath, which flooded clarity of thought back to him. He glanced down at himself—and laughed, a single peal of disbelief. He couldn't have planned that better. Her blood covered his hoodie, spattered his shorts, but they were both black—invisible, or like he had sweated through them at worst. As for his trainers? The slightly darker red specks could pass for watery mud. He used his sleeve to rub spatters of her blood off his bare lower legs.

He would have to be careful. Harry slipped the bloodied knife into the hoodie pocket—marvelling at the glossy ruby sheen on the blade, and fascinated by just how much blood had spilled from Amelia onto him as he'd attacked her. He wiped his hand on the inside of his hoodie pocket, but still, that blood refused to leave, wedged in every crack and crevice of the skin on his hands—his knuckles, the lines of his palms, around and under his fingernails.

Harry took out his phone. It was switched off, but he could see himself in the reflection on the screen. Blood spattered his face, more at the chin, deposited as he flicked the knife up each time to plunge it back into Amelia. Harry scrubbed at those stains too, until they vanished into the black fabric of his hoodie. Heat had flooded him during the attack and before, but now, cold gnawed around the edges as the morning nip set in.

A dog barked, perhaps the same one, closer this time. He had to go. The longer he lingered, the more chance he would be discovered, or close enough to be seen by a witness and placed at the scene.

Harry looked down at Amelia once more, savouring

the sight of her. She lay in a tangled heap upon the ground, her face staring into the grass unseeing. That beautiful chestnut hair scraped back into a bun, and resting in the mud. The leaves were beginning to turn in the canopy overhead, but she out-blazed them all, the crimson staining her dark and bold, brighter than any winter berry that would ripen that season. It covered the curves of her torso in splatters and blooms, a once-living canvas—but her chest was still, never to rise with breath again.

He longed to reach down, touch her cheek, but he wasn't an idiot. The less he forensically contaminated the scene, the better. There was just one thing he wanted... Carefully, Harry crouched before her and reached for her thigh, and the tell-tale lump there. He eased his forefinger and thumb into the snug, body-hugging pocket—gods, Amelia was still warm, though he didn't know why that surprised him, for it had been less than two minutes since he had killed her, though each moment seemed to stretch into eternity to bless him with the time to examine his handiwork—and pulled out her phone. A key fell out too – and he grabbed it with a swoop of excitement roiling in his belly at the realisation that it would be her house key...that maybe he could visit her place. See inside it. For himself.

He switched the phone off and slipped it into his shorts pocket. As he started to stand, a glint caught his eye. A beautiful leather Pandora bracelet with a single charm hung round her slender wrist—a flower with a glistening baby pink crystal at the centre. On a whim, he unclipped it, taking care not to touch her, and slipped that into his pocket too.

Then, he stood, and his eye was critical as he looked over the scene. Making sure that, aside from the horrific mess of her, there was nothing of his. He looked at his feet. At the mud there, and frowned. He slid in his own footprints, distorting the size and shape of them, so there would be no print they could take from it, not one that would match, and carefully picked a path through the dirt and grit before he stood upon the track once more, clear of anything that could incriminate him with a footprint.

A part of him yearned to stay. Just a little longer. The thrill inside him sang, the dare of it all, the frisson of being caught. But he didn't intend to be.

And so, Harry ran.

CHAPTER FIVE

Detective Inspector Daniel Ward groaned.

Wicked Witch flashed up on his phone.

He gritted his teeth and answered.

'What took you so long?' the woman snapped at him.

'Morning to you too. I was parking up.' He berated himself for explaining–feeling like he had to justify himself.

'Hmm,' she said sniffily, but she couldn't be mad at him for that. 'Oliver's dug up the garden again. It's even worse than last time! Holes everywhere, even through my favourite beds! He's ripped up every single geranium!'

Daniel could hear her building to a righteous fury.

'Well, did you keep him outside?' he said, trying to keep black anger from filling his own tone—it never served him well. It had rained almost all week—she'd better not have kept Olly outside with only a tiny kennel for shelter... He gripped the flat-bottomed steering wheel instead, channelling his anger out through his hands, the supple leather warming against his skin.

'Of course, I did! I have to go to work and after the sofa debacle, I'm not leaving that dog alone all day in the house again to chew up whatever he damn well pleases.'

Daniel forced the bark from his voice. 'He's a Beagle, Katherine. They get bored. They like to dig, chew—you need to keep him busy.' Katherine. It still felt so strange to call her that. Detached. Informal. She had always been Kate. Beautiful Kate. Funny Kate. Happy Kate. Until the bitter end.

'He's a dog, and he needs to learn how to behave. I'm not keeping him like this.'

'Well then I'll have him. I keep telling you, I want him with me.' He stopped short of saying that he missed Olly-dog. She'd only crucify him for it. She tried to hurt him with everything he cared about. How had it become so bad between them? He struggled to pinpoint it still–but it was irreparable. It had still felt like defeat to file for divorce, even in spite of that.

A momentary pause. 'No. I'll manage.'

Daniel swallowed all the things he wanted to say. He'd said them all already, and they'd gotten him nowhere. 'If you can't cope with him, then it's not fair to him—or you—to keep him. I want him.'

'No.' And with that, the phone went dead.

Daniel slowly lowered it, staring at it, the black screen now devoid. What had she even called him for? What was the purpose of it? Moan about the dog, and deny him any access? Just to get the blood thumping through his veins, his heart pounding in anger? She had managed that expertly, as usual.

Daniel forced himself to take deep, slow, calming

breaths. He clicked the screen on, and a picture of Olly lit up his lock-screen. The Beagle's warm, brown, liquid eyes staring up at him in a smile, his tongue lolling out, and the blur of his tail behind him as he stood, ready to fetch.

Daniel remembered that Olly had been drenched in brown mud not minutes later, having dove into a bog to fetch a poor throw. He could almost look back fondly now on the flack Katherine had given him for bringing home a dog covered in mud and debris—back to her pristine cream carpets and white-tiled kitchen floor. Now, it was the only small source of pleasure he could find—in pissing her off—when it still felt like she held all the cards. She'd gotten the house, and the dog, and he'd ended up with... well. It wasn't worth dwelling on.

The divorce wasn't helping. Between work and home, life was shite at the moment.

Gritting his teeth, Daniel got out of the car, slammed the door, and locked it, before striding into Trafalgar House, Bradford South Police Station, and home to the Homicide and Major Enquiry Team that Detective Inspector Daniel Ward served in. Frankly, solving murders seemed easier than dealing with Katherine and the divorce, half the time.

'You're late,' DCI Martin Kipling's nasal voice rang down the hallways.

Not what DI Ward needed to improve his mood. It was 8:01 am. Not that Ward made the point aloud. 'Sorry, sir,' he said instead, clenching his jaw to stop anything else coming out that he might regret.

DCI Kipling usually stuck to his office, but with the

Bogdan Varga trafficking case hotting up again, he'd started to appear far more regularly than DI Ward liked. DCI Kipling took point on the Varga case, ever since it had escalated with the lorry find last November. In principle, Ward couldn't blame him, not when the man had DSU Diane McIntyre breathing down his neck and ready to eviscerate the DCI at the first sign of failure.

The case had gone national with that find, and all their necks were on the line if HMET screwed up. Needless to say, no one wanted to find another lorry full of deceased illegal immigrants for reasons far more important than their employment. Unfortunately, shit rolled downhill. DCI Kipling would be first... but DI Ward would be next.

'We've got an update.' Kipling fell into step beside Ward, the older DCI a head shorter by comparison.

DI Ward shrugged off his jacket, looping it over an arm, and headed for the kitchen, noting the empty coffee cup in Kipling's left hand. 'Oh?'

'Customs has found another lorry potentially linked to Varga.'

Ward's full attention sharpened on Kipling. 'How? Is it here?'

DCI Kipling pushed open the canteen door and crossed to the kettle. 'No.'

As Ward followed Kipling in, the smell of takeaway from the night shift turned Ward's stomach as he breathed it in. He waited a second for Kipling to elaborate, before grabbing a mug from the cupboard and preparing his own brew.

'Could be something or nothing, with Varga, as you

well know. Might be a shipment of something he ought not to be transporting... could be a decoy.' Kipling's mouth pursed. Despite his temper being far less fiery than Ward's, his own displeasure at Varga's constant evasion of the law was no less.

Kipling cleared his throat as the kettle hissed and rattled behind him on the counter. 'There's been a duplicate CMR—road consignment note—filed with the port in Liverpool. Only picked up since we've tightened measures with them, seeing as we know Varga ships into the UK via Northern Ireland to Liverpool to avoid all the checks at Dover. There's possibly people on the take at Liverpool, though we aren't sure yet—but whatever we know, Varga will probably know too, therefore we must tread carefully.'

DCI Kipling gave DI Ward a meaningful look. A reminder that he had not forgotten the last time Ward had acted rashly when it came to Varga.

Ward stared blankly back.

'Anyway, they picked up the duplicate code, and what do you know? The CMR relates to goods entering the UK from, drumroll please...' Kipling raised an eyebrow, looking at Ward expectantly.

'Slovakia.'

'Ding ding ding, correct. The lorry that originally used the CMR is registered to a shell company in Slovakia that we believe has ties to Varga. The CMR was already used a month ago—so we've missed whatever came into the country—but if it's being used again...'

'We need to be there to find what Varga is shipping

in,' Ward said quietly, the teaspoon in his hand, the brew forgotten.

'Yes, we do.'

Ward stepped forward to pour his own brew—DCI Kipling having made his own without offering. 'What's the plan?'

'I need you and the team to prepare for the lorry's arrival, especially if it's a live shipment. We don't want a repeat of November.' For a moment, a dark shadow crossed Kipling's face. They had all been deeply personally affected by that, not just professionally.

He continued, 'As this is our case, we'll be directing this in Liverpool the moment that ship docks. Get DS Metcalfe to liaise with Customs, Liverpool's Major Enquiries Team, and their uniforms. We need cooperation and we need numbers.'

'When's it coming?'

Kipling scowled. 'There's the bad news. We're not sure. It was filed incomplete, so chances are, we'll only find out when that lorry re-files on departure. We need to be ready to move at a moment's notice. It'll be here within the next week. We just don't know when.'

Ward's shoulders sank. That wasn't good news. Needle in a haystack sprung to mind. Worst case, they would get a ping when the lorry passed through the port at Liverpool—but if it wasn't stopped there, they might be too late to catch it.

'Get on it, DI Ward. I've emailed across the lorry paperwork to you and Metcalfe.'

'Yes, sir.'

But Kipling was already gone, the back of his light suit jacket flapping as the door swung closed behind him.

'Shit,' breathed Ward, sinking against the counter, the burning hot mug in his hand. He put it down hurriedly and rinsed the teaspoon.

DI Ward still had nightmares, more frequently than he cared to admit, about the lorry they'd found last November, piled high with dead immigrants who had suffocated trying to escape the sealed compartment. It had given them no solid evidence that Varga was behind it. HMET *knew*, but they couldn't prove it. The driver was currently on trial, and some of the others in the supply chain, but they'd never even been able to press charges against Varga. Their only chance was to catch him in the act again, and before it was too late.

To DI Ward, it all seemed too much like chance to be comfortable. If they were wrong, if they were late... more people would die. And Varga would remain a free man. The shades of his prior victims would endure without justice. A familiar sense of locked down pressure built within Ward, a wave of helplessness, threatening to overwhelm.

It was so important, so *very* important that they got Varga for everything he'd done—and to stop his future crimes—yet, Ward struggled to acknowledge that reality, it seemed as though he had no control over it all. It was too painful to admit that, in this, he couldn't simply fix it. Varga was too clever to leave a trail. It was an international nightmare to pin down a man made of smoke and deception.

With a sigh, Ward pushed off the counter and

grabbed his brew to go find DS Scott Metcalfe. Scott was already stationed at his desk, a steaming mug beside him —and his first plate of biscuits.

'Morning, Daniel,' Scott said with a grin as Ward entered the shared office.

'Marie not feeding you enough?' Ward nodded to the biscuits, raising an eyebrow.

'What?' Scott said, instantly defensive. 'I'm cutting down. And these are plain, none of those fancy chocolate-covered ones.' He sounded sad about that as he glanced down at the plate.

Ward snorted with laughter and clapped Scott on the shoulder. 'Ah, mate. I feel sorry for Marie trying to slim you down, if you think *this* is what constitutes a diet.'

'She's bloody starving me, man!' Scott muttered mutinously. '*Salad* for tea, Daniel. I'm not a chuffing rabbit! Winter's coming, a man needs pie and peas!'

Ward chuckled again. 'You poor, hard done by lard arse. You are a grown man, you know. Stand up for yourself!'

Metcalfe looked at him incredulously. 'And risk her wrath? Christ... don't think so, mate. You know how it is.'

'Happy wife, happy life.'

Metcalfe winced. 'Yeah. Something like that.'

'Then don't come crying to us. Enjoy your rations.' Ward grinned. Scott looked sorry for himself, but Ward knew Scott worshipped the ground Marie Metcalfe walked on and wouldn't hear a bad word against the woman who'd raised their three kids and taken care of him in the three decades since they'd married as teenage sweethearts.

'What do you want, anyway? I presume you're not just here to mock my starvation?' Scott looked at him through narrowed eyes, his lips thinned.

'Right you are, Scott. Kipling's caught me up on the Varga update.'

'Ah yes. I was just reading the email from him. Sounds promising.'

'Hmm.' Ward shrugged, wrinkled his nose for a moment. 'I wouldn't be so sure. It's never that easy with Varga. He sai—'

At that moment, DS Emma Nowak, DI Ward's usual partner, called across the office. She was already standing, grabbing her bag and various items she'd need. 'Sorry to interrupt, sir, but there's been a murder. You've been designated as SIO, and we have to get there at once.'

Ward turned back to Scott. 'Can I leave you on this? You know what Kipling's like—we can't screw this up.'

'I'm on it. I want this bastard nailed as badly as you, Daniel. We all do.'

'Thanks. Put DC Shahzad on monitoring any chatter he can find. DC Norris can sort the lorry—find out everything you can about it. Where it's registered, where it's been, who's driving it, anything he can. Will you liaise with Liverpool to make sure we're placed to swoop in if the lorry materialises? We'll need cooperation between Customs, Major Crimes, and their uniforms.'

'No problemo.'

Ward sighed. He liked to take this sort of thing on himself, spearhead the team rather than delegate, but HMET had suffered the same brutal funding cuts as other frontline services. They no longer had the luxury of devoting an entire team to Varga. He would have to juggle it, along with the cases they were already handling. The Detective Constables, under DS Priya Chakrabarti coordinating, were already inundated with the darkening nights, for it meant an increase in burglaries—the same spates in the same areas they saw every year when the nights drew in. The same deluge of unsolvable crimes they had to process every autumn and winter.

'Kipling will be around, I'm sure, to keep you all to task.'

'Lucky us.' Scott flicked his eyes skyward for a moment, and shook his head. 'We've got this. You bring in the new case, and we'll juggle it somehow.'

'Cheers, mate.' Ward quickly chugged his still-hot brew and dumped the mug on his desk to wash later. He shrugged his coat back on, and out of habit checked his pockets for his wallet, car keys, and phone, before crossing the room to where Emma waited.

'Morning, DS Nowak.' His smile was genuinely warm—Ward cared for his team, who felt at times more like family than colleagues, for what they did together, day in, day out. Their kind of job formed an unbreakable bond of loyalty and camaraderie.

Her white teeth flashed as she grinned in response. 'Morning, sir. Not the quiet day DS Metcalfe hoped for, I think.'

'I heard that,' Scott called across the office.

'I'll bring back *proper* biscuits, DS.'

'Always knew I liked you,' came the grumbled reply before Metcalfe subsided behind his ancient, whirring computer again.

Emma smirked, and walked out, thanking Ward for holding the door open for her. 'Y'alright, sir?' she asked as they walked down the corridor.

Ward hid a yawn behind his hand. 'Fine thanks, you?'

'Same old, sir, same old.'

'How's the wedding planning going?' Emma and her fiancé Adam were due to wed the following summer after he had proposed to her that spring.

'Haven't had time,' Emma said with a laugh. 'Not with all these burglaries. Adam's happy with that though. He's not really a fan of picking cakes or flowers. Got all our suppliers booked though, and the dress is ordered.'

Ward couldn't help but smile at the excitement radiating from her. Katherine had been so beautifully innocent one day long ago too. He hoped their marriage would end up better than his. 'I'm sure Adam'll look gorgeous in it.'

Emma shot him a wicked look, but she couldn't hide the smirk, or the crinkle at her eyes. 'You're *terrible.*'

Ward winked. 'What have we got, anyway?' he asked as they left the station. In the absence of any pool cars that day, he headed over to his Golf. Emma slid inside, glancing around appreciatively—the scent of pine from the dangling air freshener beating the stained, old pool cars with the lingering odours of farts, unwashed bodies, and many meals and spillages by a long mile—before she answered, flicking out her notepad for the details.

'Okay. We have a victim, young woman in her mid-late twenties—' Ward glanced over at Emma. She was the same age, but Emma seemed unperturbed. The job was getting to her already, Ward saw, hardening her against the brutality they sometimes saw. '—found dead this morning by a dog walker. Location is Harden Beck, just outside Bingley. Police are on scene, and an ambulance nearby.'

Ward frowned. 'Alright. Put the details in the satnav.' He tapped the centre console screen onto the right mode before he slid out of the car park and joined the main road.

'Twenty minutes, sir. Looks like the best way is past the top of the hospital, over Cottingley, and on the old Bingley road.'

'Right-oh. Let's go meet our victim.'

CHAPTER SIX

Twenty minutes later, Ward parked on the narrow lane. Ahead, he could see the bright yellow of an ambulance where the lane gave way to a track. The morning fog was already lifting, but not to anything special, just more of the grey, drizzly, wet weather they had already had enough of that week. The scent of wet soil hung cold and rich in the air. Ward gladly breathed it in. He knew what he would soon smell. Death was never welcome to experience in any of the senses.

They approached the scene where police tape already fluttered, and a PCSO stepped forward to challenge them. The trees overhead seemed like tall, silent sentinels. Aside from the chatter ahead, it seemed utterly silent, as though all life had fled the place.

Ward and Nowak showed their warrant cards. 'DI Daniel Ward, SIO, DS Emma Nowak. Who's organising so far?'

The PCSO nodded them past. 'PC Lithgow—her there.' She pointed to a middle-aged woman with a neat, greying-brunette bun, and a police hat under her arm.

'Cheers. Keep the cordon and your scene log going, please.' HMET didn't have the manpower to take that over.

PC Lithgow stood with one of the ambulance staff and a very unhappy older bald man shivering with a subdued Collie-dog sat leaning against his leg. The PC looked up as they drew closer, and introductions were made, the PC running off a list of pertinent facts in a succinct, detached manner that Ward liked and recognised as coming from years of service on the force.

'This is Mr Graham Bell. At approximately a quarter to eight, he came across the unfortunately deceased body of a young woman. He called for an ambulance immediately, but they pronounced her dead at the scene, when we were alerted. PSCO Turner and myself attended, secured the scene, and alerted HMET. The paramedics are about to leave unless anything else is needed from them—Mr Bell doesn't need any medical attention.'

'Thank you,' Ward said, and turned to Nowak. 'Can you get me an ETA on the divisional surgeon—' for despite the paramedics, procedure still had to be followed in confirming death, '—and CSI?'

'Course, sir.' Nowak immediately turned away, already phone in hand to dial.

'Thanks for your help, PC Lithgow. Mr Bell, if we could keep you a very short while longer, I'd appreciate it. We'll need to take some details, and our Crime Scene Investigators may need some additional information to make sure you're properly accounted for at the scene.'

'I-I didn't do anything,' the man said, his face slack with horror as he misinterpreted. 'I just found her.' At his feet, the dog stood and grumbled, unsettled.

Ward smiled reassuringly. 'Of course.' He looked at the ground, at the mud that interspersed the trail. 'They might need to take prints of your shoes, for example, to discount you from our investigation. Stay with PC Lithgow, a moment, please.'

He nodded to PC Lithgow, and understanding crossed between them. The man wasn't under arrest by any stretch, but it wouldn't be the first time a murderer had stayed close to the scene, even called in the crime, in an attempt to hide in such plain sight as to exonerate themselves. Whatever his position, however innocent, the man had important details DI Ward needed to know.

Around the corner in the trail, just beyond the bridge, the body waited. It drew him closer with the same morbid fascination they always did. DI Ward didn't want to look, yet, he couldn't look away. First, white trainers, mud scuffed, came into view. Legs on the ground. And as Ward rounded the trail, the tangle of bushes between the trees parted to offer him a view of her.

Crumpled and limp, she was a sad sight. Dark blood marred the soft lilac of her running top. Her arms lay bent at unnatural angles—like a marionette that had had its strings cut and toppled to lay however it fell. They were covered too, in spurts and spatters of blood. It glistened on the leaves of the nearest bushes, like a cursed dew. Staining the tree against which, he presumed, she had stood, already seeming to have irrevocably soaked into that layer of bark.

A light breeze lifted the unwelcome scent of death to him too. Heavy and pungent, it sat on his tongue unpleasantly, a bitter aftertaste he couldn't shed. Ward was careful to approach no closer, for with each step, the ground sank beneath his weight. No doubt the walker who had found her might have approached closer—and he noticed dog tracks too—though the route was so commonly used that any imprints could have belonged to anyone. He hung back, although he wanted to draw closer, to examine for himself in more detail, and start to build up a picture, but contaminating the crime scene was a price too high to pay.

From what he saw, from the amount of blood in the environment and upon the prone young woman, whose face was partially hidden by an outstretched arm, she had died a violent death. It was never easy to deal with that, as a police officer or detective, they were all still human. It was a savage reminder of how callous humanity was to itself.

By the blood, it looked as though she had been stabbed repeatedly in a sustained attack, though only a post-mortem would confirm her cause of death. Her slim hands were covered in blood—her own, he wondered, or perhaps someone else's... but as DI Ward peered closer, he noticed the edge of a savage cut across her palm. *Defensive wounds.* His mouth thinned into a grim line.

Who had done this? What had caused this? A lone jogger out, viciously attacked. A mugging or sexual assault gone wrong? A deliberate attack? A random one? Had she been there since last night, or was this a fresh kill? Ward sucked the inside of his cheek, glancing around, but could see nothing obvious. He needed pathology and forensics to unlock more pieces of the puzzle first.

With his hands in his pockets to fend off the chill of the day, drizzle threatening overhead, Ward strode back to the PC, the witness, and the ambulance crew—who were just driving off.

DS Nowak nodded to him. 'Surgeon will be here shortly, CSI on route, photographer coming separately.'

'Thank you.' Ward glanced up the narrow lane, which he reckoned wouldn't have seen so much traffic in a week as it was about to, and turned to the man standing with PC Lithgow.

'Mr Bell,' he said gravely. 'Based on the nature of what you've found, we'll need to take a full statement from you. Can you describe what happened? Please include as much detail as you can.'

Mr Bell nodded, and his eyes darted to that hook in the track, where the body lay out of sight just beyond. When he spoke, there was a tremble in his voice, and Ward could see that the dog's lead was wound so tightly around his hand it bit into the skin. 'I was walking Tilly just like I do every morning.'

At the mention of her name, the dog's ears perked up, and her mouth split to reveal a lolling tongue.

'I can't say I noticed anything out of the ordinary— the mist was very thick this morning. When I came down past the bridge, I saw the purple o-of the lady's top. It was very out of place, you see. Tilly rushed ahead of me, but she had her tail right down, and she wouldn't go to the lady—she's such a friendly thing.' The man's voice had become monotone, but it wobbled once more. 'I knew something was wrong.'

'I went over to her, and tried to see if she was ok, and...' Mr Bell swallowed and clutched at the end of the dog's lead with both hands. He turned a face twisted by consternation to DI Ward. 'Then I noticed all the blood. She wasn't moving, and there was blood everywhere. I felt her forehead, is that alright?' He looked at Ward, cowed, as though he'd be cuffed and hauled off for the murder.

'She was cold—not freezing, but cool—and there was nothing, she wasn't breathing. I-I rang the ambulance straight away but... I didn't see how there was any way to save her. I think she was already gone.'

Tears glistened at the corner of Mr Bell's eyes. 'I didn't do anything wrong, did I? Was there something I could have done to help her?' He looked desperately between PC Lithgow and DI Ward.

PC Lithgow smiled sympathetically and placed a hand on Mr Bell's shoulder. 'It's alright, Graham. By the sounds of it, she was already gone, like you said, and nothing you could have done would have brought her back. Don't blame yourself. This has been a traumatic morning for you—do you have anyone I can call to come and be with you?'

'M-my wife. She'll be wondering where I am. I'll ring her now.'

'I'll speak to her too, if that's alright. Make sure that you're taken care of. This is a terrible thing to see.'

Mr Bell nodded jerkily. 'Y-you just don't see things like this here. Bingley is a nice town, a quiet place. Who would...? *Why?*'

The PC's answering smile was sad. 'Sometimes, we never know, Mr Bell, but we'll do all we can to find out what happened to this young lady. I've already got your details. Come on, let's call your wife—what's she called?'

'Sally.'

'Let's give Sally a ring and we'll get you home. I've got all your details so if there's anything else we need, we'll be in touch.'

'Th-thank you. Come on, Tilly girl, come on.' The dog stretched and followed them up the track, away from that horrific scene.

Ward hung back with a silent Nowak, watching them go. He could do little until CSI arrived. First of all, they needed to find out who she was. He'd spotted a slimline pocket on the thigh of her Lycra running pants with a flat bulge in it—a slimline purse with ID if he was lucky.

'Is it bad?' Nowak asked quietly. Perhaps, Ward wondered, it had affected her more than she'd let on. After all, they were reportedly around the same age. Nowak sometimes went running too, down the valley where she lived in the World Heritage Site village of Saltaire. Ward was aware of the disparity in how safe men and women felt when they were out alone. No doubt this would make Nowak glance over her shoulder even more.

'Aye,' Ward replied.

As PC Lithgow saw Mr Bell away from of the crime scene, chaos descended as CSI, the divisional surgeon, and the photographer all arrived at once, blocking up the narrow lane with a backlog of vehicles, and overwhelming the poor PSCO guarding the scene, who hurriedly logged everyone's details in the records.

Victoria Foster—impressively imposing for a petite woman—made sure she was at the front of the pack, to make sure any contamination to the scene by the surgeon and the photographer was kept to a minimum. In short order, a white tent popped up and her team transformed as they donned white paper suits, boot covers, masks, and hoods.

'Morning, Ward. What've we got?' She was still instantly identifiable from her usual wild spectacles—today, bright yellow plastic rims, spotted with red.

Ward raised an eyebrow. It was the most civil greeting she'd given him on a scene in donkey's years. 'Morning, Victoria. Mid-twenties, last night to this morning, possible multiple stab wounds. Haven't seen anything too obvious.'

She glared at him sharply and opened her mouth. He held up his hands and spoke first. 'Don't worry, I didn't go near her...'

Victoria narrowed her eyes. 'You're learning. Interesting. Didn't know dogs were that smart. Good.' She brushed past him without a further word.

Nowak sniggered beside Ward.

'Oi. You're supposed to be on my side,' he muttered darkly. 'I don't know why she's got it in for me.'

'Treat 'em mean, keep 'em keen, sir?'

It was Ward's turn to laugh. 'You're joking, right?

Even if she weren't married, even if we were the last two people left on planet Earth, that's a firm bloody no.'

'Oh, sir, lighten up and take a joke.' Nowak's eyes twinkled with mirth.

'I'll give you 'a joke'. Christ, you'll give me nightmares,' Ward said, glaring at her.

CHAPTER SEVEN

'Amelia Hughes. Twenty-seven.' Ward stared at the photograph of the driving licence—the original having been bagged up for evidence. He had been right— a slimline purse with a fiver and her driving licence had been tucked in the thigh pocket of the victim's running leggings.

'Too young to die, and particularly like this,' Mark Baker said, his hands tucked behind his back as he surveyed the crime scene with all the serenity of admiring the view on a stroll. The pathologist was well used to death, though DI Ward hardly saw him out of the pathology laboratory at Bradford Royal Infirmary where he was based.

'Aye. What are your thoughts?' It had been a long and cold morning. The PCSO had stood patiently, turning away walkers and a growing number of curious onlookers as word spread through the town of what had happened. Nowak had popped across the river into town for a coffee run, for though the mist had now lifted, the steely grey clouds had burst, and they were all sodden and frozen.

Ward drained the rest of the lukewarm tea, still appreciative of the slight warmth it added to his belly against the pervasive cold that stiffened him. It was a race against the clock for Foster's CSI team to capture all the data they needed from the scene, and for Mark Baker to conduct his initial examination of the victim once the divisional surgeon had confirmed the very obvious, that she would not be joining the land of the living again.

Mark let out a long exhale as he approached Ward, having taken a look at the body. 'It's as you thought, Daniel, m'boy. Multiple stab wounds, and a lot of blood. I'll conduct a proper investigation, of course, with all my tools, but it very much seems like this young lady had a very unfortunate run-in with whoever did this. It was a sustained and violent attack.'

He glanced up at the sky. 'If the weather was on our side, I might have called for a blood pattern analysis specialist, but the scene's degrading so fast with this damnable rain, I don't think there's much point.'

Ward had been for a closer look—though careful to stay a distance away from Victoria and her team who combed through every inch of the undergrowth and surrounding area. 'There's blood high up on the tree trunk, so my theory is that she was pushed against the tree and stabbed there.'

'I'd agree. I've seen the scene from all angles—' and indeed Mark Baker's usually pristine ivory pressed trousers and brogues were muddy and scuffed, '—and the blade was long enough and used with such force that it had penetrated through Miss Hughes' back. There are stains on the bark where it's pooled straight out of her from those wounds, and spatter marks caused possibly by other wounds, arterial spray and the like—I'll have to examine her to be sure—or the arc of the knife moving through the air between strikes.'

'Time of death?'

Mark grimaced. 'Fresh. Looking at the weather, the temperature, the likelihood of anyone being out here, the condition she's in... I think your walker Mr Bell just missed this. I'd peg between...' He pursed his lips, tipped his head from side to side as he deliberated. 'Five a.m. at the earliest, through half-past seven.'

'Hmm.' They would need to ask for witnesses to narrow that window down, and work from there. Perhaps someone somewhere saw something. There were houses nearby, out of sight, granted, but the killer could have passed them. Ward shook his head. 'Who the hell would do this?'

Mark sighed and folded his arms across his ample belly, his long trench coat wrinkling. 'That, m'boy, is for you to determine.'

'Thanks, Mark.' He left the pathologist waiting at the bottom of the lane for the transport to the morgue to arrive for the body, and returned to Nowak.

'Right, we have a name, so we can do preliminary checks, identify next of kin, start pooling suspects.'

'I'll ring the office, sir, get DC Patterson to pull up her files.'

'Great. Ask him to find her on social media too, build up any connections we can find for her life. Hold the next of kin—we'd best speak to them. I'll check in with Victoria.'

The CSI team were beginning to pack up as Ward rounded the bend, pulling down the tent that had kept at least part of the scene and the body sheltered from the incessant dripping from the trees above.

'Hi. Any initial findings we can go on, Victoria?' Ward said, approaching the scene.

For once, Victoria didn't bark at him to get away—perhaps because he'd left her to finish. She pulled off her blue latex gloves and mask, and Ward noticed her expression was even more severe than usual.

'She tried to put up a fight, but it didn't do her any good in the end,' she said, scowling. Ward recognised the anger in her—the anger of the injustice of a young woman fighting for her life and unable to prevail in the face of such overwhelming force and means.

'She has what looks like defensive wounds on her hands and forearms—clean, sharp slices. I agree with Baker that it's a stabbing, but we can't see any murder weapon in the immediate area—and I've had my team comb the surrounding paths too just in case. It would be a pretty big knife, possibly a kitchen knife, to create these wounds. That's missing—taken away, dumped, concealed.' Victoria shrugged. That was Ward's jurisdiction to handle, if it wasn't on-scene.

'On her, she doesn't have a phone, which is weird. I think she might have had one, because the pocket we found her money and ID inside, was large enough to accommodate one and the fabric was stretched as though it regularly contained more than what we found in it—but the other contents were still there, with a little money inside. So perhaps not a mugging. Just a theory, of course, maybe she left it at home today, who knows.

'There's little in the way of prints. I've matched foot-prints belonging to the first witness on the scene, and presumably his dog, too. There are other prints around the area, scuffed and overlaid. This is not a popular route, but it is well enough used, and there's nothing I can pull that is conclusive. Some partials, that's about it.' Victoria glanced at the black body bag behind them, the sad remains of what had, until such a short few hours ago, been a living, breathing woman.

'We do potentially have some excellent forensic data, which, given the nature of this, I'll fast track.'

'Oh?' Ward dragged his eyes away from the body bag, back to Victoria.

'She fought back. There was a curly brown hair about four inches long wrapped through her fingers. Complete with follicle, I think.' Victoria smiled darkly. 'We'll be able to pull full DNA off the follicle, if so. Plus, we took samples from underneath her fingernails. We'll test those too, in case there's anything there. We have plenty of blood samples also—a harder one to crack, but maybe it's not all her blood. Maybe she got the bastard back.'

'Excellent. Cheers. Baker's waiting on transport for her now.'

Victoria looked over her shoulder, taking a last long

gaze around the innocuous fold in the trail that had become the last place Amelia Hughes had seen. She shook her head. She didn't say a thing as she picked up a bag of her tools and left. She didn't need to.

Sometimes, their job was unspeakable.

CHAPTER EIGHT

D I Ward breezed the Golf over the top of Ilkley Moor, en-route to Amelia Hughes' parents, who lived on the outskirts of Harrogate. This was the worst part of the job by far. Afterall, there was no nice way to say, 'Hello, your daughter's dead. Any idea who might have done it?'

Beside him, Nowak reviewed the notes the PCSO had taken of everyone who had passed through while guarding the scene in order to write it up in the crime log, and all the information they'd gleaned from the scene, CSI, and pathology. She paused to take an appreciative view of the summit of the rolling moors. A wild expanse of grasses, heathers, and bracken, beautiful in its own windswept way and as changeable as the seasons, the bright colours now fading to muted browns with the turning of summer to autumn.

It was not long since they'd been up there in the dead of night for another case that had almost ended too badly to repair. Ward had no desire to turn down to Burley

Woodhead and revisit the scene at the Cow and Calf Rocks. He turned right instead, down to Menston so he could drop into Otley, across to Pool in Wharfedale, and take the fast A-road to Harrogate. Providing, of course, he didn't get stuck behind a tractor, as was wont to happen on that road, given that it was in the middle of farming country.

To Ward's relief, there were no hold-ups, but the day was getting on. He glanced at the clock in the car. 'Fancy a quick lunch stop?'

'Definitely,' said Nowak, jumping on the suggestion. 'I'm *starving*.'

Ward grinned. Just outside Pool in Wharfedale on the Harrogate road was a gem of a cafe serving local produce. 'What'll it be? I'm getting a bacon and sausage butty.'

'Mmm. Sounds good to me, sir. I'll have the same.'

'And your usual drink?'

Nowak smiled. 'Yes please, sir.' She fished a tenner out of her purse and handed it to him as he parked up just off the road in the small car park.

Ward waved it away. 'Ah, don't worry. My treat. You can get the next one.'

'Cheers, sir.'

'Don't get too cocky—next time it might be a three-course meal.'

'Not on a sergeant's salary it won't, sir.' She didn't look up from her notes, knowing he was far too decent to be that unfair, though the corner of her mouth quirked in a smile.

Ward guffawed as he shut the door behind him, and walked over to the cafe.

————

Soon, the car smelled of sausage, bacon, coffee, and brown sauce as they tucked into the large butties with gusto, savouring the warm, tender sausages and the thick, salty bacon. Proper local grub.

Ward made sure the drinks were secured in the holders between his and Nowak's seat, and belted up to set off as soon as he'd finished. Nowak put her seatbelt back on too, though she had only half-finished the butty.

'Where did you put that?' she asked incredulously, wrinkling her nose in mixed amazement and disgust.

'I don't mess around, Nowak, you should know that by now.'

'Have you heard of *chewing*, sir? Highly recommend it.'

'Nah. Takes too much time.'

Nowak shook her head. 'Honestly, with the way you inhale food, I'm surprised you're not deskbound like Metcalfe.'

'Oof, he'd have you for that.'

'He's not here, just you and your big vacuum mouth,' Nowak said primly, taking another delicate bite, somehow managing to make eating a sausage and bacon butty smothered in brown sauce look vaguely elegant.

'Next time, you're definitely buying.' Ward sent a fake glower her way.

The satnav pinged at him, interrupting their bickering. Ward looked ahead for the turning as they came into the outskirts of Harrogate. Past houses on the wide street, each one seeming bigger and grander than the last. Harrogate had its poverty like any other area, but the spa town was known for being an affluent area, on the whole. This street definitely lived up to that. Nowak gawked as they drove past a huge modern building that stood out like a sore thumb amongst the huge, but far more traditional, detached red-brick buildings.

Ward indicated and turned left in the Rossett Green area of the outskirts, where the houses almost immediately became more modest off the main road—though, no doubt still commanding an eye-watering Harrogate price tag. He slowed outside the corner property the satnav pinged as the final destination, and parked beside the kerb. Nowak brushed the remaining crumbs from her shirt and wiped her hands on the paper napkin.

It was an unassuming light-brick detached house, the kind one saw in well-to-do estates from several decades hence, possibly the seventies, Ward thought. The corner plot was unfenced, ringed by a pared-back bed of flowers and bushes that had recently been dug over for the coming winter, and a flawless, close-cropped lawn. As Ward and Nowak approached down the modest paved path to the front door, which lay tucked beside a bay window and a couple of still-flowering hydrangeas in a muted shade of pink, he saw movement from within.

The door opened seconds after his knock to a short, slim woman in her late fifties. Annette Hughes. For a moment, Ward stalled. She was the spit of Amelia, though older and... well... living.

'Mrs Hughes? Detective Inspector Daniel Ward, and Detective Sergeant Emma Nowak. We're sorry for the unannounced visit, please may we come in?' As he spoke, he held out his warrant card, Emma doing the same, and the woman looked at them, then back at Ward, frowning.

'Yes, of course. Is something wrong?' She led them inside, pausing at the bottom of the stairs to shout up. 'Bill, can you come down? There's some police officers here.'

Ward didn't correct her—police officer, detective, it was mostly the same to many members of the public, and it wasn't the time. Not with the news he had to tell them.

Bill thundered downstairs in short order, the wood creaking under his feet with every step in the ageing house, as the woman led them into a modest living room with comfortable sofas that she invited them to sit in. The faint smell of a freshly baked cake mingled with a light perfume and clean washing powder.

Bill frowned as he followed them in. 'Is this about the dog fouling? It was just a complaint, I didn't expect you to attend. I imagine you have better things to do with your time than deal with our local layabouts.'

'Quite right,' Ward said with a faint smile that quickly faded.

'Can I get you a drink?' Annette asked.

'Ah, no thank you. Please, sit.'

Annette and Bill shared a glance, curiosity turning to worry as they sat on one of the couches, Ward and Nowak perching on the other.

'I'm terribly sorry to bring this news to you, but this morning, the body of your daughter Amelia was found.'

Stunned silence greeted him.

'I beg your pardon?' Annette Hughes said, paling.

Ward nodded. Waiting. Waiting for that sentence to sink in—there was no use repeating it.

Annette Hughes, who sat tall, seemed to shrink back, down, smaller. Her hand rested on her husband's knee. His hand found hers.

'How? What happened? Is...is it her? She can't be. We spoke last night. She texted this morning. A few minutes before seven. She was just setting off on her run,' her father said hoarsely. He seemed to have aged decades in seconds, wilting like his wife as they both looked the officers up and down, finding no weakness in their credibility. Looking at each other, they burst into tears.

'She did have her identification on her, but we would appreciate it if one of you could present for a formal identification to confirm,' Ward said quietly. 'She'll be at the Bradford Royal Infirmary.'

'What happened?' Bill repeated.

Ward shared a glance with Nowak. 'Our investigations are still in the early stages, but it appears she was killed whilst on her morning run today.'

Her mother made a wordless moan of anguish at his response, staring desperately at her husband, and then Ward, as though he could take it all back. There was no way news of such enormity could be absorbed in mere seconds, but Ward had seen many responses to grief in his time.

From the photos sprinkled around the room of Amelia, Annette, and Bill, the cliff of their grief would be huge. He suspected from the photos, which lacked any others in their focus, that she was their only, and most precious, child.

'How?' Bill dared to ask.

'The post-mortem is yet to be carried out, but preliminary results suggest a stabbing.'

Annette moaned again, turning her body and face into her husband's chest.

'Why?' Tears carved rivers down Bill's cheeks.

'We don't know that yet, but we're doing everything we can to understand what happened, and bring the person responsible to justice. If you know of anyone with a motive, at this stage, any information is incredibly helpful. Did Amelia have any enemies, anyone who might have held a grudge, or had she any reason to fall foul of anyone she knew?'

Bill shook his head, staring at the floor, wide-eyed, as though he saw none of it. His arm tightly wrapped around his wife's shoulder holding her close in silent solidarity. 'No. Amelia is a good girl. She always has been. She loves her job, has plenty of friends... she really loves...' Bill winced. '*Loved* living in Bingley. It's a trendy place—far enough from us for her to do her own thing, close enough for when she needed us. Or when we needed her. Probably more the latter these days. The house is quiet without her.' He smiled sadly.

Anger and hatred cut through Annette's burning grief, and she pulled away from Bill. 'It was that... That... *ex-boyfriend* of hers!' Her hand trembled as she covered her mouth, and her eyes flicked to the heavens. 'Oh, God. What did he do to our baby?' Her hand fell to clutch the delicate golden crucifix hanging around her neck.

DS Nowak was already scribbling in her notepad.

'Ex-boyfriend?'

'Yes,' Annette spoke again, glaring at Ward with such vehemence—desperation to pin blame on someone. 'Darren Winston. Vile creature, he is. One of those ghastly men who spends all his time building the most hideous muscles at the gym, who likes to make everyone else feel small. Nasty, spiteful, immature. I don't know what she ever saw in him.'

'But they broke up?'

'She finally came to her senses. She says he never did anything to hurt her but he was controlling, and they argued all the time. We raised her to be independent,' Annette said, straightening as pride took her. 'We were glad she ended things.'

'What caused the breakup?'

'She didn't say, and we didn't press her. She was sad about it, but happy too, like she had realised getting away from him was a good thing for her. She came to ours more since—he'd kept her away, you see.'

'When was this?'

'About a month ago. When they started dating, her visits slowed and then stopped. I hated him for taking her away from us,' Annette admitted. 'When they broke up, and she started coming round for Sunday dinner every weekend again... it felt like we were a family again.'

'Do you think he could have held a grudge against her for the breakup?'

'No one else would have wanted to hurt her.' Once more, Annette subsided into tears.

'I'm sorry to have to go through all this, Mr and Mrs Hughes. Do you have his contact details?' Ward said.

'No.'

'Do you know if she had any problems where she worked?'

Bill shook his head. 'She didn't get on with everyone there, but it was just a job—I can't imagine anyone taking it so seriously they'd...' he trailed off, and pressed his face into his wife's head as she huddled into him.

Nowak took down the details for Amelia's place of work for further enquiries, but quietly interjected before Ward spoke again, 'What about any friends? Or arguments with friends?'

'She had a great girlfriend in Bingley. They were always chatting. Always racking up a phone bill.' Bill let out a mirthless chuckle. 'We paid that for her whilst she was getting started out and set up over there, to help out.'

Once more, Nowak took a name, and Annette gave her a contact number.

Ward stood. 'I'm sorry to have brought you such terrible news today. We'll do everything we can to find you answers and bring Amelia justice.'

Annette and Bill stood as one, still clutched together.

'I'll arrange FLO,' Nowak said to Ward, respectfully said goodbye, and stepped outside.

Ward continued, 'We'll send a family liaison officer around to you. They'll be your main point of contact. If you think of anything else that might aid our investigation, you can pass that to us via the liaison officer. We will also keep you informed of any developments in the same way. They're here to offer you any support you need at

this time.' He looked between them to check for compre-
hension, but they nodded dully, glazed over.

'If you need anything else for now, here are my
details.' Ward handed them a card from his pocket.
Annette had already drifted away from Bill's arms, not
paying them the slightest attention. Instead, she gently
picked up a photo of a much younger Amelia, grinning
with one of her front baby teeth missing, and clutched it
to her chest, sobbing quietly.

Bill took the card from Ward's outstretched hand.

Ward showed himself out as Bill turned to his wife.

Outside, he found Nowak, hidden from view of the
street by the open porch and a hedge, composing herself.
Tears glistened and she hastily brushed them away as
Ward appeared.

'The FLO team have put Geoff on this one,' she said
with a loud sniff, and turned away to walk down the path
back to the car.

'Great,' Ward eyed her with sympathy and followed.
Geoffrey Mason was one of the best FLOs the force had,
the elderly, broad Yorkshire man was an expert at putting
victim's families at ease and supporting them at such a
difficult time. Annette and Bill Hughes would need it.

They slid into the car and Ward turned to Nowak
before he put the key into the ignition. 'You alright?'

'No,' Nowak admitted, 'but I will be. This part of the
job is hard. The victim's a person, and they had a life, a
family. It's hard to not feel that sometimes. I know, I
know,' she said before Ward could speak. 'I need to learn
to not let it get to me.'

'Far from it,' said Ward smiling sympathetically. 'We

can't let it overwhelm us—that stops us doing our job—but you wouldn't be human if you didn't feel something. Don't lose that, that compassion and empathy are also what *help* us do our job. We keep the victim and their families at the forefront of our minds. They're gone, and they're relying on us to tell their story, find out what happened, and bring them justice.'

Nowak nodded, swallowing around the lump in her throat.

'It's also human to be scared of our own mortality,' Ward added gently. 'She was your age, that's scary. We all like to think we're invincible. Heck, I'm guilty of it too... but the truth is far more fragile than that, and when we face it... who wouldn't be scared to die when there's so much to live for?'

Nowak gave him a watery grin. 'I knew you were nice under all that grumbling.'

'Aye. I'm a big teddy bear, me.'

That made her laugh, and Ward smiled. 'Come on. Let's get ourselves back to Bingley—looks like we have an ex-boyfriend, some friends, and colleagues to question. If we can get them all today, that'll help us get ahead on this one when forensics and pathology come back.'

Nowak straightened in the seat, sniffed, and wiped her eyes one last time. 'Yes, sir.'

CHAPTER NINE

Harry had run all the way home that morning, as though the very wind lifted each step, buoying him up with euphoria. He had done it! The power coursing through him made him feel *invincible*. It pleased and frustrated him that he was clever, and he had covered all of his tracks too well. No one would ever know his brilliance.

He didn't want to go back to being a checkout boy. Ignored and overlooked. Unappreciated and misjudged.

'Fuck it,' he muttered to himself as he legged it through the corner of Myrtle Park with his hood up, startling a lady dog walker as he pounded past her. Her dog— a little ratty terrier thing—yapped at him in indignance.

Stupid thing.

He wasn't going to work today. Screw the lot of them. They could manage without him. There was no way he'd sacrifice the buzz of it all to serve fags and lotto tickets all day. He'd text in sick when he got home.

Harry left the park and darted down the back alley to

his place. The small back-to-back terrace was perfect. Well hidden from the main road a few streets away, and down the quieter end of the wide alley, it was easy to slip inside unnoticed.

Snap. The door closed behind him, the bolt locking automatically, and Harry leaned on it, pausing for a moment. The mingling relief that he had gotten away with it swiftly overtaken once more by the power buzzing through him.

The knife still hung heavy against his belly. He drew it out, almost reverently, looking at the blade, which still bore traces of her blood, though much of it had soaked into the inside of his hoodie pocket.

Once more, he was glad he'd chosen a black garment. It was *sodden* with Amelia's blood, which had soaked right through his t-shirt. It was cold and clammy on his skin, the fabric sticking to him. *How much blood had there been?*

Harry took off his trainers on the doormat and picked them up, stepping into the small kitchen. He shoved them in the empty washing machine, and stripped off his hoodie and the grey t-shirt—which was now stained a violent dark red—shorts, boxers, and socks.

He'd almost forgotten Amelia's phone, key and bracelet. He pulled them out of his shorts pocket before he shut the washer door, glancing dispassionately at the rose gold hard case on the iPhone. Without examining the garments, he poured in some detergent and set the washer on a hot fast wash. He'd run a second one later. Just to make sure.

Glancing out of the window—the alley was deserted

—Harry picked up the knife, returned to the hallway, and opened the under-stairs door. He flicked on the hallway light, pursing his lips as the light switch took on a red smear from the contact. He would clean that later.

The cellar was empty, an unused, cold, damp space with no natural light, heating, or power. The light from the hallway above was mostly cut out by his silhouette. He trod the bare steps with care until he reached the bottom, each step rough and freezing on the bare soles of his feet.

A toolbox—the landlord's, though long forgotten and never used—lay half-open on the bottom of an otherwise empty shelving unit. Harry glanced around the dark space. He opened the toolbox, buried the knife, key, and phone deep inside, being sure to cover them with some of the tools, and shut the box, pushing it back onto the shelf to wedge the lid down.

Some trophies for him.

A smirk tweaked the corners of his lips.

No one would ever know.

With self-satisfaction putting an extra bounce in his step, Harry went upstairs to the bathroom. Squeezing through the small door, which wouldn't fully open thanks to the pile of mucky washing on the floor behind it, he closed it behind him.

The bathroom mirror afforded him the first glance of his reflection.

His deep brown eyes glared impassively back at him. A slight sheen of sweat gleamed on his forehead, but in the cracks at the side of his nose, and on the edge of his cheek, by his ear, there were tell-tale dark smears where he'd not managed to wipe off all of Amelia's blood.

Harry held his hands out before him. They were ingrained with it, already darkened and dried, crusting around the edges of his fingernails, clinging stubbornly to every fold of skin in his knuckles. As he glanced down, he saw the way it darkened his chest, the liquid having bled through his hoodie, through his t-shirt, and clung amidst his chest hair. His knees were smeared red too, though he had wiped them the best he could, and on one shin, a line where a blot of her blood had dribbled down to soak into his socks.

As he took in his body, he could see her before him too. Scrabbling at him uselessly. Him pushing her hands out of the way. Covering her mouth so she couldn't cry out. Driving that knife again and again into her shuddering form. The way her eyes glazed over in shock and pain. The way they dulled as that light and life within her was extinguished.

Harry took a deep breath. Those bloodstained hands felt like a baptism. One of death, not God. One that seemed dizzying. Addictive. Arousing.

Harry knew then that he couldn't be done with just one.

———

Aside from ignoring the half-dozen calls from work, Harry spent the rest of the day reliving the high, smoking weed, and scrolling Matchmaker as his alias James Denton. He wouldn't be hasty—he wasn't stupid—but he wanted to scratch the surge of arousal that his act of murder had caused.

Every time he scrolled past someone who looked like Amelia—long, glossy dark hair, clear skin, fine-boned, light eyes—it caught at him, as though he were seeing her all over again. Euphoria at his kill and anger at her rejection surging together within him.

There were three candidates—but only one seemed up for a one-nighter that evening. Sara Pearson, twenty-three, petite, spectacles, and a bit of fat around the edges. Not his usual type, but she'd do. The opposite to Amelia. He wanted such contrast that night, though he couldn't say why. He didn't want to get to know the lass anyway, he just needed a quick shag to release that pent up energy. Then, they'd go their separate ways, job done. Maybe she'd be up for another hook-up later down the line.

———

Sara's body was *beautiful*, even Harry had to admit that, pale in the darkness of the room, only a nearby streetlight outside the blind-covered window to cast anything in relief. He'd already had her, fast and rough from behind, but it hadn't been enough.

Now she was on her back and at his mercy.

Plumper and more petite than Amelia, she had curves and a good handful of arse for him to enjoy, just the way he liked. She moaned under him as he splayed her legs further, plunging in once more. One arm supported him above her. The other hand teased her, rolling up her body, across her chest, closing those fingers around her neck and caressing all the way back down again.

Power.

Harry had power and he liked the way it felt.

Once more, he traced a line around her throat, grasping again and squeezing just a little tighter as he thrust. A moan escaped her and she clutched him closer. Towards the point of no return.

Harry released his hold on her throat...with more than a little reluctance.

As they rolled apart a minute later after the second round, however, that itch still burned. Gone was the arousal, sated for now, but that *niggle* still wormed through him.

He could barely hear Sara's breathless laughter next to him, her high voice prattling on about who-gave-a-shit-what, as that annoyance surged again. He wasn't done. The purpose surged through him.

He was still so angry that Amelia had rejected him— even in the end, when she had resorted to lies to try and stop him—and humiliated him. Now, he realised why he hadn't wanted his hook-up that night to look anything like Amelia, because he couldn't bear to think of her, rejecting him again with such callousness. Over and over.

'Are you alright, James?' Sara said, breaking through his reverie. He sat on the edge of his bed, elbows propped up in his knees.

'What?' He glanced at her blankly.

'You looked miles away then.' She giggled again. That irritating sound seemed to screw into him. He glared at her, but turning away to pull her skirt on, she didn't notice. 'Fancy doing this again sometime?'

'Yeah, maybe.' He stood and tugged on his boxers, feeling strangely self-conscious—as though Amelia's judging eyes were on him right in that moment, and finding him wanting all over again.

Sara gathered her bag, slowly looping the handle onto her arm. 'Sure you don't want me to stay the night?' She cocked her head, smiling suggestively. 'That's the kind of wake up I like.'

'No.'

Hurt and indignation flashed across her face.

'I have work early tomorrow,' Harry muttered. It was a lie. He didn't care what she felt, but she was right. Maybe he'd want her again. She wouldn't come back if he pissed her off. 'Sorry.'

Sara's face softened, and she pushed her glasses up her nose. 'No worries. Show me out?'

Harry held the door open and followed her downstairs, opening the front door. She squeezed past, brushing purposefully close, her fingers trailing across his chest—now coated in sweat, not blood, though to him it seemed just as cold and clammy for a moment—and grinned. 'See ya, James.'

He closed the door behind her and stood in the dark hallway, his head hanging, his eyes slipping shut, as he took a deep breath in, and exhaled slowly. That anger was still there. The beast within that he had awoken, untamed and unassuaged.

Amelia wasn't enough.

He would never see her again—but he didn't want to

see anyone that reminded him of her either. He strode upstairs purposefully, snatching his phone up from the side of the bed and flicking to Matchmaker once more. Now actively seeking those he had flicked past earlier.

He wanted to end them all.

Get rid of *her*. Amelia.

Lingering in his mind.

Taunting him.

Humiliating him.

Rejecting him until the end.

CHAPTER TEN

D I Ward and DS Nowak were back in Bingley and parking up outside Amelia's workplace whilst DS Shahzad worked his magic tracking down Amelia's ex-boyfriend who Ward had moved to the top of the suspect list.

They entered *Smythe & Winter* estate agents through a charming old fashioned shop front that had been well preserved on the high street since the mid-1900s into the poshest estate agents Ward had seen. It didn't match what he knew of them—practical carpets as soft as grit, battered wooden desks, gaudy boards advertising houses in every available space, and garish colour schemes like bright yellow and green, or navy and orange. This place was sleek, cream, minimal, and with touches of ornate elegance in the decorative frames on the wall picturing some of the nicest houses Ward had seen. A few stood resting on an easel artfully placed on an angle in the front window. Inside, three oak desks—two filled and one empty—stood, each with a vase of white flowers upon them.

'May I help you?' a young woman said brightly, standing from behind the front desk—a few years older than Amelia, Ward thought, with blonde hair in a high ponytail and a smart office dress paired with a short, light wool cardigan.

'May I speak to the manager, please? Detective Inspector Daniel Ward. Detective Sergeant Emma Nowak.' Ward showed his warrant card.

'Of course,' she replied after a pause, looking between them, immediately curious and apprehensive. 'Olivia?' she called, retreating to the back of the shop, where a private office was sectioned off.

They followed as she beckoned, and filed past her into the room, where plush chairs sat opposite a grand, statement desk. A woman rose behind it, middle-aged, with shrewd brown eyes. 'How may I help you?'

'We have some questions to ask about one of your employees, Amelia Hughes, Ms...'

'Olivia Winter,' the woman supplied as Ward paused. 'Gemma, please would you fetch our guests some drinks. What can we get you?'

'Ah, that'd be grand, thanks. Tea, milk no sugar, please.'

'Coffee and a sugar please,' Nowak added with a smile.

They sat, Olivia sinking into an executive leather chair and almost lost behind the desk. 'What can I help you with, Detectives? I'm afraid Amelia isn't in today, it's her day off. Is something wrong?'

Ward cleared his throat. 'I'm afraid Amelia's body was found this morning, and her death is being treated as suspicious. It appears she was killed earlier this morning, possibly between about five and half seven.' Though, given Amelia's father's text history with his daughter, Ward wondered if they could shorten the window to a mere half-hour after seven that morning.

Olivia gaped.

'I appreciate this will come as a shock to you and her colleagues here. We're conducting initial investigations to understand what happened to her and bring whoever is responsible to justice.'

'I-I just can't believe it,' said Olivia, shaking her head, staring into nothing. 'She was here just yesterday—I mean, we were messaging in the work WhatsApp just last night. What happened?'

'I'm afraid we can't comment on an ongoing investigation. At this stage, I'm here to build a picture of her day-to-day life and relationships. How long did Amelia work for you?'

'She's been here three or four years now—one of my rising stars. I'd pegged her for management, perhaps opening her own shop, in a year or two, to branch out the business.'

'So she got on well with everyone here?'

'Yes, of course.' Olivia huffed. 'Well, except for Gemma. The woman who you just met—and, speak of the devil.'

A clatter outside. The door opened and Gemma entered, her attention on the tray of drinks she carried. She set down the tray on the desk, the crockery *chinking* together, and served the mugs to each person, leaving a plate of biscuits between them all. Ward couldn't help his stomach rumble. His favourite, chocolate Hobnobs.

'That'll be all, Gemma. Hold my calls, please.'

Gemma nodded and glanced curiously at the two detectives but didn't dare linger. She shut the door quietly behind her. Olivia waited a second, the pregnant pause stretching between them. Her eyes flicked from the door back to DI Ward.

'They're a funny pair, either thick as thieves or fighting like cats. Both ultra-competitive, you see. On the whole, it works well. They push themselves and it's great for the business. Their competitiveness can be a force for greatness both in the office and out—they jog together most days, and they're always bickering about personal bests this and that. Last week, they were both surprisingly unprofessional, though.' Olivia pursed her lips.

'Both were working on the same property, and client, as it turned out. Both claimed the sale—both wanted the tally on their monthly totals, and the commission. It was quite the to-do! We nearly lost the client and the sale. In the end, I had to step in to salvage it.' She shook her head.

'What happened?'

'It nearly came to blows, which, let me tell you, is *not* acceptable in my store.' Olivia's voice rang out sternly and Ward had no doubt that she had put paid to Amelia and Gemma's conflict. 'It was settled. Amelia had worked with the client first, and so I assigned the sale and commission to her. Gemma shouldn't have interfered.'

Nowak and Ward shared a glance. 'Do you think that Gemma held a grudge for that?'

Olivia's eyebrows rose into her fringe. 'You think...? Oh gosh, no. They were both fuming all week—they've only just started speaking again, but goodness, no. Gemma wouldn't do something like that. She's been here since seven this morning, anyway, I mean, surely, she couldn't, if you said it happened this morning?'

Ward sighed. 'You're right. Seven—you're certain?'

'Yes, I came to open up early. We have an event this weekend that we're preparing for. I think Gemma was trying to get back in my good books, to be honest.'

Gemma's early time of arrival at the office discounted her, in all likelihood, given that Amelia's father had received a text from Amelia just before seven, still apparently alive and well near her home address, a good distance away from the murder location on foot. 'Thank you for that. Is there anything else you can think of, anyone else that might have wanted to harm her?'

Olivia's lips thinned into a line. 'Only that arsehole of an ex-boyfriend of hers. He came by the shop a few times after they broke up. I had to threaten to call the police on him to get him to leave—harassment like you wouldn't believe. I felt so sorry for her. He was difficult enough, but the breakup was worse.'

'I don't suppose you have any information on where we might find him?'

'Sorry, no.'

'Would you mind if we spoke to Gemma in private in here for a few minutes?'

'No, of course,' Olivia murmured. She stared at the steaming mug on the desk, her fingers linking around it, but she didn't seem to see it. After a moment, she stood. 'I can't believe it.'

At Olivia's summons, Gemma entered, her expression closed and wary. Ward wondered how much she'd eavesdropped. 'Please, sit.' Gemma drifted to Olivia's chair, the only free one, and perched awkwardly on the edge of it.

Ward could see she felt uncomfortable sitting in the boss's chair, as it were. *Good. Put her on edge. If she has anything to hide, perhaps it'll be easier to tell.*

'Where were you this morning between five and seven-thirty, Gemma?'

Gemma swallowed. Her mouth hovered open—about to ask why it mattered, before she thought better of questioning the two detectives before her. 'At home. Asleep. I got up at a quarter to six, showered, dressed, ate breakfast, and drove to work for ten to seven.'

'Where do you live?'

'Riddlesden.' A village just up the Aire Valley between Bingley and Keighley.

'Thank you. Unfortunately, this morning, we discovered the body of your colleague, Amelia Hughes.'

Gemma's mouth fell open and her hand flew to cover it. 'What?'

'We can't comment on an ongoing investigation, but I have to ask you some questions, as you knew Amelia. Did you get on well with Amelia?'

'Yes,' Gemma said, glancing between the detectives with the bewilderment they had seen a thousand times before at the impossibility of the news they'd delivered.

'Always?'

Gemma hesitated. 'Well, I mean mostly.'

'Did you ever argue?'

She winced. 'Yes. Last week. I guess Olivia told you.'

'What happened?' Ward didn't confirm or deny—one of the best interview tactics he'd been taught. Never to give until he saw what they offered. And, when it was needed, tempt them with irresistible bait to get them to reveal more than they intended to.

A momentary flash of anger flickered across Gemma's face, quickly suppressed. 'I followed up on a client who'd gone cold on Amelia. The long and the short of it is, I did a load of leg-work and secured the sale, but Amelia claimed it and Olivia sided with her for awarding the commission and sales tally.' Gemma gritted her teeth, glaring mutinously at the floor.

'And how did that make you feel?'

'I was fuming!' Gemma spat out, and then subsided. 'But that doesn't mean—I would never hurt her! It's just work, just a house sale. I mean, sure, we all want our bonuses, but it's only money. I didn't... *kill* her.' Gemma's voice had fallen to a whisper, in case just by saying the word she would damn herself.

'Did you do anything together out of work?'

Gemma nodded. 'The occasional drink every now and then. Mainly we go running together—most days, actually.'

'But not today?'

Gemma frowned at him. 'No. Never on a Thursday. Thursday's my rest day as far as running goes, and it's her day off work so she runs later, and on a longer route than we usually have time for before work, across the river.'

'And does Amelia take her phone on these runs?'

'Yeah, of course. We track all our routes in Strava.'

Beside Ward, Nowak stilled, before she scribbled something else down hastily. If Amelia always took her phone with her... They would have to search her house to know for certain. But perhaps the killer had taken it, for whatever reason. It was a small lead, but one nonetheless.

Unaware, Gemma continued. 'We see who's tallied the most at the end of each month—loser buys the winner a drink. Why?' Understanding dawned on her. 'What happened?' she asked in a hushed voice.

'I'm afraid we can't comment on an ongoing investigation. Do you know of anyone who would have wanted to hurt her?'

She shook her head mutely.

'Thank you—you've been very helpful, and we are sorry to bring such terrible news.' He stood.

Gemma nodded, her eyes sliding to her hands in her lap.

'Just one more thing,' said Ward, turning back to her. 'Would you have her ex-boyfriend's contact details?'

'No.' Disgust curled Gemma's lip. 'I do know where he works though. Down the gym by the bypass near Damart Mills. You'll probably find him there admiring himself in the mirror or pumping himself full of steroids.'

This guy sounds like a real charmer. 'Thanks.' With a glance at Nowak, they left, thanking Olivia for her time. Ward gave her a card and asked that she call if she thought of anything else that might help them. They left as the ladies inside broke into a hushed furore over the unexpected news.

'Who next, then? Best friend, or ex-boyfriend?' Shahzad had found the ex-boyfriend's home details.

Ward chewed his lip. 'Did DC Shahzad get ahold of the friend?'

'He did. She says she can be free any time today, and sent her work address—an office in Crossflatts.'

'Let's try her, then. We don't want to spook the ex—not until we know more. I reckon her friend will be best placed to dob on anyone who had a motive.'

'You're hoping it will be the ex, aren't you?'

'Yep,' replied Ward grimly as they strode to the car park. They still had absolutely no evidence of who might have killed Amelia, save for a conveniently placed ex with a temper. The friend would hopefully confirm and add to what they had, allowing Ward and his team to draw the net closer around Darren Winston before he realised they were onto him. Then, they could pounce. 'Nice and easy to nail. We get answers quickly for the family, and we can start getting justice for Amelia.'

'Hear, hear.'

CHAPTER ELEVEN

D I Ward and DS Nowak pulled into another car park soon after, down the valley in Crossflatts, where a fairly recent development of office blocks stood at the end of the Bingley Bypass. In one stood a firm of insurance brokers where Sacha Lavigne worked.

Reception buzzed them quickly through into a waiting area, where a young woman in a sharp pinstripe suit greeted them. 'Hi, Sacha.' She stuck out a hand, shaking Ward's first, and then Nowak's as they introduced themselves. 'Please, follow me.' Her accent had a hint of French, Ward thought. He and Nowak followed as she led them into a small boardroom and closed the door.

'Annette told me. Please, how can I help?' As she faced Ward and Nowak, her hands wrung together. She'd been crying, her eyes puffy and bloodshot.

'You were her closest friend, is that correct?'

Sacha nodded. 'Yes. I just don't understand. What

happened? Why would anyone do anything like this to Amy?'

'That's what we're hoping you can help us find out. It looks as though she was killed on her morning run today. A dog walker found her shortly after,' Ward replied. He gestured to the table. 'Shall we sit?'

'Yes, of course. Sorry.' Sacha slid into a padded chair at the head of the table, and Ward and Nowak took the nearest ones to her.

'Can you think of anyone who might have wanted to harm Amelia? Anyone who'd argued with her, held a grudge, threatened her, that sort of thing?'

'No. She isn't the life and soul of the party, a bit abrasive if you don't understand her, perhaps, but everyone likes her.' Sacha thought, and lapsed into silence. 'She argued with Gemma at work last week, but they made up a couple days ago, by the sounds of it. A minor snipe over who got a bonus or some such thing.'

'Mmhmm,' said Ward, inviting her to continue. That was progress. It added promising weight that Gemma wasn't involved.

'The only person she didn't get on with was Darren—oh, that's her ex.'

'What makes you say that? You didn't approve?'

'God, no. They met at the gym. She had a trial membership—it wasn't her thing, but she met Darren there, he was one of the personal trainers she worked with. She has awful taste in men.' Sacha's serious expression broke into a smile that was half a grimace for a second.

'Not that she'd believe it, but when do people, you

know?' Anyway, he charmed the pants off her, which is impressive, the guy is an ape without two brain cells to rub together. It was a miracle he could form full sentences. She's never gone for a bulky guy before, so perhaps she wanted to see what the fuss was about, if you catch my drift. Things were great for a while, a few months, but he was a complete dickhead, and you can't fake that, you know?'

Nowak nodded sympathetically, and Sacha gave her a look that said, '*Men, am I right?*'

'No offence,' Sacha added quickly, glancing at Ward.

'None taken,' said Ward, a small smirk tugging at his lips. 'I meet my fair share in this job. What happened?'

'Well, like I say, he's a dickhead. There were only so many bunches of flowers he could buy, or drinks and dinners, or whatever, before she had to accept that he had a temper as short as you've seen, and when he got mad, he got *loud*. He'd smash stuff up, all sorts. Never laid a finger on her, that I know of. I'd bury him if he did.' Suddenly, she glowered, looking a good deal more frightening than her demure appearance had suggested, though Ward didn't think she would be able to take a steroid-pumped gym-bod as big as he was imagining. Still, he respected how protective Sacha was towards her friend.

'And they broke up?'

'Yeah. At last. *Bon débarras!* Good riddance.'

'Did he take kindly to that?'

'What do you think?' Sacha cocked an eyebrow. 'Of course not. He went through the whole range of emotions he had—sad, mad, back to sad, back to mad.' Her hands gestured emphatically as she spoke.

'Emotional maturity of a teaspoon.' She rolled her eyes. 'He was an absolute psycho, like a yo-yo. He smashed a few bits up...then he'd penned her a love letter...then he had a sit-down protest outside her door for a day, and after that, he went to win her back at work.'

'Sounds charming. When was this?'

'Oh, about a month ago. He's backed off now. Thank God! Think he finally got the message.'

'Do you think he'd hurt her?'

Sacha fell silent, chewing her lip. She knew what they were asking, what was unsaid. Did she think that Darren could have killed Amelia? 'I'm not sure.' She met Ward's eyes, and when she spoke, every word was carefully weighed. 'To my knowledge, he didn't hurt her before, when they were together, or since. But... he was wild. *Volatile.* And I'm not sure what he would be capable of if he lost his temper so far that he couldn't find it again.'

'That's very helpful.' In damning the ex-boyfriend, at least. 'Do you know where we could find him?'

'Sure. I don't have his home address, but I know where he works.' She pulled out a phone and Googled the address. 'Here.'

'Thanks.' Nowak recorded the company's details. They matched the brief description Gemma had given them.

'Is there anything else you can think of, Ms Lavigne?' Ward asked, straightening in his chair.

'I don't think so. I'm sorry.' Her dark eyes were grave

as they regarded the detectives, all trace of other emotion gone from her. 'Was it quick, do you know? Did she suffer?' She clamped her lips together, and Ward could see the well glistening in her eyes.

'I can't answer that yet,' he said quietly.

Sacha nodded and sniffed, dragging the back of her hand across an eye.

'Hey—there was one other thing.' Sacha looked troubled as Ward pivoted to look at her. 'It's probably not even worth mentioning.'

'Even the smallest thing can help.'

Sacha hesitated. 'Look, I'm sure it's nothing. Just... Amelia had this guy bugging her for a while. She didn't want to talk about him much, said he creeped her out. I only mention it because he catfished her on Matchmaker —you know, that new local dating app—for a date last week. It was a rebound after Darren, nothing serious. They chatted on Saturday and she thought why not go on a date that night? She was fuming when she realised it was the weirdo. Put him in his place and all that. I mean, it can't be connected—there's no way for this guy to have known exactly where she'd be, you know? But it's the only other thing I can think of.'

'Sure.' That was highly unlikely at best. They needed Amelia's phone to check that conversation—the one piece of evidence they didn't yet have. Ward hoped that on that day of all days, Amelia had left the phone at home. 'Did she say who this creep was?'

'No, only that he'd bugged her on her way home from work a few times. If it was serious, she would have told me. That's why I say it's nothing. I shouldn't have mentioned it.'

Ward handed her a card. 'If you think of anything else, please, ring.'

Sacha took it, staring down at the card for a second. 'Please find out who did this to my friend.' she said quietly.

Nowak answered before Ward could speak. Woman to woman. An unspoken sisterhood to protect each other —stranger and friend. 'We will.'

CHAPTER TWELVE

D I Ward and DS Nowak drove in silence back to Bingley, crossing over the bypass and turning off just on the other side, as the road pulled up the hill to Eldwick. An unassuming mill on the corner of the main road and a small, cobbled side-lane housed the *Fit Start* gym where Darren Winston worked. Ward parallel parked in a gap in the single line of cars wedged against the wall.

'Let's see what he has to say for himself,' Nowak said. Ward looked at her, an eyebrow raised at her dark tone. He let her lead as they approached a small stairwell that led down into a cellar level, the sign for the gym emblazoned above the door. She turned the worn and scuffed brass handle and pushed it open, stepping inside to momentary darkness before moving into a pool of fluorescent light from the strips on the ceiling above.

A dim corridor led to a large room where a series of huge weights were stacked against one wall, reflected into the room by the wall of mirrors behind them. Grunts emanated from all corners, as the gym members, five in total, spread out across benches and equipment on their various exercises.

Ward had never felt like more of a lard-arsed tub of misshapen fat in his life, compared to the sweat-slicked muscles in there. He sucked in his gut. It wasn't that he was unfit, *per se*, but he didn't go to the gym.

Perhaps he should start, he reasoned. His youth was fading after all, along with the ease of losing weight and staying fit. The microwave dinners right now weren't exactly helping his 'sausage stuffed into casing' physique. He wasn't sure if he could even run from one end of the rugby pitch to the other anymore.

'Can I help you, sweet 'eart?' One of the buffs ambled over, casually wiping the sweat from his brow with a rolled-up towel. His focus was all on Nowak, as though he didn't even see Ward. He towered over her, though she wasn't short, bulky in every way in contrast to her slender form silhouetted against him.

Nowak introduced them both, and the man's attention flicked to Ward. His eyes narrowed. '...Is Darren Winston here, please? We need a word.'

Equipment screeched as it scraped against the floor. A blur barrelled through the gym.

Ward moved at once, darting past the monolith of a man before them with a speed and agility that surprised even himself—and slightly reassured him that he wasn't beyond help physically—to give chase. He caught a brief glimpse of tanned skin, unnaturally bulging muscles, and short, spiked blond hair on a profile that matched Ward for height before the door slammed shut behind him.

Ward crashed through it a few seconds later, the door clattering on the wall from the force of his entry and the sound echoing like a gunshot down another hallway that turned at the end. Ward gave chase, and reached the fire door at the other end just as it flapped shut.

'Police! Stay where you are!' A voice bellowed, and Ward saw with grim relief that Nowak had already gone to flank him, having left the gym by the front door and bolted around the building to try and cut the man off.

Darren halted, his giant head swinging this way and that as DI Ward closed in behind him on the narrow lane.

'Darren Winston.'

'Yeah? Who wants to know?' the man said, wheeling on him, every word spat out.

Ward eyed him warily. They might have been the same height, but Ward was no fool. The guy would crush him like a fly if he tried to take Darren down—and he wasn't about to let Nowak in harm's way against the brute either. Ward couldn't arrest him—not without any evidence to go on other than speculation, but he didn't fancy trying to detain the guy in cuffs and cause a scene with a police van and PCs coming to help them subdue him.

'We need to chat. Care to come back inside quietly and tell me why you ran? We can do this the civil way, or you can have a brawl in the street and end up in cuffs. Your choice.'

Ward could see Darren's mind whirring as he looked between Nowak and Ward who flanked him on either side, drawing steadily closer. 'Fine,' he ground out, flexing his fingers into fists.

He led them through the still-open fire door that flapped against the wall, rattling with every strike. Nowak pulled it shut behind them, cutting off the road noise outside with a *clack* that echoed down the quiet hallway.

'In here,' Darren grunted, taking them into a small, dark room that smelled of stale sweat and weak cleaning products. He flicked the light on to reveal half a dozen exercise bikes pushed up against one wall and slouched across the room. He turned to face them, and folded his arms. 'What do you want? I didn't do anything.'

'Then why did you run?' Ward asked evenly, folding his arms too. Beside him, Nowak stood with her feet planted shoulder-width apart, exuding quiet confidence even in the face of the brute before them, who could quite probably tear them both a new arsehole if he chose to.

It was a chance to examine him in the poor light of the fluorescent tubes overhead, and the light filtering down from the high-set windows that emerged at kerb-level outside. Chiselled, muscled, Ward figured he'd appeal to some women. Short, spiked blond hair sat above carved cheekbones. Ice-chip eyes were set in shadow under thick brows. His muscled arms were sleek and blemish-free, bulging across his chest. Triangle shoulders met a short, thick neck with veins standing in relief.

He did not offer Ward an answer.

'I'm guessing you thought we were here about some steroids?' Ward took a stab.

Darren's narrowed gaze became venomous, and he gritted his teeth, shifting on his feet. The scent of cheap deodorant—Lynx Africa, that old classic—wafted across the small space. Ward had struck a nerve.

'Don't worry. We're not. Whatever stupid things you choose to put into your body, feel free. As long as you're not dealing the stuff, that is?' Ward left the question hanging.

Darren gave nothing.

Ward let out a dry chuckle. Smarter than he looked then. Maybe. 'Alright. Where were you this morning between five and half seven?'

'Why?'

'Answer the question.'

'Home. Bed.'

'Do you have anyone who can verify that?'

Silence. Darren's jaw clenched as he gritted his teeth. 'No. Why?'

'Were you at home?'

'Yes.'

According to Shahzad, that meant the bottom of Eldwick village, just up the hill. It placed him in the right area—not far enough away, anyway. 'Do you ever go running, Mr Winston?'

'Huh?' That caught him out. 'No.'

'Do you ever go across the river, say, up the Harden side of the valley?'

Darren stared at him blankly. Shook his head just a fraction.

'So you wouldn't have been there this morning, then, between say five and half seven?'

'No.' Ward could hear the frustration in Darren's tone. 'Look, I don't know what you're talking about. What the fuck do you want?'

'Easy,' Ward warned him. 'Do you still have any contact with Amelia Hughes?'

'What? No. Why? Did she report me? I didn't do nothing!'

'That speaks of a guilty conscience. When did you last see her, or contact her?'

Darren looked away, scowling. 'A couple weeks ago. She stopped returning my calls and texts. Haven't seen or heard from her since.' His voice was thick. Perhaps he had genuinely cared for her. Perhaps he still did.

'Did you ever have reason or desire to hurt Amelia Hughes?'

Darren's attention snapped back to Ward. 'What? No! Did she say that? Look, I know I get angry but I would *never* lay a finger on her.'

'Amelia Hughes was found dead this morning,' Ward said gravely, watching Darren for his reaction.

All the fight left the bigger man. 'What?' he murmured, his clenched jaw falling slack as he gazed at Ward with growing horror. '*Amelia?*'

Ward nodded.

Darren stared right through him for a long moment. 'I don't understand. She can't be,' he said at last, wetting his lips with his tongue. 'You think I did it?' he asked slowly, his focus coming back to Ward.

Ward said nothing.

'I didn't. I wouldn't ever hurt her. I love her! I want her back,' Darren insisted, his hands raising to tangle in that slicked hair, his eyes closing as his face contorted in anguish. 'No...'

'You have no alibi, a known temper, and according to your record, a history of drunk and disorderly, and steroid abuse. And, you ran,' Ward said quietly.

Darren covered his face with giant, meaty slabs of hands for another long moment before they dropped to his side. 'Fine. You got me. I know I shouldn't do steds, but I do. There you go. Bang me up for that. But Amelia...' his voice was surprisingly soft, a low growl with no bite, '... I'd never ever harm a hair on her head. What happened?'

He looked at them, pain evident in his eyes, the creases in his face, wanting answers. Answers that Ward could but wouldn't give him. Not when he was the only faint suspect they had to go on.

'We can't comment on an ongoing investigation. Stay close, Mr Winston. We might need to *chat* again.' Ward laced the word with a threat.

But Darren didn't rise to it. It was as though the giant had been struck dumb and rendered mute. He stared at the floor in the corner, as though unaware they were still there.

'Come on,' Ward murmured, and Nowak left with him. As they left, a guttural roar of pain and grief reverberated through the building behind them.

'What do you think, Nowak?' Daniel mused. His fingers drummed on the Golf's steering wheel and he gratefully inhaled the faded pine-fresh air freshener scent; a far more pleasant aroma than the stench of the gym.

'I think he's too rash to be able to act that well.'

'We have nothing to connect him.'

'Nope. Just that temper of his, which I can appreciate, but it doesn't make him a killer.'

Ward sighed. 'Bugger.'

'Bugger is about right, sir. I don't know that we have any other decent leads right now.'

Ward glanced at the clock on the dashboard. How was it past five already? 'We have more digging to do before we can discount him. I think we should check out his phone records, and search his home address. He is the only known antagonist for Amelia currently in the picture.' Ward sighed.

'I'll get on a warrant in progress right away, sir.'

'We've stayed late enough for now, anyway. I think we've done the rounds for today. Let's get back to the station, write all this up, see if Victoria managed to find anything else for us yet, or whether any of DC Shahzad's work's paid off. Hopefully, someone's done better than us, anyway. Hmm.' Daniel's phone buzzed insistently in his pocket. His fingers, on the keys and ready to turn on the ignition, withdrew. 'Hang on. Let me check this before we set off, in case it's urgent.' He fished in his jacket pocket for the phone.

'Oh, for fuck's sake...' Daniel ground out as he flicked out the phone to check the notification. It wasn't work, as he'd assumed.

CHAPTER THIRTEEN

'What's up, sir?' Nowak raised an eyebrow.

Seven missed calls and thirty-three unread texts greeted Ward. All from Katherine.

'The wicked bloody witch, that's what...'

DS Nowak had the good sense not to reply.

He quickly flicked through the texts, each one becoming more irate than the last at the impossibility of putting up with the damned dog and his destructive tendencies.

Daniel's heart sunk.

On the whole, most days, he had two worries on his mind. Firstly, the divorce falling through. Secondly, his pup.

Katherine had never been able to handle the boisterous Beagle. He'd always been Daniel's pride and joy, the child they'd never had. It had crucified him to leave the dog behind, but Katherine had been certain to leave him no choice in that either.

He checked the most recent voicemail last, not wanting to listen to the rest. Her shrill voice filled his ear.

'...come and get this damned dog right now or he's going out on the street. I've had enough!'

Daniel sighed, his eyes momentarily slipping shut.

'Everything alright?' Emma asked, although she'd probably heard Katherine's every word.

'Mind if we take a short detour?' Daniel smiled weakly.

'Not at all. Do I get to finally meet the famous Oliver?'

Daniel sighed, and started the ignition. 'Looks like it.' Looks like his pup was getting a late-night escape from prison pass—but Daniel was happy to attend if it meant he got to see Oliver, or better yet, take him away. He wouldn't get his hopes up yet, though.

———

He drove as fast as the speed limits allowed down the Aire Valley, past Keighley, past Bingley, past the World Heritage Village of Saltaire, gritting his teeth through the painfully slow twenty-miles-per-hour section and sped to upper Baildon. Through the maze of streets he drove, to the charming semi he had once shared with Katherine. A 1930s build with a generous bay window, arched open porch, and hydrangea-filled front yard that bloomed vibrant pinks and blues when in season.

The forever-home that he could no longer call his, once the divorce went through. Katherine still hadn't put it on the market, judging by the absence of a sign outside. She sure as hell wasn't taking the lot and leaving him penniless—with the dog a hostage to boot. She knew exactly how to make him sweat, damn it. *Stay cool, Daniel.*

'Nice house, DI Ward.'

Daniel grunted noncommittally. 'Stay here, DS. Sorry.'

'Not a problem, sir. I can go over my notes.'

The curtain twitched, and the door opened before he'd even closed the car door behind him. Katherine flew out in a blaze of fury and fluff—wrapped in a giant cream dressing gown against the autumn night's chill.

'What on earth are you doing turning up with another *woman* at my home?' she hissed at him, blue eyes wide and a snarl on her face.

'Well, I'm working. And I'm a police detective. Draw your own conclusions,' Daniel said flatly, stopping a good six feet away on the driveway and folding his arms. 'Why doesn't the house have a For Sale sign yet? We agreed to this weeks ago.'

'I've been busy. Some of us have to work!'

Daniel laughed mirthlessly. 'Oh, sorry, Katherine. Was it too stressful working from eight 'til four today on your marketing clients? Boo fucking hoo. You know I work longer hours, at all times of day and night, and we agreed *you'd* deal with it, because *you* can do the viewings, *you* live here not me, and *you* wouldn't trust me to sell a packet of crisps.' He raised his arms momentarily, gesturing at the night around them to make his point, then crossed them again. 'But if you can't be arsed, I'll handle it.'

'Fine,' she retorted through gritted teeth, her crossed arms matching his. 'I'll do it this week.'

'See that you do. Now, what's so important that you've pulled an on-duty detective off his murder investigation?'

She flinched at that, but pursed her lips and drew up indignantly. From inside the house came a howl and a bark. She whirled, rage pulling her features taut. 'Shut up, Oliver!' she shouted into the open doorway.

Daniel gritted his teeth, trying not to rise to it.

'Take the damn dog. I can't deal with him this week. I need to get the garden repairs done before we can get the house up for sale.' Daniel refrained from taking a cheap shot there—that if she had listed it when they'd agreed, she wouldn't have her present problem. 'And I'm getting a crate to put him in whilst I'm at work.'

'No, you're not.' The retort slipped out before Daniel even thought about it.

'Yes. I am,' she said flatly, with the hint of a smug smirk flitting across her lips.

'That's cruel,' Daniel forced out, his voice devoid of the rising ire inside him.

'It is what it is. It's happening. Deal with it. But since you want him so badly, he's all yours. This week only. I'll have him back Monday evening. Seven.'

'I'm not bringing him back if you're going to cage him.'

'Oh yes, you will. All his paperwork's in my name, Daniel. If you don't bring him back, I'm well within my rights to report him stolen. A police officer getting done for stealing a dog?'

'He's my dog too!'

But Katherine hadn't ceased talking. 'Wouldn't look good at all, would it? So, if you want me to call the police on you, by all means, do keep him.' It was a taunt as much as it was a threat. He didn't need the aggro of calling her bluff.

'I am the police. And if *you* want a prosecution for animal cruelty, keep talking,' Daniel growled.

'You're not the law, tough guy. It isn't illegal to crate a dog.' Katherine laughed that tinkling laugh that he'd used to love for its lightness, but now loathed for its self-satisfied smugness that made him want to punch walls. She turned and disappeared inside, returning a moment later with a bundled-up lead in one hand, and a knee-high Beagle held back by his collar in the other.

The moment Oliver saw Daniel, he lunged, almost pulling Katherine off balance and onto the ground before she yanked him back, a yelp cutting through his excited volley of barks. She let go of the collar and Oliver launched at Daniel, who dropped to his knees to accept the dog and a hail of snuffles and licks and whines.

Katherine forgotten for a moment, he smiled, filled with joy, a laugh escaping him as he swept the dog close for an embrace, rubbing his head and patting his flank. 'Hey, boy! Hey, Olly-dog, I missed you, little bud. Hey, I know. I know. Hey hey, alright, I don't need a bath, buddy, thank you.'

The lead hit him squarely on the shoulder as Katherine threw it at him, and Daniel's mood soured in an instant. 'He can shit all over your dump all week and rip your furniture. Might improve the place.' And then, she was gone, the door slamming behind her, leaving him alone on the darkened driveway with the sound of Oliver's tail wagging so fast it slapped against his leg.

'Come on then, Olly.'

Olly paused, and squatted.

Daniel turned away the moment he realised what Olly was doing–hiding his vicious grin from Katherine no doubt watching him through the spyhole on the front door. A nice little parting gift for her. He could have cackled.

'Come on, Olly!' he called innocently, opening the back driver-side door of the car mounted on the kerb. Knowing she couldn't accuse him of dog fouling if it was on their own private property. Out of the corner of his eye, he just glimpsed the offending turd sat proudly on the middle of the driveway. He wanted to guffaw, but held it in.

A moment later, Olly flew past him and leapt into the car, all paws and ears and wagging tail, to greet a delighted Emma who fussed and cooed over him. Olly tried to scramble from the back to the front.

Only when Daniel had shut the door did he relax into the car seat—letting out a belting laugh at Oliver's parting shot—and Olly scrambled over the centre console into his lap. Daniel breathed in the familiar scent—dog, mixed with the scent of what had been his home.

'It's good to see you too, little bud.'

Oliver plonked his bum down in Daniel's lap, and Dan guffawed. 'Mate. I can't drive with you there.' Oliver looked up at him, tail wagging and his tongue lolling out, seeming to grin too.

'Think he's happy to come back to the station with us?' Emma asked, raising an eyebrow.

Daniel snorted. 'Anywhere's better than with her. I'm sure he'll be made a fuss of.'

'Hmm. Well, good thing DCI Kipling doesn't pull night shifts or you'd be hung out by your balls for bringing him in.'

Daniel winced. 'Yeah, well, the less said about this to him, the better...'

'No one would, sir. You don't have to worry about that.'

'Oh, I'm not worried about your loyalty, I'm worried about DC Patterson's fat mouth blabbering things it shouldn't...'

'Speaking of DC Patterson...'

'I know. I know. He's a good kid.'

'Oh no, I'm not defending him. He's a prat,' said Emma primly. 'Just cut him some slack right now. I over-heard that his mum's ill and he's running her to the hospital all the time for tests and whatnot. So if he's a bit tardy, don't be too hard on him, sir. If that's alright?' she quickly added on the end, as though DI Ward would pull her for disrespecting a superior.

Daniel regarded her quietly for a moment, his hand resting on Oliver's neck. 'Nothing escapes you, does it, DS Nowak? Thanks for that. Good to know. Right. Let's get you back to the station, Olly-dog. Get you booked in. I think a nice spot under my desk'll have to do you for tonight. We have a murder to solve.' Daniel wouldn't be clocking off til long past the dog's bedtime with the stack of paperwork awaiting him. Long after his, if he were honest.

Dealing with the wicked witch always took the wind out of his arse.

CHAPTER FOURTEEN

The sad little pile of flowers mourners had left had grown since last night, the overnight rain had battered them mercilessly. Harry paused for a moment, pretending to stretch as he surveyed the scene.

Part of the bark had been harvested from the tree against which he had ended her—the part stained with her blood. Crime scene tape fluttered, though no one manned it. Aside from that, there was no other sign of what had taken place. It was as though all traces had gone, in just a day.

Her body was gone, the mud churned up around where he had let her fall. Busy with the passing of many feet—her death would be investigated. Harry wasn't stupid. He hoped he'd done enough to avoid suspicion, and that he hadn't left any forensic evidence behind. She hadn't even known his real name. He smiled. They'd never catch him. Now, or for the next ones.

Harry stood, letting that same rain drench him without mercy. He would have wondered whether the heavens cried for her loss, had the rain not been so angry and driving. He was angry too at the sight of all those flowers. The bitch didn't deserve them. He wondered if any of them knew what she had really been like. *Stuck up cow.*

It was strange to think that he had been here with her just a day before, and what had transpired in this quiet, unassuming place. He wore the same things—black, with those red trainers—all fresh from the wash. But what would not happen in the mirror of the previous day, was Amelia Hughes running into him again. He breathed in the damp, earthy scent contemplatively.

Morbid curiosity had drawn him back, though he wasn't sure whether it was a good idea. He turned to jog back the way he had come—across the bridge, through the corner of the park, and home. He dared not linger too long, in case anyone saw him. As he took the path to the river, bordering the field, he passed a dog walker and a pair of female joggers—all of whom he smiled at in a semblance of friendliness, so as not to arouse suspicion.

Drenched, he'd need to dry off before work, and his hair would be a frizzy nightmare because of it, but he didn't care. He didn't work at a Sainsbury's Local to have a glamorous job. He worked there because it was the only place that would take him after getting no A-levels and only a handful of GCSEs.

———

'Where were you yesterday?' hissed Jamal from the checkout, mid-serving, as Harry sloped into the store. 'I had to cover, missed my mate's birthday drinks, you knob!'

Harry shrugged. 'I was ill, sorry.'

'Yeah right,' muttered Jamal as he continued serving, scanning goods with one beep after another. 'Hangover more like.'

The day passed excruciatingly slowly between his breaks, though Harry had snuck his phone onto the shop floor to fix up his next Matchmaker—a hook-up and a body in one, he hoped. He flicked open an incognito tab. *How long does it take for someone to suffocate?* he typed. And then, *How long does it take to kill someone by strangulation?*

The only break in the drudgery was the frisson of horrified excitement passing through the town at the murder of one of their own, and a bright, pretty, young thing at that. It filled him with satisfaction to know the news of his act had spread already.

He gleaned what information he could from each passing customer who brought it up. The police were investigating. They had already spoken to someone in connection with it—that was a pleasant surprise he hadn't expected. They weren't even looking at him—not that they would have known where to look. Rumour was, it was the ex-boyfriend. Even better.

Harry made sure to pass on that helpful rumour with each customer he spoke to. He wondered if there was any truth to the stupid ex-boyfriend being blamed. He could have laughed.

The dickhead had that coming. He still felt strangely protective of Amelia in that regard—the man had treated her like crap. *He had this coming, even if he didn't do it.* It was nice to feel like he had a one-up on the man who she had seemed to think was his better.

———

Later that day when Harry had clocked out and returned home, it was more morbid curiosity that drew him down into the cellar to look at Amelia's phone. He took it up into the kitchen, using the dampened sponge in the sink to wipe off the traces of blood that had found its way into the cracks in the phone case.

It sat in his hands for a long few minutes as he contemplated, but he was too curious not to. *Can they find me, if they're looking?* He knew about cell towers—but they were imprecise.

He turned on the phone as a flicker of daring adrenaline rushed through him at his cockiness. The phone loaded—and a lock-screen showed. Pin protected.

Damn. Harry chewed his lip. He picked up his own phone and Googled for a hack, until he found one that would work.

He held down the home button and waited for Siri to appear. 'What's the time, Siri?' he asked, glancing at his phone for the next step. A few seconds later, and he was in. He grinned slowly. *How stupid. All that security, and you can bypass it with Siri and a few clicks? Idiots.* He snorted.

The phone buzzed in his hands as messages racked up—from unsuspecting contacts in the morning, and later that evening, nothing. A few concerned messages wanting to check she was okay... and plenty of notifications from social media feeds that Amelia Hughes would never see.

Harry flicked through her phone, totally absorbed, the screen's backlight the only illumination in the room as the sun set quickly over the deep valley. He was careful not to directly go into the messages—it would be impossible for Amelia to check her phone after she had died—he didn't want to alert anyone to his prying, the police least of all. He knew switching the phone on was a taunt of his own towards them, but they'd never find him off the cell tower triangulation.

Instead, Harry scrolled through her camera feed. Plenty of selfies, many of which he had already seen on her Instagram, and if he went back far enough, there were some more private images of a more suggestive nature that presumably she'd shared with her boyfriend. Altogether too much skin and lace for public viewing, but Harry rather enjoyed them. He'd have liked his own copies, but he wasn't stupid... sending them to himself would be far too obvious. With a sigh, he switched off the phone again.

That need was hungry anew. The need for power and control—and the desire to kill again.

CHAPTER FIFTEEN

It had been a funny old night. A late-night trip to the supermarket to pick up a couple cans of dog food and biscuits, some dog toys, a bone, and a microwave lasagne for himself. They had a quick meal and wind down before bed and settled in with the dog snuggled at his feet and soon snoring gently. Just like old times. The once-familiar weight now felt strange, and Daniel tossed and turned, his thoughts flipping between Oliver and the murder.

As yet, the team had absolutely nothing to connect Darren Winston with the murder of his ex-girlfriend Amelia Hughes—aside from a notorious temper, which didn't make him guilty. Would they find anything? Ward hoped that Victoria Foster's CSI team had found something useful in their investigation, or Baker in the post-mortem, for him to go on in the morning.

Then, his worries turned to the ever-present demon lurking in the darkest recesses of his mind. Bogdan Varga. And the lorry that would reach British shores sometime in the next week. Would they find it? Would they find it *in time*, if it contained live cargo? Would they be able to pin it on Varga? Or, like usual, would he walk free and disappear back to Slovakia until his crime empire in Yorkshire needed him again?

As usual, when it came to Bogdan Varga, DI Ward felt like he was sinking not swimming.

————

With regret, Daniel left Oliver the next morning, having tidied away everything chewable he could find, and leaving the dog with a bone. Oliver whined as he shut the door. Sealing away those brown, begging puppy-dog eyes that pleaded with him to stay. Howls followed him down the stairs from the first-floor flat. He fled before Ms Burrows from the flat underneath could figure out it was him that she'd be having a go at for the racket.

Ward yawned as he slid into his car. It was Friday, but that didn't matter, not really, to the police, who didn't work a traditional Monday to Friday. When was the last time he'd had a proper weekend? Ward couldn't remember. He worked six shifts on—two earlies, two mids, and two lates. Though, if he were honest, he worked a lot more hours than that to get the job done. More each year, as well, with the worsening of the funding cuts to the department. His day off was a fleeting thing, quickly come and gone with nary a moment to rest properly before his still-battered mind and body went straight back to it.

Today was allegedly a mid-shift, but he was still going

in for nine am. That was the problem with working in the CID field, and especially in the more serious HMET department, he could never really leave his work on the desk. Amelia Hughes and the victims of Bogdan Varga followed him home feeling almost viscerally present. They were spectres that sat waiting in his living room, stood at the foot of his bed, hovered in his kitchen, ever there in his waking and sleeping hours, calling him back to bring them justice.

They followed him all the way to work, sat quietly in the recesses of his mind. Waiting for their turn. For once, he was just grateful they'd allowed him a nightmare-free sleep, for a change. He couldn't remember the last time he'd slept so deeply and undisturbed.

'Morning all,' Ward called as he stepped into the blessedly warm office, a welcome heat against the autumnal nip outside.

'Morning, sunshine. You're chipper today, what's up?' Metcalfe said through a giant yawn from his desk.

Ward laughed mirthlessly. 'I'm not always a grumpy git, you know. Got a good night's sleep for a change.'

'Oh-ho, did you now?' Metcalfe winked suggestively.

'Mind out of the gutter, mate. Like I have time for any of that these days!' Dating was the very *last* thing on Daniel Ward's mind. Ward shrugged off his jacket, slipping it onto the back of his chair before easing into the worn blue fabric and switching on the machine. 'Anyway, sorry—I never made it back before you left yesterday. This murder's a bugger of a case. Hoping CSI or pathology can give us some leads. How did you get on with Varga?'

DS Metcalfe leaned back in his chair, crossing his hands across his belly. 'It's not arrived, and we haven't heard a whisper of it, if that's what you're asking. DC Shahzad hasn't found anything from his usual channels—if there's a big shipment coming in, the low-lifes on the street don't know—yet. He'll be in later to chip away at that.'

'Hmm.' Ward stretched his neck over the screen to call over to DC Norris. 'David, how are you getting on with the lorry?'

David stood and ambled over, spoon in hand and eating a small breakfast porridge pot. 'Morning, Daniel. Right. I did some digging and we might have a crumb, but I'm not sure of more than that. The registration of the lorry on the last shipment, and the one marked on the paperwork this time, belongs to an LLC—uh, Limited Liability Company—registered in Slovakia. Bratislava Logistics Solutions. A well-known shipping business there, reputably run, held in good standing. Except, there have been a spat of crimes lately with lorry plates being cloned.' Norris regarded him meaningfully before he continued.

'I've confirmed with CCTV from the last shipment arriving that the lorry that entered the UK did not match the lorry owned by this LLC. There was no company livery, the make and model were inconsistent, the age too.'

'So he's running a shadow shipping business?' Ward said, raising an eyebrow.

'Looks like it, sir. It would appear as though he has his own transport, and he uses legally registered plates from actual haulage firms—we don't know if there are others out there that he mimics—to travel on apparently legitimate business, according to the paperwork. But, obviously...'

'Fuck.'

'That just about sums it up, yes.' DC Norris had a far cleaner mouth than DI Ward, one of the few in the building who didn't swear at all, the result of a highly conservative upbringing. A quality Ward respected, but didn't know how on earth he managed. 'We may have just uncovered precisely how Varga transports all his illicit goods in such huge numbers without us realising.'

Ward blew out a long exhale. 'How the hell do we catch him? We don't have the capacity to check every single plate for every single haulage company at every single checkpoint, to see if the vehicles are legit. There are what, four to five million lorries a year going through forty UK ports—and more that we probably don't know about coming through smaller ones?' He groaned.

'Well, this is the thing. I don't know that we have to look at all of them. We already know he ships in via Northern Ireland and Liverpool—easy way to slip through the EU-UK border, right?'

'What's on the declarations?' Ward asked, straightening in his chair.

'Ah, well that's the beauty,' replied David, immediately catching his drift. 'The Customs paperwork is impeccable—Varga must have a specialist working on this —and all taxes on alleged goods inside are prepaid to the penny. It's all *legitimately* shipped items, it would seem, so I suspect he's cloning actual import paperwork from elsewhere on that count. If the lorries were opened, obviously the contents could vary, but of course, with a probably unregistered or stolen lorry running on cloned plates and no doubt an innocent or low-level lackey driving, there'd be no leads.'

'Varga would do what he does best—disappear, leaving no trace.'

'Exactly, sir. It makes me wonder if we don't have a wider shipping problem here, because if he can import immigrants without detection, then he can import cigarettes, narcotics, all sorts.'

The three of them—Ward, Norris, and Metcalfe who'd drifted over—fell silent at the implications. Varga could be a bigger criminal than even they had dared to dream—yet they had no way to catch him.

Ward tugged at his close-cropped beard and shook his head, his lips a thin line. 'It's the perfect setup. With border control as lax as it is, they can't check every shipment, and let's face it, it's a numbers game. He only has to get most of his shipments through—probably a small number, to be fair, though it'll be a lot higher than that—to make bank on it all. He can afford some collateral damage, and he probably expects it.'

Metcalfe leaned heavily on the desk beside Ward's. 'So, that means it doesn't even matter if we find this lorry. Not really. Not to him. It's worth a fraction of a percent of his operation.'

'Yup.' Ward gritted his teeth. Yet again, Varga seemed to brazenly taunt them with his audaciousness. Was there anything the bastard couldn't get away with?

'Er, I'm not done yet, sir,' DC Norris said sheepishly.

'There's more?' Ward said, grimacing.

'Afraid so, sir. That's just the *accompanied* cargo. There'll be unaccompanied cargo too—shipped in freight containers. Dropped at the port by, presumably, one of Varga's cloned lorries. Picked up on this side by...well, we have no idea. Could be a legitimate firm, or not. Either way, the cargo is less likely to be checked. The freight takes longer than an accompanied cargo, so if anything, I'd say if he's transporting live cargo, it would be via accompanied truck, but unaccompanied cargo opens him up to be able to transport a wider variety of things undetected.

'These containers *should* be checked by the driver to confirm they match the CMR document: the border force prefers that the drivers watch loading and lock the containers themselves, and they *should* also be checked at the port... but we know most of this doesn't happen in practise. Unaccompanied containers are not searched, unless there's a suspicion or reason to. Again, it's a numbers game, with the numbers skewed even more in Varga's favour.'

Ward leaned back in his chair, deflated. Some days, it was hard not to feel defeated by the tide of darkness that seemed so impossible to fight off.

'I mean, we can put a pin in that, sir. We don't have evidence to suggest he's doing that.'

'Oh, he will be. He's not stupid, I'll give him that.'

'Well, I didn't want to say that. Yes, probably. But there's no point worrying about it now. Not yet.'

'Right you are. We have this lorry, and it's a lead,

however small.' Ward smiled, but it was more of a grimace. 'How did you get on with Liverpool?'

'All ready, sir. We have their Major Crimes Unit on standby, and Customs and port policing will beef up numbers so we're ready when it drops. I'm on standby waiting for that CMR to be allocated to a ship. Expecting today or tomorrow, to be honest, with the current turnaround.'

'Cheers, David. Stay on it. Scott, when Kasim gets in, keep him on the chatter anyway. You never know, perhaps someone this end will be getting ready to receive whatever shipment Varga is moving.'

'Aye.' DC Norris and DS Metcalfe returned to their desks.

A frisson fluttered through Ward at that—the promise of the chase, however hopeless it felt with Varga weaving loops around them all.

CHAPTER SIXTEEN

D I Ward stood, stretching his neck and shoulders and wincing at the crack. It was time to get back to his other pressing case—Amelia Hughes. He grabbed a brew from the canteen and returned to his desk to open up the pathology report waiting in his inbox from Mark Baker, who had finalised the report that morning at seven am. Ward was grateful the man worked hard to help out the CID where he could.

He scanned the report. Amelia Hughes had indeed died from exsanguination. Blood loss caused by multiple stab wounds, several of which had pierced vital organs and major blood vessels. The dog walker Graham Bell had just missed the murder. From what Ward had already pieced together from Amelia's last contact with her parents, and the time of discovery, she had died probably minutes before his arrival. And yet, he had seen nothing. Heard nothing. Perhaps the killer had smothered Amelia so she couldn't cry out. That morning's fog had shrouded the killer's departure in such close proximity. Given the brutality of the attack, perhaps that had ended well for Graham Bell.

Baker had also noted the multitude of defensive wounds on Amelia's forearms and hands. She had tried, however fruitlessly, to defend herself. From the angle of the stab wounds, and the sites of the defensive wounds, Baker had established that the killer had been taller than Amelia, predominantly striking down at her torso. That further ruled out the dog walker, then, Ward realised, for Graham Bell had been a diminutive man. It did not, however, rule out Darren Winston. He would have towered over Amelia, and been strong enough to restrain her with ease. Incapacitate her.

Ward leaned back in his chair. They needed the search warrant for Darren's property to be approved.

Baker also noted that the victim and attacker were likely in extremely close proximity from the depth and force of the wounds that had penetrated right through her in some cases, with the long, bladed article the killer had used. Another tick against Winston, in Ward's eyes, the huge, muscled man was definitely capable of such brute strength.

The weapon was a large kitchen knife, Baker reckoned, though CSI hadn't found anything at the scene. Either way, the attacker would have been drenched in Amelia's blood—hard to hide. Impossible, Ward would have argued, had their killer not then simply vanished.

An appeal had gone out yesterday afternoon for witnesses and information, but as Ward scanned the information that had so far been reported and collated, there was little to go on. There had been several runners out, male and female, all ages, in the park across the river, at the time. The killer could have been one of them, or none. Ward could hardly imagine anyone blending in, covered in blood and wielding a huge knife.

He tapped his fingers on the desk, deep in thought, as DS Nowak entered the office. 'Morning, sir.'

'Hmm? Morning, Emma. You alright?'

'Yes, thanks. Are you on with the Hughes case?'

'Yeah.'

'Oh, by the way, Jake is back,' Nowak added as she filed past to her desk.

Ward glanced at her and nodded. DC Patterson had taken a few days of unexpected holiday to care for his mother after her discharge from hospital following surgery. No doubt the lad would be knackered and in need of rest, but Ward couldn't give him that. 'Good. We'll need all hands on deck with this one.'

'No doubt. I arranged with Amelia's parents to meet them at her house today to hand over their spare key. CSI will be heading over too to do a full sweep on the place, see if we can find her phone or anything else. I forgot to mention last night, her parents forwarded her contract details, so I've requested more information from the phone company. If the phone's not at her home address, then we might be able to track it to some degree, or see if the person who attacked her has accessed her data on there, or contacted her in any way. You know, if she was backed up to the cloud or anything, we might have plenty of content to go on.'

'Excellent. Can you get Jake on with tracking her last movements? Contact the running pal at work for

Amelia's Thursday route, and see if there's any CCTV to back up the timings of her being in that area, and perhaps find something more.'

'Of course!' Emma lit up. 'She said they used Strava to track their runs. It might be that Gemma can see it in *her* running app—maybe friends can share their routes.'

Ward nodded, unconvinced. 'Sure. Worth a try. Stay on the phone company—that could be critical. I'll meet with Amelia's parents and take a look at the house with Victoria and her team. Chase up the search warrant too. I'll be close to Darren's and the profile of this attacker fits him perfectly. We need access to his home to search for any evidence.'

If he's not already destroyed it. The man's show of grief had seemed so raw and real, but that didn't mean Darren hadn't done it, deliberately or in a momentary lapse of control.

'Course, sir. I'll let you know if there are any developments.'

————

Ward remained in his car parked behind the CSI van outside Amelia's home address, a new-ish development of modern terraced houses that he recalled seeing one of which for sale on Rightmove when he and Katherine had split. He'd passed, knowing he couldn't afford it without their house sale to fund a deposit, but they had been excellently done out. He remembered admiring the view onto the canal behind the houses.

Whilst he waited, he scrolled the news, but didn't

pay attention to the headlines—one depressing sentence after another. He flicked onto Facebook instead. Most of his colleagues were on there, a few school friends he never spoke to anymore, and some family too, including his brother over in Manchester. Daniel paused over a picture of a sloshed looking Sam—younger than Daniel, but with bigger shadows under his eyes, and a smile that never reached them—with his arm around a different woman to the week before.

Daniel made a point to message Sam every week, though he rarely got anything back. Sam had never really found a way to deal with their mum's death, or their father's abuse. He'd succumbed to drugs and drink, mostly living month to month with this girlfriend or that, or couch surfing. Daniel had tried to help him. But he'd had to accept that he could only ever lead the horse to water.

He fired Sam a text anyway.

Hey bro. How are you?

He didn't wait for a reply—he'd be lucky to get one.

A text did ping from Nowak. *Got the warrant on Winston's home address. You're clear to search.*

Ward's stomach flipped at that. He had to wait for Mr and Mrs Hughes, and Foster from CSI, but as soon as he'd scoped Amelia's house, he'd search Darren's. The hulking figure of the man loomed in his mind. Ward wasn't daft enough to think he could take the man on. He hoped he'd not need backup.

A grey estate pulled onto the street, and Ward looked up, to spy Amelia's parents, Bill and Annette Hughes in the front. He slipped out of his car, raising a hand to greet them as they pulled up onto the kerb outside Amelia's house.

'Morning. Thank you for coming,' he said, making no attempt to comfort them as Bill opened the door for Annette and helped her out of the vehicle. They were both red-eyed and waxen, looking as though they'd aged a decade overnight in their grief. 'I'm afraid you won't be able to come inside, not until our Crime Scene Investigators have gone over everything, just in case there's anything pertinent to our investigation. When we're finished, I can return the key to you and you're free to make whatever arrangements you need.'

Bill nodded, Annette sniffing loudly beside him. They looked at the house for a long moment in silence, before Bill took a deep breath. 'Here you go.' He handed a key over with a keyring attached—a basic plastic thing with an estate agent's branding on it. Most likely Amelia had never used it.

'Thanks.'

'We'd best go, then,' said Bill, though he dithered. Ward understood why with a rush of sympathy at Bill's next words.

'I'm going to formally identify her.' His voice sounded hollow and lifeless at the prospect of attending the hospital to confirm what he never ever wished to— that his daughter was dead in the most awful way, and they would have to bury their own child. Worse still, that they would have the indignity of a drawn-out wait to do so, whilst investigations were ongoing.

There was nothing to say to that, but Ward murmured his condolences anyway, empty though the words felt. Bill and Annette drifted back to the car, and without a further word, or a look towards Ward as he raised his hand in farewell, drove off.

Victoria slammed the van door shut, her attention following him before she walked over to Ward. 'Morning.'

'Hey.'

'You open up, I'll grab my things. We can chat inside.'

'Oh?'

She didn't reply.

Ward did as she'd instructed, unlocking and opening the door. He froze as a beeping emanated from the panel, and looked down at the key in his hand, with relief noticing a small tag that had hidden behind the keyring. A fob. He waved it at the control panel, which beeped at him once more and flashed, before falling silent. Ward relaxed. The last thing he needed was to have to call Amelia's grieving parents back to disable the alarm.

He stepped inside, the fresh vanilla scent of a diffuser plugged in at the bottom of the stairs washing over him. For a moment, he looked around, picking out little details in the still, silent house. Cream carpets lined the stairs to an upstairs landing. Rich wooden laminate stretched throughout the ground floor, pulling him into a long, slim living-come-dining space with a cream leather sofa and chair, and oak dining furniture. A sleek, modern, white bookcase stood against the wall, housing a variety of titles he couldn't read from where he stood. Above a simple, modern fireplace hung a flatscreen tv, perfect to watch from the recliner sofa.

'Ahem. Shoe covers. Gloves. Come on, do we have to do this again?'

'Ah, sorry.' Ward had the good sense to wince.

Victoria simply thrust some at him, staring him down whilst she waited, already fully garbed in her paper suit. When he straightened, ready, she nodded him in. 'Go on, then. And don't touch anything.'

Ward moved into the living room and stood aside so Victoria could pass. They swept the property in silence together, looking for anything out of the ordinary—but it was as though the house were frozen in time. In her bedroom, Amelia's clothes were laid out neatly—underwear on the bed, a cream chiffon top and pale-blue skinny jeans hung from the mirrored wardrobe door.

In the bathroom, a folded towel lay on the sink with Amelia's watch—that she had presumably taken off to go running. Though he couldn't see a phone anywhere, the charging cable next to the bed snaked out across the carpet. The bed was already made, ready for the next night, though she hadn't returned to it, with no sign that anyone else had been there. The second bedroom, an office space, lay still and undisturbed.

Downstairs, the lounge was tidy, a blanket strewn across the sofa the only sign of messiness in the otherwise pristine space. In the kitchen at the back of the property, Amelia's breakfast awaited. A crusted, dried-up bowl of overnight oats that had sat waiting for her a day too long, a spoon neatly laid next to it on the work surface. An empty mug with a spoon of coffee and a dash of milk in it. The kettle was heavy with un-boiled water. It was all organised precisely how Amelia liked it, no doubt. Ready for her to return from her run and pick up her life.

Nowhere was there any obvious sign of a disturbance, or anyone else in the property who might have accompanied Amelia on that fateful last run. Ward glanced around the open-plan living area. Aside from the touch of breakfast and that messy blanket, it could have been a show home, for there was no soul in the place. A different kind of empty to Ward's apartment, which he'd simply neglected to make into any kind of home. The flat was nothing more than a place to sleep, eat, wash, dress. Perhaps he ought to make a better effort. This house, on the other hand, was flawless in its cold lack of personality. Modern and minimalist was how Amelia had felt at home. Ward perused the titles on the bookshelf by the television. Titles on the Danish concept of *Hygge*, Marie Kondo's minimalist theories, and some women's fiction jumped out at him.

Victoria's paper suit rustled as she passed back through the kitchen towards him. 'I'll drop the key off with your lot when I'm done. You don't need to be here.'

Ward turned, raised an eyebrow at her. 'Nothing suspicious?'

'No. Same conclusion as you—I don't think the killer was here, or with her when she left the house. There's nothing I can see to point to that. I will, however, go over things with a finer tooth comb before I leave it. Bins, bedsheets, that sort of thing. Always useful to double-check, then there's no doubt later.'

'Alright, thanks. I'll canvas the neighbours before I

head off, see if anyone heard or saw anything. Do you have any updates from yesterday's material?'

Victoria adjusted her surgical mask. 'Sure. Not everything's come back yet, hence why you don't have a report, but we have some preliminary findings, perhaps they'll help. Don't touch that!' she snapped as Ward reached out for one of the books.

He held his hands up in surrender.

She glowered at him. 'Honestly, I *just* think you're getting somewhere and then you go and do something daft.' She waited until he stepped away from the bookshelf.

'Right. The victim had on her a small purse with her driving licence and a five-pound note in it. There was no phone present. You know all this?'

'Yes.'

'Best to check. Now, we found no murder weapon on or around the site, and no one has reported anything unusual—I checked with HMET on that this morning in case we needed to pick anything up. I also checked with Baker for the likely size and shape of any weapon, and we haven't found anything that could cause the wounds he saw. So, we're short on that count, which is a shame. It might turn up.'

Ward shrugged.

'We do know that the site where the victim's body was found was the kill site, purely from the blood analysis there. There's no escape of blood anywhere else, no trail, and the amount is consistent with the death occurring there. That's still important to note, though it closes some avenues of possibility.'

'She wasn't transported there and dumped already dead.'

'Exactly, and that's key. We would have found tyre tracks, heavy footprints, drag marks or blood elsewhere, for sure, if that was the case.'

'The killer still could have left by vehicle, though.' To a point, both sides of the beck were accessible by a track.

'That's up to you to figure out.' Victoria regarded him coolly.

Ward pursed his lips. 'Anything else?'

'Yes, two key things, which is why you haven't already got the full report. Firstly, we were able to capture a partial fingerprint from the attacker left in Amelia's own blood on her arm, possibly as he moved her arm out of the way to give himself another clear shot. I have someone working on translating that and then comparing it to any suspects you can hand us.'

'Might have one. The ex-boyfriend is at the front of the line. He has priors—his prints are already on the system.'

'Send them over. We'll take a look as a matter of priority. That could really help, but it's not the best piece of evidence we have.'

'The hair?' Ward remembered her triumph the day before.

'Yes. In the struggle, the victim managed to capture some excellent evidence. A hair that definitely doesn't match hers. It was tangled in her fingers. It's long, a few inches, curly, dark, and coarser than hers, which was all pulled back into a bun anyway. So, the only logical conclusion I can draw is that it's most probably her killer's. Upon further examination, it *did* have the follicle attached, which means we could send it off for DNA profiling.' Victoria smiled smugly.

'When will we know?' Victory or not, the data was all that Ward wanted. Even as he thought about the ex-boyfriend, and thought about how it would damn him, the man's short, spiked, blond hair came to mind. Very different from the longer, curly, darker, coarse hair Victoria had described. Either way, it would give them answers. Perhaps just not ones they wanted or liked. And perhaps it would only bring more questions.

'End of today.'

'Great. Anything else?'

'No. You're *welcome*.'

'Cheers.'

Ward left to knock around at the neighbours', and see if anyone had heard anything, wondering if Victoria would ever see him as anything other than a nuisance— and wondering if he would ever feel at ease in her crotchety presence. The woman reminded him far too much of Katherine to be comfortable—outspoken, confident, and entirely disdainful of him.

The neighbours revealed little, for it seemed to be a quiet street and not like the streets of old where everybody knew everyone's business. Half didn't even know who Amelia was, or which house she lived in. However, it took what felt like an age to disentangle from the man next door, who complained vociferously at Ward for a good ten minutes solid about the noisy sex and shouting that came from Amelia's house sometimes, and the fact she dared to park across the halfway line between their driveways sometimes without thought or consideration for him. *That* brought on a rant about the 'youth of today' and 'bloody snowflakes.'

Shameful, lazy, disgraceful—Ward took each of the comments and criticisms and filed them away, wondering if the man had any empathy when it came to the dead and speaking ill of them. What good would it really do for the man to moan of her now? The things he spoke of didn't matter one bit when Amelia Hughes had lost her life—and in such an especially cruel way. People would never cease to amaze him with their ignorance and callousness.

When Ward had at last detached from the man, with no small amount of relish, and with Foster having no further need of him, he raced up to Darren Winston's home in Eldwick. He hoped that, with it being mid-morning, the man would still be home so he wouldn't have to batter down the door, as unlikely as it was. He rang Darren from the car, only a few minutes out as he sped up the hill towards the village of Eldwick.

'Hello?'

'Darren, it's Detective Inspector Daniel Ward. We met yesterday. Are you home right now?'

'What? No. I'm at work.'

'Can you get home, please? I have a search warrant for your address, and I think we should talk.'

'You *what*? You're not going in my house, you have no right!'

'Sorry, Mr Winston. I have a warrant. I can either enter with you or without you. I'm giving you the courtesy of letting you know so you can come and open up, and I don't have to the batter the door down.'

'It's a shared house, you can't—'

'I'd get home quickly, please.'

Ward cut off the call as a string of expletives fired down the line. *Well, there goes the notion of doing this calmly, then.* He rang Nowak and updated her—that he'd be meeting an irate Winston and hoping to search around and have a chat single-handed.

'Well, rather you than me,' she sniped.

'Gee, cheers.'

'Good luck, sir,' she said with mock sweetness, after establishing that he didn't want any backup. He'd reasoned that by the time anyone from the office arrived, he'd be beaten to a pulp anyway if he needed the help.

Ward pulled up outside a nondescript semi-detached house in the charming village. A house share, Winston had said. Ward wondered who else lived there. He'd find out before Winston turned up, after all, the warrant gave him the right to search.

He knocked on the door and a young man, early twenties, wearing a slouchy hoodie, joggers, and with rumpled blue hair, answered.

Ward showed his warrant card. 'May I come in, please? I have a search warrant for this address in relation to Darren Winston.'

The man tensed.

'I'll need to search any shared living areas, and his private room.'

'Not my room?' the man queried, his eyes narrowing.

'Not unless you're doing something you shouldn't be, sunshine,' Ward replied flatly, staring at him.

'Nope,' said the man lamely, and stood aside to let him in. The faint smell of weed inside was Ward's clue as to why, but with a murder to solve and the likes of Varga on his books, Ward wasn't about to try and take the kid down for personal possession.

'What areas does Mr Winston have access to?' He glanced into the living room next to the entrance hall, and he could spy a dining room and kitchen at the back.

The man hung back in the shadowed hallway, beside the stairs. 'Er, all downstairs, and he has one of the rooms upstairs. Oh, and we share the bathroom.'

'How many people live here?'

'Three, um, me, Darren, and Fiona. We house share.'

'Who owns the house?'

'Landlord.'

'I see. Anyone else stop at this property in relation to Mr Winston?'

'No.'

A conversation with a plant pot would be more forthcoming. 'Right. Well, I'll take a look around down here, then upstairs in Mr Winston's room or any shared areas.' He pulled on latex gloves, glad for once that he'd remembered some, and swept through the living spaces downstairs. If the house had a theme, 'messy' would have been it. Used cups and plates scattered about, alongside the detritus of living—receipts, boxes, bills, gaming stuff, DVDs, coats, and hoodies laying on the back of sofas and chairs like lounging cats. Wooden horizontal blinds shaded the room from view from the street outside and cast the space in a dull half-darkness. In the back, the dining room was much the same, the table piled high with detritus and a battered couch shoe-horned into a corner next to a bookcase stuffed with random items, ornaments, and stacks of books. It looked like any other home where people shared space that he'd seen, nothing jumping out at him as out of place or recently moved to conceal or dump something.

The kitchen was surprisingly tidy, though there was hardly room to swing a cat. *No knife block*, Ward noted, and an assorted jumble in the cutlery drawer of knives with one small sharp kitchen knife.

Large tubs of protein dominated one corner of the counters.

'These Darren's?' Ward jabbed a thumb in their direction.

'Yeah.'

Ward carefully opened each of them, peering inside, the contents exactly as stated on the exteriors. Still, the chocolate, vanilla, and strawberry scents rising from the protein powder inside was a pleasant interlude to the tang of cannabis permeating the air.

The bin was almost full, stuffed with ready-meal containers, paper, cellophane, foil, and some crumpled beer cans. The usual trappings of a home.

'Take me to Darren's room, please?'

'It's locked. We each have a lock on our doors. Only he has the key.'

Ward would have to wait for Darren to return. It would be soon, if the big man had any fear the police would batter down his door. 'The bathroom then.'

The man traipsed up the stairs after him. Ward poked around a small bathroom, finding no hint of anything untoward there either. Of course, he hadn't expected to in a shared house. Anything Darren had that was personal would be behind the locked door on the landing, that led into the front bedroom.

The front door crashed open downstairs. 'Steve?' Darren bellowed.

The blue-haired man winced. 'Up here, Daz. Police are here, mate.'

Darren thundered up the stairs, nostrils flaring.

Ward held his hands up. 'I'm not here to cause trouble, son. I need to take a look in your room, that's all.'

Darren's knuckles cracked as his fingers flexed into a pineapple-sized fist. Slowly, he held out a bunch of keys and barged past Ward to open the bedroom door. 'There. I've got nothing to hide.' As he stepped back, Ward noticed Darren shaking with fury. As expected, perhaps, given what others had said about Darren's short temper, but the man didn't seem stupid enough to try and obstruct Ward, physically or otherwise.

'Thanks.'

He went into the bedroom, flicking on the light, for the curtains were drawn, cutting out all light except for a thin crack that crept in around the edges. The bedroom wasn't huge but it was tidy, unexpectedly so. Perhaps Darren wasn't the culprit for the mess downstairs. The double bed was neatly made, the navy covers plain and clean. Underneath the bed, assorted boxes containing shoes, clothing, and some bric-a-brac from Darren's childhood, Ward surmised from the collection of child-like trophies dated over ten years prior.

Behind him, Darren paced the small upstairs hallway like a caged beast, the floor creaking under him with every step.

In the wardrobe, Ward found an assortment of clothes and more shoes on the bottom. A chest of drawers held underwear, socks, day-to-day clothes, and gym gear. Weights, resistance bands, kettlebells, and some smaller gym equipment were wedged between the wardrobe and the window.

Ward approached the bedside. He carefully peeled back the bedding, looking around the corners of the mattress.

'What are you even looking for, anyway?' Darren burst out angrily, pausing his pacing.

'Evidence,' said Ward grimly. 'Or lack of it.'

'You think I did it, don't you?' Darren turned back to him, his face in a monstrous grimace.

'I can't comment on an ongoing investigation, son, but we have to explore all possibilities.' Ward met the man's eyes levelly.

'I couldn't hurt her. I never could!' he burst out. 'I loved her more than anything. I just...She couldn't cope with my temper. I was trying to work on it. I *am* trying to work on it. I wanted her back.' The last sentence came out as a pained whisper.

Ward saw the true raw pain in his eyes. The man was telling the truth, he was sure of it, and yet...that temper was nasty. It would take so little for Winston to lose control, to do something he regretted. Ward wrestled with his instincts. The natural path was to chase the loud, angry ex-boyfriend. It was an obvious choice. But that long, brown, curly hair that Victoria had found on Amelia's body didn't fit Darren and his short, spiked, blond hair. Not at all.

Ward replaced the bedding, and turned to the bedside drawer. The way Darren tensed, shifting towards him, though Ward stood across the room and bed from Darren in the doorway, made Ward tense too.

Pills rattled in the small drawer as he opened it. He raised an eyebrow at Darren.

'Steroids,' muttered the man, glaring. 'Personal use.'

Ward estimated the number of pills—a couple dozen —in the drawer. He nodded. 'Alright. I won't lecture you.' Darren was big enough and ugly enough to take care of himself, whether he wanted to put stupid things into his body was his own choice. It wasn't illegal to own them for personal possession, at least.

Inside the drawer was a passport, Darren's, Ward checked, a half-used pack of condoms, and some bills, Vaseline, a small assortment of knick-knacks like rings and hair wax. A small black box caught his attention, right at the back of the drawer.

He pulled it out. Flicked open the hinge. Inside, nestled on a bed of soft navy velvet, was an engagement ring. A solitaire of white gold with a single diamond gleaming in the centre.

Tears flowed freely down Darren Winston's face as he saw that box.

You were going to propose to Amelia Hughes,' Ward said quietly. It wasn't a question.

Darren nodded.

Ward's heart sank. He couldn't help but pity the man, pity his predicament, and now, he would never get the love of his life back. His thoughts on Darren Winston's guilt were wavering, a deliberate attack seemed unlikely. A momentary lack of control still possible, but... he looked at the ring in the box in his palm once more. He wasn't sure anymore. Ward slipped the box shut and placed it back where he'd found it in the drawer, before closing it.

Ward's gazed passed around the room once more. He hadn't missed anything. There wasn't anything to find— no bloodied clothing, nothing that could match the black fibres Foster had found transferred to Amelia in the struggle, and certainly no bloody knife. Only an engagement ring that Amelia Hughes would never wear, and her ex-boyfriend's broken heart.

CHAPTER SEVENTEEN

In pensive silence, without even the radio on for a change—because for some reason, he couldn't stand to listen to the peppy presenter and upbeat pop that day—Ward returned to the police station to log what little updates he had, and check in on the team's progress. DC Patterson sat hunched at his desk, three empty coffee cups next to him, and uncharacteristically dark shadows under the young man's eyes.

'Alright, Jake?' DI Ward greeted, for once, sparing him a ribbing. Jake had spent a long night at the hospital with his mother, Ward surmised.

'Yes, sir,' Jake said wearily. At Ward's prompt, he launched into an update.

Patterson had come up blank on CCTV in the area, though that was unsurprising. Some of the town was covered, but not in the rural area across the river. Contact had been made with each of the houses nearby, but again, nothing—no noise, no sightings, nothing out of the ordinary, and nothing on the home CCTV systems a couple of the larger houses had.

There had been one sighting of a possibly suspicious male in the immediate timeframe. A dog walker had reported in that a young Caucasian man in his twenties, dressed in a dark hoodie and shorts with red trainers, who'd had his hood pulled up even though it wasn't raining at the time, had nearly trampled her and her dog off the path as he jogged through the trees in Myrtle Park. Average height, average build, maybe dark hair. No other sightings of the man had been reported, however, nor more identifying details, as he had passed in a blur.

Ward sucked the inside of his cheek. *Could be connected. Could just be a snarky dog walker pissed off at someone being rude.* There was no CCTV around that area of the park, nothing to corroborate her account of the jogging man. *But it doesn't sound like it could be Darren.*

Then, Ward checked in on DS Nowak, who returned to the office just after him. She had been to take a statement from Bell, the dog walker, to detail his story further, and confirm timings, plus verify his alibi with his wife—as much as one could without any further corroboration. The man was a wreck that day, and his wife beside herself with worry, according to Emma. Understandable, given what he'd found. As Ward listened, he wondered at the man, could he be the culprit?

After all, first on the scene, and having not heard any disturbance or screaming... it was *too* neat. And yet, when Ward thought about how the man had reacted, and seen the shock setting in, he didn't think Graham Bell was a cold, calculated killer able to put on an act like that. Not to mention, the man would have been covered in blood, impossible to hide in such a short time without CSI finding some evidence.

And Graham Bell was a diminutive man. Baker's autopsy had details that the arc of the knife wounds had come from higher up, as though the perpetrator stood taller than Amelia. The man was in the right place at the right time, but Ward was more inclined to believe he had been the very unlucky first witness on the scene, not the perpetrator. Mind, Ward had been wrong before. Perhaps best not to discount him completely.

Nowak had also spoken to Gemma, Amelia's work colleague, about the running app they used to compete each month on miles run. 'Not good news, I'm afraid,' admitted Nowak. 'Gemma can only see the runs that Amelia completes and shares, so an incomplete run isn't logged. Without Amelia's phone, we would have no idea where a particular run ended.'

'Alright. I suspect it ended where she was murdered. We know her phone went offline shortly afterwards, so I highly doubt the app could tell us anything we don't know. We have enough of an idea of when the murder occurred, from Bell's discovery and Amelia's texts to her parents just before. That'll have to be enough. I suppose there's nothing more the app would have told us, except to shorten an already brief window.'

'Darren's still number one for now,' Nowak mused, staring into nothing as she perched on her chair with Ward leaning against the desk beside her.

'Aye.' He shared Victoria's promising forensic leads. Yet, however much he hoped they would neatly pinpoint

Darren, he agreed with Victoria's gut feeling that it was the murderer's hair. If that was the case, just on the physical description of the hair, and what he had observed of Darren's appearance, then the murderer wasn't Darren.

'But it's such a small piece of evidence, it might be entirely coincidental. It could be him after all.'

'I agree,' said Nowak, sighing. She reached forward to take a sip from her glass. 'If only we had her phone. It would give a much clearer picture.'

Ward agreed, though he also felt repelled by the amount of data they could seize on a phone. The ability to download all the content in minutes, they had everything in the palm of their hands from location tracking, to messages, to photos, deleted or not. It felt cruelly invasive to hold such intimate details of a person's life in his hands —without a warrant, and sometimes without the full understanding, knowledge, or consent of the phone's owner. Data had become a grey area for such invasions in the digital age. It was one reason why Ward was cautious as to what he used his own smartphone for. Someone was always watching, and legitimate or not, he had no desire to see his every move tracked, possibly to be watched back at a later date by strangers, outside his control.

'Did you get the warrant to engage with the provider yet?' Despite his resistance to using Amelia's phone's content, it would have been helpful, and a darn sight quicker than having to procure a warrant, and wait for the network company to comply with anything pertinent. Ward wanted to know more about the stalker Sacha Lavigne had mentioned—messages would be recorded on Amelia's phone, if there were any pertaining to the man.

Plus, it would give an invaluable insight into Darren and Amelia's communications post-breakup that no statement of Darren's could ever come close to in terms of the gritty truth.

'I did. I should have something back today.' She sounded as unhopeful as he did, but still, better than nothing. 'Darren's came back already, and I've started going through. So far, I can't see that he's tried to make contact with her in the past couple of weeks.'

Just like he'd said. 'Just because he's telling the truth about that doesn't mean he didn't kill her, though.'

Nowak had no answer, except a deflated sigh.

'Right, well, best break for lunch then and we'll get back to it,' said Ward, annoyed that they still didn't seem to have any concrete leads, save for an ex-boyfriend who perfectly fit the bill, but forensics evidence and a gut feeling that would suggest otherwise. 'Anyone fancy a butty from the van?'

For the past few weeks, a mobile sandwich and break-fast bar had been parking down the road to take advantage of the school traffic there. It was about as good as anyone would expect from a sandwich van, but their sausage and bacon butties beat a slice of toast hands down.

'Yes!' came a chorus of answers back at him. Ward sloped around the office taking orders on a post-it and collecting change. 'Want owt, Patterson?' he stopped at Patterson's desk. Much as the young lad had pissed him off upon joining HMET—seeming all too jokey and far more concerned about getting his hair right than doing the job properly—Jake Patterson was beginning to wear down Ward's annoyance. Jake had a knack for numbers and patterns, and finally, he seemed to be showing he was dependable, plodding away at his caseload.

'Er, yes sir. Please.' Patterson looked up at him —suspiciously.

'This once, I'm being nice to you. Don't get used to it.' Ward winked.

When he'd taken Patterson's order, he jogged to the van to the tune of his rumbling stomach. He returned not too long later with an armful of white paper sandwich bags, the grease just beginning to seep through to make the white translucent. Soon, the open office carried the fragrant aroma of bacon and sausage, and the blessed sound of silence as everyone tucked in.

'Thanks, sir,' said Nowak, sitting back with a groan. 'Twice in two days. Think I'd better lay off for the week, now.'

'Ha—and I forgot you owed me this time, Emma,' Ward replied, chuckling.

'Ey?' Patterson's head was up. 'How come she gets that kind of treatment?'

'I keep telling you, lad, if you work hard, you'll go far. I might get off your back and make you a brew once in a while,' Ward replied with a wink.

Patterson subsided amidst mutters of 'unfair treatment', 'discrimination', and 'favouritism'.

'Hey, sir.' Emma sat up, and at the tone in her voice, Ward did too. 'The network's come through.'

Ward rushed over to her desk, leaning over her shoulder. 'Go on. What have we got?'

'Sir...' Emma's voice was hushed. 'Amelia's phone

disconnected from the network yesterday morning—
several minutes or so before Graham Bell found her. It
reconnected. Last night.'

'Do they have a location?' Ward searched the ream of
data on the screen—but realised that the file attachment
was a call history—a painful thing to have to cross-check.

'No, sir.' Emma scanned the email in a small pop-up
over the call record. 'Bingley area—I mean, that's something, I suppose. But nothing more exact than that.'

'How come it's not more accurate?' interjected DC
Patterson over Nowak's other shoulder.

'This isn't James Bond, lad,' Ward said. 'We don't
have a satellite hovering overhead triangulating, or
anything daft like that. They can tell which cell towers
it's pinged, and based on the signal strength make a
reasonable guess at location, but aside from that...' Ward
sighed. 'We need that phone ourselves. The location
history on the device is the only way we'd be able to track
its exact movements.'

'But, sir?' Patterson asked, his brow scrunching in
puzzlement. 'How can we access the location history on
the device if we don't know where it is?'

'Jesus Christ,' Ward muttered, flicking his eyes
skyward. Regretting his kinder thoughts about the lad
immediately. 'I swear you were sent to test me with your
stupidity. That, lad, is a paradox beyond your ability to
solve, I reckon.'

'Well I don't know, I'm still new here. You might have
a Z hiding downstairs, you know?'

'I think you mean Q—and I wish. The only thing
hiding downstairs is the grimmest locker room I've had

the misfortune to see. I'd take gadgets and an Aston Martin over that any day.'

'Oooh, no—Lambo all the way,' said Patterson.

Ward huffed and rolled his eyes. 'You know nothing about cars, Jake.'

'I watch F1!' Jake retorted.

Ward winced. 'And you think that makes you an expert? Yeah. Nah. What do you even drive?'

Jake looked away and reddened. 'Fiat Punto,' he muttered.

Ward boomed with laughter. 'A Fix-it-again-tomorrow Punto? Bloody hell.'

'Yeah, alright, I can't afford anything better right now. My insurance is two grand a year as it is. One day I'll have a nice car.'

'Not on a constable's salary.' Nowak chortled.

The rest of the afternoon passed in a depressing inch towards freedom of combing Amelia's phone records for any clues—to no avail. Nowak matched numbers to Amelia's parents, her friends, colleagues, and various entities like her bank, or a takeaway for the calls made and received. There were no text messages from an unknown number that could have been the stalker Sacha had mentioned, which led them to another dead end.

Patterson continued to comb through the CCTV, and Ward waited on the forensics results from Victoria. The house sweep had provided nothing of note, save for a brand new and still-boxed bottle of perfume in the kitchen bin. Perhaps a gift from Darren, Ward wondered, in an attempt to reconcile. Or perhaps an older reminder of him that Amelia didn't want lingering.

The forensics results finally arrived in Daniel Ward's inbox, and he opened them eagerly. But his shoulders fell. The partial fingerprint was no match for the ones they had on file, not even Darren Winston—but then, it was a partial, smudged, and not ideally produced. There was room for error, as Victoria had noted, in such an instance.

Her team had also searched Darren's home as soon as she had finished at Amelia's that morning, confiscating items of clothing that might provide fibres to match the microscopic black fibres transferred from Amelia's killer's garment to her top during the assault, but further analysis had proven inconclusive, the fibres didn't match. Which meant Darren Winston, if he had killed Amelia, hadn't worn any of the garments found at his home address.

The DNA profile of the hair taken from Amelia's hand was completed too. Ward's heart lifted. The DNA was male. He scrolled quickly to the markers in the DNA that were compared with those from the voluntary sample Darren had provided Ward after the search.

No match.

It wasn't a match for Darren, or to any known samples on the police database. In fact, Foster had found absolutely no forensics they *could* match to Darren.

Ward's jaw set. *Damn it!* He had worried as much but... to see it outlined in black and white, irrefutably, was still a large blow. He'd been hoping beyond hope, that somehow, it would give a solution. That it would confirm, beyond doubt, that Darren Winston had murdered his ex-girlfriend in cold-blooded revenge. Or, at the very least, it would match someone else, another serious criminal on file, so they could at least have a speedy resolution.

Now, they were up shit creek without a paddle.

He knew exactly where Amelia Hughes had met her end, and they could narrow it down to such a precise, short window... and yet her killer had escaped scot-free. Unless new evidence came forward—they found her phone, or the murder weapon, or perhaps a sighting was reported—DI Daniel Ward had precisely the square root of nothing to go on.

Was it worth pursuing the ex-boyfriend? The forensics pointed away from him... but the hair could have been a misdirection. Perhaps it had been on Darren's clothing as he attacked her, and in the struggle, had transferred?

Ward groaned and his eyes slipped shut for a moment—but no longer. His phone buzzed into life, playing a cheery rendition of a Spice Girls song that DI Ward most definitely hadn't put as his ringtone. Ward shot a venomously smiling DC Jake Patterson an equally poisonous glare before he picked up. He didn't have the heart to lash out—not with who was calling.

CHAPTER EIGHTEEN

'Afternoon, DCI Kipling.'

'An update, Ward,' Kipling said. 'I have DC Norris and DS Metcalfe with me now.'

Ward glanced up—he hadn't even realised that Norris had slipped out. David's desk was in the corner, in a nook that gave him about as much privacy as anyone could have in a shared office. Metcalfe, Ward had assumed, was busy on the shitter, or in the canteen—the man made an event of everything entering or leaving his body, much to the grossing out of everyone there.

DCI Kipling had a cushy office upstairs, away from the busyness of their shared office. Ward preferred it that way, to be frank. None of them wanted the DCI breathing down their necks all day long—not one as unlikeable as Kipling, anyway.

'Oh?' Ward straightened, all thoughts of revenge on DC Patterson gone for the moment.

'The shipment will be an accompanied load, driver coming through with it, and it docks in Liverpool tomorrow morning. We'll be there to meet it. Full response from Liverpool's CID and uniforms to lock down the vehicle as soon as it passes Customs, then it's over to us to secure what we need from it.'

A spike of adrenaline shot through Ward at the prospect, electrifying him with anticipation and nerves. 'What do you need from me, sir?' He grabbed a pen and slid his notepad across the desk.

'Everyone on board. I don't care what shifts everyone's supposed to be on tomorrow—cancel everything. Need the whole team in Liverpool for seven in the morning. Make the arrangements. I'll brief here at four, we move out at five.'

Ward scribbled it all down. It would give them ample time to coordinate with Liverpool on the other end.

'Metcalfe and Norris will give you all the pertinent details. Make it happen. See you at four tomorrow.'

The line went dead.

Ward stared dumbly at his phone for a moment. This was it, he realised. This was their chance—to catch Varga in the act, hopefully add evidence beyond weight, beyond avoidance to the case they had so slowly been scraping together. He stood slowly, rolling the chair out behind him.

Expecting a backlash, Jake already half hovered over his own chair, prepared to flee. His grin faded at the unnerving bleakness on Ward's face.

'Everyone.' Ward's loud voice stilled the office at once, and the DCs and DS Nowak all turned to look. 'We have an update on the Varga case.' He relayed Kipling's instructions, that they were all to assemble for a briefing before the crack of dawn the next day, to take down the kingpin in the act.

As he finished, and strode out to find DS Chakrabarti and the other DCs in the Incident Room, which they had taken over with their burglary caseload, the office erupted in a furore behind him as his team took in the news that, finally, they would be going head-to-head with Varga's operation.

———

That Friday night, Ward returned home gratefully, weary to his bones, but charged with the dull anticipation —both worry and excitement—at the chance HMET would have next morning to find the next piece in the puzzle to nail Varga.

A hail of barks and a blur of fur and claw and tongue greeted him as he opened the door. Ward shoved the dog back inside, slipping in himself and shutting the door behind him before he dropped to his knees.

'Good to see you too, buddy.' His eyes slipped shut for a moment as he let the dog fuss, dropping a heavy palm on the pup's head in response. 'Come on. Let's get you out for a walk.'

He'd been out all day and needed to rest, but the weight of it all seemed oppressive. Fresh air would help. A walk across the old viaduct and through the fields to blast away the stranglehold his present cases had on him, tugging this way and that at his attention.

In a few minutes, they were into the fields, walking a path towards the dark shape of the viaduct stretching across the small valley ahead, a relic of the Victorian industry heritage of the area, long gone and leaving only a semi-rural village behind to be slowly swallowed in the growing suburbs of Bradford city.

There was a nip in the air and Ward shrugged his jacket closer, Olly straining at the lead. He let the dog off, and Oliver shot across the viaduct eagerly, looping back and forwards. Ward wished he had the pup's energy. He drifted to the edge of the viaduct and rested his hands on the wall, looking down into the dizzying depths of the valley over a hundred feet below.

It was a beautiful valley, winding all the way down into Bradford eventually, but up in Thornton, green and lush, though now starting to turn to autumn. So different to the barren moors of Baildon where he had lived with Katherine.

It had been need and circumstance that had seen him choose the flat in Thornton, but for the first time, as he looked down upon the beck, and the village of Thornton stacked up on the hill to his left, he wondered if perhaps this would be a place he could call home. He had to make one somewhere, after all. Why not here?

It was a decision for a different time. For now, Ward was still trying to find his feet, a hard task in the ever-changing maelstrom of cases at HMET that saw him working all hours. He returned home with Olly after a short time, with homeliness in mind for a change, and only one thing meant home to him. His mother's paintings.

Ward shut the dog out of the bedroom with an apology before he unrolled the poorly kept canvases on his mattress—deciding as he knelt, that he would upgrade and get himself a bed frame. He couldn't live like a pauper forever. Couldn't live as though Katherine would agree to share anything from the house with him. It wasn't going to happen. He had to stop waiting, stop living in limbo, and start again.

He unrolled each painting reverently. Watercolour on thick paper stock. Yellowing and fading with age. It was a sad sight to see that the passage of time had marred them so much, and yet, he could still remember each one, fresh as the day they were painted.

One of Ingleborough, the striking profile of the peak stark against a pink and peach winter sunrise. One of Burnsall, the river snaking through such bright green fields and under the old stone bridge. One of Filey Brig, jutting out into the steely grey-blue North Sea with seagulls soaring overhead. He remembered his mother painting them with her steady hand, leaning close to the paper to dab them on. Each stroke of the brush *just so*.

His lips curled in an unconscious smile at the thought of her tender ministrations to that canvas, slowly teasing the artwork to life. He missed her fiercely in that moment, a painful aching gulf opening in his chest.

It had been his father's fault—Ward was certain of it. That day still haunted him too, when nightmares of Varga's lorry of death abated. He had returned home from school to find her crumpled at the bottom of the stairs. A fall, his father had said—when the bastard had shown up later that night, so drunk he could barely walk —but Ward knew it had been a shove.

The monster had left Daniel and his younger brother

Sam to walk home into that. The coward had fucked off to the pub to drown his sorrows and his guilt and left her there. Who would have known, had he stayed to help her, whether she could have been saved? But by the time Daniel and Sam had found her, she was long gone.

Something inside him had snapped that night. He'd beat his father senseless and left with Sam in tow. It wasn't something he was proud of, but even now, he wasn't sure that he regretted it. The bastard had battered them all for years without reprise—and Daniel's mother had paid the ultimate price for loving her husband faithfully for all those years. Angela Ward had been buried in a pauper's grave with a small attendance a couple of weeks later. Her death had been ruled as accidental.

Daniel and Sam had bounced between aunties and uncles in the couple of years after that, before they were deemed to be 'adults'. Then, Sam had moved out of the area and Daniel had joined the force as a way to channel his grief and fury. The paintings were all he had kept from that house over the years, lugging them faithfully from one home to the next, though they had never seen the light of day—first, from his still-raw grief, and then from Katherine's unyielding refusal.

Daniel stroked the canvas with a finger. He would change that. His past was dark, and yet in there hid light too—his mother's lasting, loving influence.

He reached for his phone and tapped into the browser. 'Framers near me,' he typed and scrolled through the top few results. A shop called *Griffith's Fine Art and Framing* caught his eye—fairly local just over the hill in the small but pretty village of Wilsden, with opening hours until eight some weekdays, meaning he could go after work if he made it out early enough—and remembered. *Perfect.*

Hoping it was for the last time, Ward carefully rolled up the last of Angela Ward's legacy and re-wrapped them in the black bin liners, before putting them out of the dog's reach on a pile of boxes in the corner that he still hadn't unpacked. He resolved to do that too. Buy a bed, get himself some decent furniture, unpack everything... with his mum's paintings, perhaps this could feel like home one day soon.

A whine sounded outside the door—and paws scrabbling at the wood.

'Can't have a minute's peace with you, eh, lad?' Ward said as he opened the door and Olly bounded in. *Not that I'd change it for the world.*

He made himself and the dog a late dinner—nothing fancy, just a pan of chicken arrabbiata that would last him a few days, and a can of Pedigree's finest meat and gravy for the pup—before retiring to bed, with Olly tucked into him on the mattress. Even that made the place seem more homely, and he laid a hand on Oliver's back, smiling as the dog huffed in contentment and wriggled closer.

Yet, worries crept in around the edges of his contentment. Worries of Amelia Hughes—and her hulk of an ex-boyfriend, who had no alibi, potential means, motive, and opportunity, yet didn't match the small shred of forensic data they'd gathered.

Worries of Varga too. Tomorrow, Saturday, would dawn soon—a scant few hours of sleep lay ahead for

Ward at best. His eyes ached with the weight of tired-ness, and yet, he stared at the ceiling above, wide-eyed, unable to fall into slumber.

Nerves jittered through him, the sickening see-saw of anticipation and dread that accompanied anything to do with Varga. As usual, it was the waiting that was the worst. He wished he could already be in Liverpool, cracking open that lorry and finding a happier ending inside than the one they'd had last November.

Would they find the truck?

Would it be a live shipment?

Would they be too late to save anyone again?

———

Daniel Ward was one of them again. One of the bodies piled in the lorry. This was the very worst of his night-mares. He laid on his back and the cold floor of the lorry shuddered under him, in motion as it sped towards its final, fateful destination.

Above the rumble of its engine, he could hear the chok-ing, gasping, desperate moans of those around him. The stench of their acrid fear and the excrement in the van choked him as much as the lack of air to breathe, and his chest tightened in panic.

In the faint light of a tiny lamp fixed to the inside of the truck, they were nothing but shadows lumbering over him. They clutched at each other, some clawing at the door behind his head until their nails bled, dripping hot blood on him, some hammering the walls with broken-down crates—each strike becoming weaker, slower, than the last.

Bang...bang...bang...

He couldn't move, his limbs leaden. Weighed down by his fear and the bodies piling upon him. One by one they fell, never to rise again, covering him in limp limbs, slack faces falling into his periphery, contorted by suffering and terror, their bloodshot eyes seeming to bulge out of their sockets.

Ward struggled under their dead weight, but his limbs wouldn't obey. It was as though he were clamped there by force, unable to move, command of his limbs having fled. He could only endure as the dead mounted, with him at the very bottom of the pile, until they crushed him to the floor so deeply that he couldn't even expand his chest to fill his lungs with the life-taking air.

Light appeared above him, faint, but enough to outline a silhouette familiar to him in nightmare and waking. Bogdan Varga. The man's teeth glinted as he smiled at Ward.

And then, the bodies atop him compressed him further. Through the very bottom of the lorry, they all seemed to sink with Ward still buried under them, a great mass of tangled limbs and bodies, into blackness and cold and silence. The faint light inside the truck faded away, and with it, so too faded Daniel Ward, with his last, gasping breath.

Into another inky blackness—a dark hallway, unlit save for the faint orange streetlight outside that pooled inside the front door, casting Daniel Ward's shadow into the narrow hallway. Across the heap crumpled at the foot of the stairs leading up to the pitch-black upstairs of the small terraced house.

Daniel rushed forwards, but his limbs were lead, as though he pushed through treacle, and he couldn't reach her with his clumsily outstretched hands. For now, he was at his family home, and the body at the bottom of the stairs would be his mother, her neck broken, her body beaten, her blue eyes gazing unseeing at the peeling wallpaper above the battered skirting board at the bottom of the stairs.

CHAPTER NINETEEN

Harry—or rather, James Denton—had managed to charm Charlotte Lawson into a date that evening, last thing. Glad he was of it too, for he was all prepared. Adrenaline rushed through him, putting an arrogant swagger in his step.

He'd changed his Matchmaker profile picture to match his own appearance, but he'd kept the cover story —a marketing expert working in Leeds, living in Bingley. He needed to charm the pants off her, quite literally, if he were to stand a chance.

What were a few little white lies sprinkled here and there anyway? They wouldn't matter to Charlotte Lawson in a few hours. She'd be dead.

Harry stepped off the train at Saltaire station, not stopping to admire the quaint arch designs that marked the World Heritage Site's unique style of architecture, only his own reflection in the train window on the way past. He smoothed his hair and ran a hand over his freshly shaved chin, every step he took filled with self-assurance. He wore the same outfit he'd bought for his failed date with Amelia—it filled him with the bad memories and encouraged him to embrace that darkness within him—and carried a single rose for Charlotte. All part of the charm.

Charlotte awaited him outside the bar, a long navy coat elongating her tall, slim figure. As she turned to him, he had a flash of Amelia all over again, before he drew closer and took in the subtle differences. Charlotte was slightly shorter than Amelia, slightly less petite in her build. Her glossy brown hair slightly shorter, her skin paler, a smattering of light freckles across her cheeks. Her darkened lips parted in a smile as she saw him.

'Hi, James.' She extended a hand.

He took it, bowing his head to kiss the back of it, before whipping the rose out from behind his back and presenting it to her. 'For you.'

She blushed as she took it. 'Such a gentleman. Thanks.'

'Shall we?' Harry laced his fingers into hers, having not dropped her hand, and gently pulled her into the restaurant doorway.

He charmed her all night, plying her with compliments and engaging stories that didn't belong to his own life, keeping her wine glass topped up, although the cost of the full bottle made him wince—especially when he ordered a second to keep her sweet. He made his own pint last as long as the first bottle before he ordered his next.

It gave him the edges of a pleasant buzz, and a tad more courage, but no more than that. He would have to remain clear-headed. More than that, he wanted to. He wanted to remember every second of this.

He smiled again as she paused to take a sip, their eyes grazing, and locking. She really was very pretty, and if he was so inclined, sociable, entertaining, and interesting. It was a shame, perhaps, that he was not inclined.

A pity that she met a monster like me. Yet, Harry grinned back nonetheless, the picture of open easiness, until she had drained the last of the second bottle.

'Whoops!' she said with a giggle as she stood up and nearly stumbled over her chair leg.

Harry caught her with strong, gentle hands, steading her. 'Are you alright there?'

'Yes, thanks. Sorry. I shouldn't be making such a tit of myself on a first date, I know. That wine's just delicious. Are you sure you don't want me to pay towards?' She nodded at the bill on the table, under which he'd already left the full amount, and a little tip so she didn't think him a miser. He had to get her back to his for any of it to be worth it. What was an extra fiver in the grand scheme of things?

'My treat,' Harry assured her. 'What kind of date would it be if I didn't cover it?' He winked, and she melted into his side as he hooked an arm around her. She fit so comfortably there. He led her outside and along the pavement, into the shadows, before he kissed her. Clumsily, she opened to him, tasting of wine.

After a long kiss, he pulled away and nuzzled his mouth into her neck, planting a teasing kiss. 'Come back to mine?' he murmured.

She moaned. 'Oh, I shouldn't. I'm not that kind of girl, James!'

Harry chuckled into her neck, with another kiss, that frisson of excitement nothing to do with bedding her—well, only a *little*—and everything to do with the thrill of another, darker chase. The one she didn't see coming. Not from nice, respectable, gentlemanly James Denton.

'You know you want to...' he murmured, his breath hot on her neck. Another kiss to tease her a little more.

She groaned again. 'Fine...What can I say? Tonight's been amazing. I don't want it to end here.'

Harry chuckled, and with another deep kiss, this time on the lips once more, pulled her back to the kerb. He hailed a taxi and helped her inside.

'Sycamore Avenue, Bingley, please.'

A nod was his only response from the taciturn driver. That suited him. He scooted Charlotte over to the middle seat and tucked her under his arm, laying his other hand on her leg and sliding it slowly, suggestively, upwards.

He had the taxi driver drop them just off the main road into Bingley—far enough away from home so the driver wouldn't be able to identify where he lived, close enough to walk back. Or stagger, in Charlotte's case.

The cold air seemed to have hastened her inebriation, and Harry supported her as he walked them down Sycamore Avenue and turned off into the back street. It was dark as he led her inside, but he'd made sure to tidy up in anticipation that he'd be able to tempt her back.

It was easier than he'd hoped, with the wine to help—she couldn't keep her hands off him as he helped her into the hallway and locked the door behind him. He had a lot more on his wish list than snogging at the bottom of the stairs, so he manoeuvred them upstairs, one step at a time, shedding garments in a trail all the way from the bottom to the top.

Now the arousal had taken him, steering his brain in a different direction to murder, but he had no intention of coming this far only to give up. He pushed Charlotte back onto the bed where she fell in a giggling heap, her lithe, naked form tempting him, that chestnut hair spread like a fan on the duvet—but there was one more precaution he had to take. He slipped on a condom. After all, he had no intention of being caught. He'd double-checked that semen would be able to be forensically identified.

'Come on,' she moaned, wriggling across the bed and pulling him on top.

'If you insist,' he murmured, grinning devilishly.

In the dark, with her moaning under him, it was a fantasy to believe that it could really be Amelia, and he wished it was, after all the effort he'd put into wooing her... but the fantasy soured to anger once more. Amelia had been a fool. It hadn't had to end the way it did—it was her fault, really. And it would be because of her that Charlotte would die too.

'*James*,' she moaned, pulling him closer, her hands traversing across his body so he moaned too.

Harry made sure he took his pleasure before his hands found Charlotte's slender neck.

She retched as her breath caught; as she tried to speak and couldn't. Drunk and clumsy, her hands beat at Harry's chest, gentle at first—and then harder, as she realised that he wouldn't stop. Her nails scratched at him, tearing into his chest, and with each stinging, burning trail she left on him, his euphoria and sense of power only grew.

Charlotte struggled fiercely under him, pinned by his weight as he straddled her, her hands unable to prise his away from her throat as he squeezed, and squeezed, and squeezed.

Her fist struck his face, sending a stinging blow through his skull that had stars dancing across his vision. He pushed down on her, placing all his strength and weight on her neck.

Her movements slowed. Her hands glancing off like feathers caressing him, so weak was she. Until at last, they fell limp with a soft *thump* onto the bed.

Harry released her slowly, waiting, watching, listening, feeling for any sense of her. She was so warm between his legs, as though still alive. Of course, moments ago, she had been. Now, Charlotte Lawson lay still, spread out on his bed, never to breathe again, her bulging eyes glazed over, unseeing. Her hair rumpled on the pillow. Her elegant hands limp.

Harry admired his handiwork in the pillar of light cast by the streetlight nearby outside.

CHAPTER TWENTY

The nondescript white minibus thundered off the motorway, part of a convoy of two transporting DCI Kipling and the HMET, Ward included, to Liverpool docks to intercept the lorry marked as Varga's. The day dawned with their passage west over the Pennines.

Liverpool's Major Crimes Unit awaited them, waving them through port security once DCI Kipling had shown the port authorities the relevant paperwork, and escorting them to a space reserved to take and examine the lorry. It was all too familiar to the previous November for Ward's liking, and shivers crawled down his spine at the bare concrete, surrounded by a maze of shipping containers.

In silence, just as they had travelled, Ward and his team filed off the minibus, to an immediate blast of cold air—refreshing after the stuffy confines of the van, but cold, too. They would all be frozen before the lorry came, but the DCI was taking no chances that they would be ready and waiting to intercept. They all stood, stretching with muffled groans of relief after the journey over the Pennines, past Manchester, Ellesmere Port, and to Birkenhead, where the Stena Line Freight ferry was due to dock at the terminal there shortly.

Liverpool's Major Crimes awaited too, and DCI Kipling conferred with his counterpart in a mutter, as the two forces huddled in their separate groups, breathing plumes of white into the cold, pre-dawn air. The sun teased the horizon with a slight lightening already, though the dreary grey heralded yet another plain autumn day. In the distance, far up the estuary, Ward could see the hulking ferry coming to port, one slow inch at a time.

His nerves ratcheted up another level. He shifted from foot to foot, impatient to get on with the job. But Liverpool's Major Crimes would handle disembarkment —they would be the ones to identify the lorry and apprehend the driver, so that the Bradford team could escort it from the ferry to the side yard where it could be examined.

Liverpool's CID dutifully filed off—and it was time for Ward and his team to wait as the sun rose in full, the ferry docked, and the first lorries thundered off.

'Gods, this is the worst part,' growled DS Metcalfe, folding his arms and clamping them to his chest, the collar of his coat turned up to shelter his neck from the insidious breeze.

'Aye,' Ward replied. This time, there was no CSI backup, no medical waiting...they had no credible evidence that there were people on the lorry, or that there was a threat to life, only the knowledge that the lorry was Varga's and that meant it was most likely something illicit, at least. But Ward feared if it were anything worse. He didn't want to have to make the same calls as last time, around to the several local morgues, trying to find enough spaces for all the bodies.

DCI Kipling's radio crackled. 'Come on,' he called to the team, his tone steel. 'It's time.'

They marched to the lane where lorries were already starting to pass.

'White lorry, registration plate Brava Alpha nine one three Delta Zulu, coming shortly.'

'There,' Metcalfe's sharp voice alerted them as he spotted it first, filing off in turn behind another lorry.

'Ward, go.'

Ward stepped out to halt the lorry in front of it, flashing his warrant card. The driver frowned, until Ward gave him a thumbs up and hopped up by the window. 'Just a sec, fella. Just stopping the lorry behind you, but don't think he'll be so good as to stop. Hold for a moment until we clear you, please?'

'Nae bother,' said the lorry driver, his Glaswegian accent strong. He shrugged and glanced in his mirrors as the plain-clothes detectives swarmed the lorry behind him, with Ward catching up.

The driver had already clambered down with his arms held up, empty-handed. 'No English, please, no speak English.'

'For fuck's sake...' Ward heard DCI Kipling mutter. DCI Kipling marched forward and cuffed him with DS Nowak's assistance. 'I'm detaining you and your cargo for the purpose of a search. Follow me.' Kipling turned to Metcalfe. 'You're HGV trained, right?'

'Yes, sir.'

Ward gave Scott a sly side-eye. It had been a *long* while since Scott had updated his vehicles training—but he wasn't about to dob Metcalfe in. He was more experienced than the rest of them, in any case.

'Bring it over.'

Ward jogged forward to release the HGV in front. 'Cheers, mate.'

The driver raised a hand and rumbled away, leaving a red-faced Metcalfe in the white lorry, triple-checking his gears before he set off in the HGV that far outsized his usual Renault Mégane.

DCI Kipling commandeered one of the minibuses to hold the driver in, guarded by DC Patterson for the moment—who was more than a little annoyed to have to babysit instead of getting stuck in, stripping the lorry. The Liverpool Major Crimes Unit returned after Metcalfe navigated the lorry into the centre of the yard.

Ward's stomach flipped again, and he clamped his mouth shut against the rising nausea. This was such a different scene to the previous November, and yet the memory felt as fresh as the present, the likenesses too uncomfortable, especially after last night's nightmares. He just wanted to get the damned lorry open and be done with the agony of not knowing.

'Ward, Shahzad, get it open,' barked the DCI.

Ward and Shahzad marched forwards and wrangled the handles on the back door into place. For a moment, they shared a look, one filled with the same, unsaid fear of what they would find inside. And then they pulled the doors open.

Ward was almost scared to look, but he forced his eyes up, to the lorry's interior. His heart seemed to quiver in visceral relief.

No people.

No immigrants.

Dead or alive.

Just stacks of boxes.

'Thank God,' Shahzad murmured next to him.

'Right, thank you, ladies and gentlemen,' said DCI Kipling, clapping his hands together. 'Let's get to this. Liverpool, please stand down for now, HMET will do the initial search. Most grateful for your assistance.'

'No worries, mate,' Ward heard one of the Liverpudlians nearby mutter in his strong accent. 'We'll just 'ang about 'ere, nothin' better to do on a fookin' Saturday.'

The shipment inside was, per the CMR note, packaging. Which was *loosely* accurate, in that everything inside the lorry was packaged. That was about as far as the similarities went when the HMET examined the contents of those boxes. Counterfeit designer clothing. Another pie they didn't know Varga had his finger in.

'I think it's about time we had a chat with our driver here,' remarked Kipling as he surveyed the contents, far more innocuous than the previous lorry they had seized. 'Ward. With me.'

Ward followed him to the minibus, leaving the rest of the HMET team to unpick the contents of the lorry—peeling back side panels, the dashboard, upholstery, for any more illicit goods. They climbed inside, relieving DC

Patterson, who joined the search party instead—scuttling off at speed before the DCI could change his mind.

The driver sat in the middle of the back row, watching them with a face darkened by suspicion and mistrust. He looked to be in his early forties, his jet-black hair thinning slightly on top, with silver strands threading through his combover. He wore a simple black Adidas tracksuit, a hole in the fabric showing a hairy knee. His dark eyes flitted between them, under bushy, back brows, his thin lips set in a mutinous line.

'What's your name?' The DCI started with a relatively simple question.

The man didn't answer.

'Your *name*,' Kipling said lounder, enunciating each syllable.

Ward glanced at his superior, stood with his arms folded beside him at the front of the minibus. 'If I may, sir?'

Kipling glared at him, but didn't object.

Ward advanced on the man and slipped into an aisle seat a few rows in front of him. '*Si Slovak?*' *Are you Slovakian?*

The man looked at him sharply. It was always a surprise that he had bothered to try and learn their language. Most people didn't. '*Áno,*' he replied slowly. *Yes.*

'*Ako sa voláš?*' *What's your name?*

The man paused for a moment. Swallowed.

'*Je to v poriadku,*' Ward reassured him. *It's ok.*

'Miroslav.'

'Miroslav...?'

'Ferenc.'

'*Ďakujem, Miroslav. Hovoríš po anglicky?*' Ward raised an eyebrow.

'A little,' the man admitted.

'Ok, now we can get somewhere. Is this your lorry?' Ward gestured outside.

Miroslav shook his head.

'Who does it belong to? Whose lorry?'

'A man,' said Miroslav, scowling at Ward's resulting glare. 'I no know his name. Man call 'boss man', yes?'

'Right then; the boss man. He pays you to drive this lorry for him?'

'Yes. Some before, some after when I go back.'

'We'll need more than that.' Ward sighed and turned to Kipling. 'We need an interpreter. We can't question him in broken English.'

Kipling held up his hands in an open invite to progress as he saw fit. Ward took out his phone and dialled back to the station, to get him on the phone with an interpreter. Fifteen minutes later and he finally had one. *Now*, they could talk properly. His broken Slovakian could only get him past the niceties. Ward placed the phone on his knee, with the woman on loudspeaker.

Kipling set his phone to record and joined Ward in the aisle seat opposite, reciting what was needed to interview the man under caution.

'Who owns the lorry? Ward asked again.

He got no fresh information back from the translator.

'Who is the man that hired you? What does he look like?'

A brief description that could have belonged to half

the male population in the man's home country followed —medium height, medium build, middle-aged, no distinguishing features, Slovakian.

For Christ's sake. 'Have you worked for this man before?'

A hesitation. And a delayed, 'Yes.'

'How often?'

The man swallowed. 'Sometimes.'

'Do you know that this lorry is registered on cloned licence plates?'

The man shook his head, but he wouldn't meet their gaze.

He knows he's doing something wrong.

'Did you supervise the lorry being loaded?'

'No. I was a last-minute change. The original driver got sick.'

'Do you know that it's a crime to use cloned licence plates, and to ship goods into the United Kingdom that have not been properly declared on your CMR?'

'I don't know about these things,' said the man desperately, the interpreter translating his words into English. 'I just drive here, drive back, all is good for the man.' He looked rattled, his eyes slightly wide, his movements agitated as he shifted on the seat.

'How much do you get paid to do this?'

'Five hundred Euro now, five hundred Euro again later.'

Ward raised an eyebrow. He knew from prior research on the country, that average wages in Slovakia were around fifteen thousand Euros a year...if the man earned a thousand Euros for every shipment he delivered on top of his normal wage, well, what a difference that would make to his life.

'How many of these journeys do you make?'

'One or two a month.'

'And you work elsewhere too?'

'Yes, I drive lorry every day.'

'Who do you work for?'

'Bratislava Logistic Solutions.'

Ward shared a glance with Kipling. He'd heard that name before. It was one of the companies that Varga used as a front for his shadow industry. He stole their licence plates and used their branding to do his dirty work across Europe. Ward navigated to a photo of Varga on his phone and showed Miroslav. 'Do you know this man?'

Miroslav stilled. He squinted at the photo, making a show of examining it. 'No.'

'For the record, I am showing Mr Ferenc a picture of Bogdan Varga.' Ward was certain the man was lying. 'You know there is a prison sentence for smuggling goods into the United Kingdom? Your CMR declares you carrying packaging, you're bringing in counterfeit goods instead.'

'No! I didn't know what was in the lorry. That's not my business.'

'As the driver, *you* are responsible for checking your shipment.'

'It's not my lorry. I was a last-minute replacement for the driver who was sick. I had no choice!'

'And why is that?'

That had him. He looked between the two hard-faced men, his lips flapping but nothing emerging.

'You know Bogdan Varga, don't you?' Ward still held the photo out to Miroslav. The man looked anywhere but.

His eyes darted to Bogdan's picture and away again, before he nodded, one sharp jerk of his head, his lips clamped shut.

'Did Bogdan Varga threaten, coerce, or bribe you to drive this lorry?'

Miroslav swallowed, and cleared his throat. 'I don't know.'

'Come on, you can do better than that.'

Miroslav glanced out of the window at the lorry, whose contents were now scattered all over the yard, officers pouring through them. His eyes scrunched closed.

'The more you can tell us, the more we can help you, Miroslav. You want that, don't you? Do you have a family back home?'

Miroslav nodded shakily. 'Wife. Three boys. A daughter.'

'And I bet you want to get this all cleared up and get home to them, right?'

Miroslav nodded, slumping forward to rest his elbows on his knees. A hand tangled through his hair.

The man didn't have the air of a criminal mastermind, just a normal man, caught up in a business that he probably didn't know the half of. One who, if he did have a wife and family, was probably doing his damned best to provide for them all. A thousand Euro job every few weeks would have been a lifeline to make that happen.

Ward knew how these things seemed—it was *just* driving a lorry from A to B, no need to know what was inside. No harm, no foul. But it was a long and slippery slope from there. Especially for the likes of Miroslav, who was nothing more than a sacrificial pawn, a piece easily lost and replaced in Varga's operation. Bogdan wouldn't even know the man's name, let alone give a shit that Miroslav had taken the fall for Varga's smuggling operation and that his family would suffer the consequences.

'Help us to help you, Miroslav. Tell me *more*.'

CHAPTER TWENTY-ONE

Miroslav whispered, 'Once you start these jobs, you cannot stop them.' His eyes met Ward's guiltily before he returned his gaze to the floor.

Ward waited, questions wanting to spill from him, but he held them all back. Giving Miroslav the chance to continue. He did.

'First one little thing, then another, and another...but you cannot say no. The money is good, it helps, but if you do not take it, they punish you.'

'Who? Who punishes you?'

'His men.' Miroslav gestured to Ward's phone.

'Varga's men?'

Miroslav nodded. 'Yes. They will report you to the police for doing criminal things, or maybe they will beat you up, or set your car on fire, or hurt your wife, threaten your children...' He trailed off, his face utterly hollow, horror lurking deep in his eyes, a scar upon his soul.

'What did he do?' Ward asked quietly.

Miroslav wrung his hands together. 'They beat up

my boy. He was so bad, he was in hospital for three weeks. Ten years old, a child, and they beat him like a *man*. They watched my daughter's school and followed my wife home one night. We were all so scared. I could not say no after that.'

Ward sighed. 'You do the jobs now because you have to, not because you want to.'

Miroslav nodded miserably, hanging his head. 'I don't ask questions. It's not my business. I drive where they tell me, and I do what they say. At least we have some extra money to help out. And no one gets hurt.'

Ward swore under his breath. 'Do you have any specific details you can give us—times, dates, names, people, places, any official documents, or bank transactions? If we can track these people down, put them behind bars, we can free families like yours from his influence.'

Miroslav looked at him, a desperate hope lighting his eyes, but it was quickly veiled. 'If I talk, he will kill us.'

'We can protect you.'

Miroslav laughed, but it was bitter. 'No, you can't. Not from him.'

'You're scared, I understand that, but I promise you. Help us bring him to justice.'

'I have already said too much,' Miroslav said sadly, and he covered his face with his hands. 'If he finds out what I've told you, he will hurt them.' His voice was muffled, but the interpreter managed to share his words.

Ward sighed. The man was right, he was in an impossible situation. But so was Ward. 'Miroslav Ferenc, I'm arresting you on suspicion of illegally importing goods into the United Kingdom.' He recited the police caution. 'You'll be taken to a station with us to be questioned further, and then we'll go from there. You may be remanded in custody. Do you understand?'

Miroslav nodded into his hands.

'I'll get Patterson,' Ward said, standing. Bitterness filled him. It wasn't fair. Miroslav was, as an adult, responsible for his own choices and actions, but it was clear he'd been backed into a corner, forced to work for Varga to protect his family. Yet, Miroslav would take the fall, and his family would suffer for Varga's criminal empire, whilst Varga would remain free and untouchable.

And they were still no closer to having anything like substantial evidence to charge Varga with, for any of it. The lorry and Miroslav Ferenc, were just two pieces in Varga's game, so far beneath Varga's notice, Ward doubted Varga would even care to know they were compromised. He probably didn't even know Miroslav Ferenc's name.

Had they won, or had they lost this round? They hadn't found a lorry full of bodies, or immigrants, to Ward's relief, but their seizure would make no difference to the crime lord.

'Damn it!' Ward growled.

CHAPTER TWENTY-TWO

B ack at Bradford South Station after a long few hours processing the lorry's contents and the return journey, they booked Miroslav Ferenc into the custody suite downstairs. Kipling had taken point on questioning the Slovakian, with DS Metcalfe in attendance, to find out what other details they could about the lorry's intended destination and the cargo's handover, in addition to trying to cajole anything more out of the petrified man about his involvement with Varga's operation.

Ward returned upstairs to the main shared office for the last of his shift to catch up with Nowak on any progress in the Amelia Hughes case. They marched to the Incident Room to go over all the details they had so far, standing side by side in front of the Big Board to run through.

'We know that she was killed between about seven and seven-thirty, on her Thursday morning run. The location is just past Harden Beck,' Ward said.

Nowak answered, 'There were no sightings of anyone running *with* her through Myrtle Park on her route prior to her murder. She was sighted alone by one witness, so it appears she was running solo, which is consistent with her usual routine.'

'Right. OK, so the attack. It was quick, brutal, and effective. The killer either had a lucky break on the timing and location, or it was very well planned. Which do you lean towards?'

'Planned, sir.'

'Why?' He agreed, but he wanted to hear her theory too.

'Well, sir, if it was unplanned, then it was incredibly well *prepared* for, in that the perpetrator had the means necessary to commit the act. So to a degree, they had planned to harm someone, right?'

Ward tilted his head. 'I see what you're saying.'

'People don't just wander round with great big kitchen knives, right?'

'On the whole, no. We haven't found anything suspicious in her background checks to suggest she was running with the wrong sort of crowd who might carry weapons.'

'Quite the opposite, sir. She seems to be squeaky clean.'

'Indeed. I'd agree that it points towards being premeditated. If it was a random attack, I reckon we'd have caught someone by now. No one commits an act like that and gets away without leaving a massive evidence trail.' Ward scratched his beard. 'This seems to be a crime of passion, no matter how we look at it. The frenzied nature screams that the killer knew Amelia. Love or hate, there were strong feelings there.'

'Strong enough to kill for,' Nowak murmured, her eyes fixed upon the picture of Amelia Hughes at the top of the board.

'Right, so Amelia jogs along her usual Thursday morning route, listening to her music—Foster has her earbuds—so maybe she doesn't notice or hear anyone, and the next minute, she's forced off the trail.'

'Backed against the tree,' Nowak continued, staring at the photo of the bloodied bark.

'Perhaps there's a struggle or scuffle—reasonable to assume so—before she's overpowered, by the killer. We have black fibres from his on her top from that contact. She was stabbed repeatedly from front to back, mainly in the upper torso area, by a large-bladed article, as yet unrecovered.'

'From the evidence we have, the killer is suggested to be larger and stronger than her—in order to overpower her, and from the angle and force of the wounds inflicted,' Nowak interjected. 'I mean, sure, it could be a woman the size of Miss Trunchbull, but that's unlikely. There'd definitely be some reported sightings.'

Ward chuckled. 'Aye, indeed. I'll go with that for now. We're looking for a male. That's the most likely. In the struggle, black fibres from the killer's clothing transferred to the victim's top. There's a partial smudged fingerprint on her arm, which is inconclusive. The victim also managed to snag a hair, most likely from the perp, although we can't be certain *yet*, which forensics found wrapped around her fingers. The DNA profile of that hair follicle is male. No match on file.'

Nowak nodded. 'But it's described as several inches long, brown, and curly, which doesn't fit with Darren.'

Ward grimaced. 'We'll get to that. Then, she was left to bleed out, which, due to the severity of the wounds, happened incredibly quickly. The perp left immediately —perhaps disturbed, perhaps planned, but they didn't stop to take in the scenery or whatever. I reckon if it was planned, that they didn't stay was down to Graham and his dog approaching—maybe the dog barked, and alerted the killer, who fled.'

'Luckily for Graham, if it was a guy with a massive knife.'

'Aye. Foster noted scuffed footprints in her report, as though tracks in the mud had been deliberately obscured, so the killer was smart enough to do that.'

'They knew what they were doing, trying to remove evidence.'

'Aye.'

Nowak folded her arms. 'They'd have been *covered* in blood though. I just don't understand how he could have melted into thin air, drenched in it.'

Ward huffed. 'A good question. I wonder if the black garment he was wearing helped to obscure that. From a distance, you wouldn't be able to see it, the blood would blend into the dark fabric. At worst, it'd look wet.'

'But even so. He couldn't have gone far. Not like that. His face, hands, everything would have been covered.'

Ward sucked the inside of his cheek and examined the map printed of the area. 'There are plenty of ways to get out of there without being spotted—rural area, lots of tree cover. Close to Bingley too. Is it reasonable to assume the killer lives there? I agree, they wouldn't be able to travel a huge distance looking like that, and the time-frame is so tight.

'She was discovered an extremely short time later—minutes—by Graham Bell and his dog.'

'Graham Bell has been questioned,' Nowak inter-jected, 'and there is video footage of him that corrobo-rates his journey and timings from a household with a Ring doorbell further up the lane.'

'Good work.' Ward smiled at Nowak. That had been her idea to check, since there was otherwise no CCTV in the area beyond private video feeds and devices.

Nowak inclined her head. 'Cheers, sir.'

'And aside from that...the killer disappears into thin air. We have several suspects. Graham Bell likely wouldn't have had time to kill Amelia, then hide the evidence of his attack, totally clean himself up, etc., etc.

'For a time, we suspected Gemma, Amelia's colleague, with whom the victim had a disagreement at work. Gemma's movements were confirmed by their boss, placing her away from the scene.' Ward stroked his beard before he continued.

'The only suspect who does *not* have a suitable alibi is Darren Winston, Amelia's ex-boyfriend, who has a known history of anger management issues and who claims to be at home at the time of Amelia's murder. Their relationship was tempestuous, and in the words of

Amelia's closest friend, Winston was 'volatile'. When we attempted to speak to him, he fled—a natural reaction that does not read well.'

'Agreed, sir. Potentially, he has motive, but I'm not so sure about means or opportunity. He's a big guy. I'm sure he would have been noticed, as he lives a distance away from the site of the murder, and doesn't drive. In addition, CSI found no bladed articles matching the potential murder weapon—a kitchen block with a knife missing, for example.'

'That doesn't mean anything, though. Could have had a separate single knife, could have bought one just for this purpose,' Ward countered.

'Aye, but I also received the triangulation data from the mobile phone company. I've been looking through it on the way back from Liverpool. In addition to his phone records, which show no calls or texts between himself and Amelia Hughes in the two and a half weeks preceding her death, the triangulation of the signal at the time of the murder shows his phone was switched on. At that time, it was present at or around his immediate home address, with a very low margin for error due to the high concentration of masts in the area.'

Ward sighed and folded his arms. 'He might have left it at home.'

'The hair Foster found on Amelia's body isn't his.'

'Could have been on either of their clothing for another reason.'

'There are no fibres matching any of his garments to the ones on Amelia's clothing at the time of her death.'

'Any idiot knows to dump, hide, or destroy clothing like that if they don't want to get caught.'

'Then where is it, sir?' Nowak challenged, glaring at him.

Ward regarded her impassively. 'We're getting nowhere with Winston, are we?' he admitted after a pause.

'No, sir.'

'Ok, so he remains a suspect. We have some evidence to suggest he wasn't there—phone records, no sightings. We have some forensic evidence that doesn't match—the hair, the fibres.'

'We have a hunch and nothing more, that he could be involved due to the acrimonious ending to their relationship, but nothing anywhere near strong enough to meet the threshold for charging,' said Nowak.

'Nope. It's like you want him to get off.'

Nowak snorted. 'I'm being thorough. We don't cut corners, sir.'

'No, we do not,' agreed Ward with a nod, and returned his attention to the Big Board. 'Known offenders in the area?'

Nowak winced. 'Crap. Sorry, sir. I overlooked that one.'

'Get on it now, then.' Ward stared after her as she hurriedly left, blooming red at her oversight. Nowak was exceptionally skilled at what she did, but still young, with lots to learn.

He looked over the big board again, taking it all in. Amelia's parents and her friends, all pointing towards Darren as the only antagonist in Amelia's life.

There was only one word circled and finished with a question mark that Ward couldn't add any information to —not without Amelia's phone. The one Sacha had mentioned as a passing remark. Perhaps it was more than that after all.

Stalker?

CHAPTER TWENTY-THREE

I t was soon time to finish, for they had started the day
cruelly early to begin with. Ward had spent the short
remainder of his shift completing paperwork for the lorry
and Miroslav Ferenc's questioning, and chewing over the
mystery of Amelia Hughes' killer.

*Was it Darren? If not Darren, then who? Who was
Amelia Hughes' stalker?*

Nowak had chased up any known offenders in the
area, with no luck on any likely candidates. Some drugs-
related offenders, and plenty of drunk and disorderliness
thanks to the roaring nightlife in Bingley, but no known
hardened criminals with a penchant for violence that
would make a list of suspects worth checking out.

———

Daniel kicked off his boots whilst trying to fend off Oliver's enthusiastic greeting, shushing the baying dog as he
closed the door behind him. He hadn't ingratiated

himself with the neighbours yet—and frankly, he had no desire to, but he didn't need any trouble. He had enough of that in his personal and professional life.

He was glad to return to the relative warmth of the apartment. Outside, a miserable drizzle, the kind that permeated through all layers of clothing, had begun to fall, and Daniel had been daft enough to not bother with a coat.

He crouched in front of the Beagle and clamped a hand around his muzzle gently to quiet him. Oliver only wriggled free, whined, and burrowed into Daniel's chest just the way he had as a puppy, laying his head at Daniel's neck, and leaning on the DI, rolling to expose his belly for rubs, nearly knocking Dan over with the weight of him.

'You're just the same as you ever were, eh bud?' Daniel obliged with a belly scratch. 'Glad that life with the ice queen hasn't hardened you up. Come on, Olly. Tea time.'

It was a little early, but Daniel didn't care. The day had been long enough. He slung a ready-meal lasagne into the microwave and doled out a can of dog meat for Oliver into one of his own bowls, since he still hadn't had a chance to get the Beagle anything more permanent. By the looks of it, the dog had quite happily curled up and slept on Daniel's bed that day, judging by the rumpled, fur-covered state of it.

Oliver fell upon his food at once, and was done by the time the microwave pinged a couple minutes later. Daniel juggled out the burning hot plastic container, and grabbed a fork, taking it directly to the sofa resting on a tea towel so he didn't burn himself. No point making extra washing up, he figured. He flicked on the TV for a bit of background noise, not caring what was on.

The first mouthful nearly burned him, but he swallowed it nonetheless, and chewed through his next one more carefully, crunching through a corner of uncooked pasta. Peril of microwave cooking, but he wasn't about to become Jamie bloody Oliver working all the hours that he did. Besides, Katherine had been the better cook, and he'd been happy enough to leave her to it. When she'd first tasted his cooking, so had she. He'd been devastated, considered himself a *decent* cook, and had liked being in the kitchen, but there hadn't been much point after that. Maybe he'd pick up a cookbook and give it another go, knowing there was no one else to judge him now.

Oliver's head poked into his lap and the dog whined softly, all gooey brown eyes and pleading, his tail thumping on the floor as he sat squarely in between Daniel's legs.

'You can't have this, Olly. It's not good for me, God knows what it'd do to your insides, mate.'

As he finished, Oliver whined softly and jumped up on the sofa beside Daniel, his warm weight settling across Daniel's lap. Daniel lay an idle hand on the scruff of his neck. 'It's good to have you here, bud. Missed you.'

It had been several long months since he'd moved out, since she'd sworn he'd never see the damned dog again, and all the rest of it. It was painful to think about, so he tried to seal that wall back up again. It had been a lonely few months, and Daniel Ward had done what he did best —poured every part of himself into work. Every case he could take, every hour of overtime he could manage without burning out. All to avoid dealing with it, if he was being perfectly honest with himself.

He realised with a groan that technically, his time with Olly was already half gone. If he didn't want to call Katherine on her bluff, he'd be returning Oliver to her in a few days' time. Whether he liked it or not. And he didn't. The flat would once more be drab and empty without the dog, who already seemed to have filled it with his smell and boisterous presence.

Despite it being an early start, Ward had no intention of going to bed early, and there were still a couple of hours left before dark.

'How about we go for a good long walk, eh?' It'd been an age since he remembered taking the dog out on Ilkley Moors. The last big walk he'd taken the dog on was the one where he'd decided at last to stop running away and have the conversation both he and Katherine needed. It had been over for a while. And bitterness would have consumed them both if they'd left it too much longer. He remembered envying Oliver that day for his complete ignorance of such things. The dog had been happy to belt around the moors in the sunshine, chasing ground-nesting birds and rabbits who exploded out of the heather around him as he frolicked.

It was only a five-minute drive to Ogden Reservoir, with Google Maps to help him figure out precisely where the car park was—down a long, narrow, and twisting lane. The reservoir was dark under the rain-bloated sky, but with his hoodie on, Daniel reckoned he could survive if they had to dash back to the car.

Daniel eased out of the car and Olly shot out behind him a second later. Daniel lunged for Olly's collar, yanking the dog short of bolting off, with a cut-off yelp. 'Nice try, bud,' he muttered, clipping Olly on the lead until they had left the puddle and pothole-filled car park, following a track up onto the deserted moors.

Up there, the wind blasted at him—savage and yet refreshing, scouring the day's fatigue away from him—and he gratefully took in the vista around him. Tangles of gorse, heather, and bracken, with small game and sheep trails crisscrossing the moor. Crumbling drystone walls piled here and there. Above them both, on the next hill, across a small ravine-like gulley, vast windmills turned silently, drowned by the gale.

Daniel let Olly have a good long leg stretch, bounding around the moor after sticks. The sheep weren't out at that time of year, so he was permitted to run Olly off the lead. Oliver cocked a leg against a bush, before Ward whistled for the dog to come back.

They'd made it to the summit of the hill and he could see in every direction, from Calderdale to the south, the Pennines to the west, to Ilkley Moors to the north, and all the way to the Vale of York in the east. He didn't know where the paths led. Something for him to learn, he realised, if he settled there, for him and Olly to adventure in future perhaps, Katherine permitting.

For now, it was time to return home. Tomorrow was Sunday, but that meant nothing to him. He'd be back at HMET trying to figure out if they could save Miroslav Ferenc from his unwitting fate... and determining who the hell had killed Amelia Hughes.

CHAPTER TWENTY-FOUR

'Sir?' Nowak's voice greeted Ward as he made it into the office the next day on a mid-shift. 'There's been a *misper* reported in the Shipley area.'

'Oh?'

'DCI's assigned it to us, sir. Charlotte Lawson, early twenties, nursing student. Sunday morning now, and she hasn't been seen or heard from since approximately eight on Friday evening. Very out of character for her to be uncontactable, so her family officially reported her missing.'

Ward frowned. 'Why's it taken them so long?'

Nowak grimaced. 'They thought they had to wait twenty-four hours to report her gone.'

'For fuck's sake,' Ward breathed, his stride momentarily hitching. 'Why do people do this?' he asked, but it was rhetorical.

Nowak simply shook her head.

TV had a lot to answer for. It was often the impression that a person had to be missing for twenty-four hours before they could be reported, but in fact, the sooner the better. Those first twenty-four hours were often the most crucial to capture leads with the greatest chance of finding someone safe and well.

'Right,' said Ward with a sigh. 'Another one to add to the pile, then. With Amelia, Varga, and now this young lass, we'll have to divide and conquer. Can you get contact details for any key friends and family? I'll take her parents, you take the friends, and we'll see what we can piece together of her last known movements.'

'Aye, sir. I've just forwarded you an email with her details and a picture on.'

'Excellent. I'll get DC Norris to start circulating it. Can you put DC Shahzad on her phone too, please? We won't have a warrant, I know, but see if he can squeeze anything out of her bank too whilst he's at it, if there's anyone there on a Sunday. We need her last known location, then perhaps we can track her from CCTV or someone might recall seeing her.'

Hopefully, the lass was out on a weekend bender and hadn't told her parents. Wouldn't be the first time, wouldn't be the last. Miroslav Ferenc would have to wait, Ward realised with a groan. The man had been in custody for long enough, but the missing woman had to take priority, when there could be a threat to her life or safety.

Once more, Ward berated the cuts to the policing service over the years. It was a bloody nightmare being pulled in so many different directions on so many different cases, each just as important as the others. The Incident Room served them all, a Big Board for each case

—though Bogdan Varga's spanned several now. Charlotte Lawson's would take up a new board, though hopefully not for long.

Ward had a curl of unease in his stomach. He did every time they had a missing person case. They never knew whether they'd find the *misper* alive or not. Well or harmed. Shipley, where Charlotte Lawson lived, was only just down the valley from Bingley, where Amelia Hughes had been so brutally murdered. It was a little too close for comfort.

Nowak was already back at her desk, a frown illuminated by the light of her monitor as she typed away at lightning speed. Ward opened up the waiting email from her, scanning through Charlotte's basic details and viewing the attached photograph. She had a passing likeness to Amelia Hughes, he noticed immediately, which was somewhat coincidental.

Charlotte's parents heard from her every morning and evening, and had not had contact with her since Friday teatime, the email stated, and it was they who had reported her missing. She was a diligent and committed nursing student who worked and studied plenty of hours, and who had an active social life outside that. No boyfriend to speak of, though she occasionally went on dates. She was an open person, but kept that side of her life private when it came to her parents. They were worried sick, obviously, and had visited her apartment on Saturday evening but she wasn't home—and had not been there for a day or two, they thought, judging by the washing up and laundry. The last they'd heard, Charlotte was planning to go out with a friend on Friday night, a girl named Grace Tanner, but they didn't have a contact number for her.

That was where Nowak had already stepped in, trawling through Charlotte's social media until she found Grace, and then using social media and the police database to find contact details.

'Sir,' Nowak said, as Ward came off the phone with Charlotte's worried parents, who were unable to give him anything else pertinent. 'I may have something.'

'Go on,' Ward said, looking at her over the partition between their desks.

'I've just spoken to Grace Tanner, and she told me that her and Charlotte had planned to meet on Friday night, but that Charlotte cancelled because she'd found a date using the Matchmaker dating app.'

Ward's ears perked, and he frowned.

'She doesn't know much about the date, except that he was called James, and that they were meeting in *Don't Tell Titus* for dinner and drinks in Saltaire on Friday night. She texted Charlotte to ask how the date had gone at around ten, and to check she was ok, but never heard back. Charlotte didn't answer any calls or messages since.'

'Shit.'

'Yeah.' A missing young woman after a date with a stranger didn't bode well.

'She doesn't know anything at all about the guy?'

'Called James, that's it. Handsome. Charming. That's all Charlotte told her.'

Ward leaned back in his chair and huffed. 'Not much

use. Alright. Can you get the CCTV from the restaurant if they have any?'

'They have cameras. Adam and I go there all the time. I'll get on that now, see if we can get a visual of the guy at least.' DS Emma Nowak and her fiancée Adam lived in the village of Saltaire.

'Great. I'll check with Kasim on the phone now.' Ward eased out of his chair and visited DC Shahzad at the other end of the office. 'Alright, Kasim?'

'Hi, sir. What can I do you for?'

'How are we getting on with Charlotte Lawson's phone?'

'Just looking at it now, sir. I don't have detailed records, but the network triangulated the last known location, which was somewhere in Bingley. The phone was switched off from the network at eleven twenty-four Friday night.'

'Bingley?' Ward frowned. 'She allegedly went on a date in Saltaire that night. You're sure?'

'Yes, sir. Waiting on a warrant now to access messages, call history, and a more detailed location history, but it was definitely Bingley.'

Ward had an uncomfortable feeling in his gut. The two women—Charlotte Lawson and Amelia Hughes— were uncannily alike in appearance. Each of their last known locations were unusually close in Bingley. He didn't want to voice the thought that perhaps they were connected.

Do we have a predator on the loose?

Don't Tell Titus came through with the CCTV within the hour, given the urgency of the *misper* investigation into Charlotte Lawson. DC Kasim Shahzad was already trawling through the footage to find Charlotte Lawson and her mystery date.

Meanwhile, Nowak was putting together a social media campaign with DC Patterson to go out immediately in the hope that viral sharing could piece together Charlotte's last known movements, and find her before anything untoward happened, in case she was in some kind of danger.

'Sir.' Kasim's voice rang out across the office.

Ward rushed across. 'What've you got?'

'Charlotte,' Kasim replied solemnly, gesturing to his screen.

Ward stood behind DC Shahzad. 'Go on.'

'So, we have them both in the bar area from around eight-ish. You can see Charlotte on the left there—' Shahzad pointed her out, '—next to a man she's talking to, so I can only assume it's her date. I've jumped through the footage and they move to a table shortly after, stay there for about ninety minutes, and then leave. At this point, it's around ten o'clock. Outside, the footage shows them getting into a taxi almost off-camera, and heading south up the street, presumably to turn at the top towards Bingley, where the final location of her phone ends up.'

'Right. Pull stills of the pair of them—I want as detailed as you can get on that man, and find out who the taxi firm is. We need the next piece of the puzzle.'

'Yes, sir.'

Ward stared at the image for a long moment—at the

blurred face of the man who stood next to Charlotte Lawson with casual ease, who had led her to a table with an arm around her waist.

Who is he? And is he connected to Amelia Hughes? Where is Charlotte Lawson?

He crossed the office to return to his desk. 'Did you speak to the staff on shift on Friday night, Emma?' He asked DS Nowak.

'Yes, sir. They don't remember the couple, it was busy. There wasn't anything unusual about their behaviour or their appearance to mark them out as worth notice.'

'Alright.' Ward tutted. Not unexpected, but disappointing nonetheless.

'Right. I have to go and tidy up Miroslav Ferenc,' he said reluctantly. 'Make sure the appeal for Charlotte goes out on social media ASAP, but I want a picture of the man she was with on the posts too—get the blown-up version from Kasim. He's on with tracing the taxi they used too—I want an update on that when I've finished with Ferenc. We'll need to check out the driver. I'm not liking where this is going. We need to trace both of them before this gets out of hand. Still no contact?'

'No, sir. Nothing from Charlotte yet.'

Ward sighed. 'Right. Cheers, Emma.'

'Good luck.'

Ward grimaced. What could he say? No matter what Miroslav Ferenc told him, he was either going down for smuggling, or being put six feet under by Varga's crew for getting caught and possibly grassing.

CHAPTER TWENTY-FIVE

Ward strode down to the custody suites, bracing against the detestable stench of the place—sweat, vomit, piss, shit—and that was just one sense. The noise—moaning, screaming, shouting—was a constant jarring on the nerves. It wasn't a pleasant place to be holed up, to say the least, and he didn't envy Miroslav Ferenc. He waited as the desk staff unlocked Ferenc.

'*Ahoj. Pod' so mnou prosím,*' Ward said to him. *Hello. Come with me, please.*

Miroslav regarded him impassively. The Slovakian looked dog-tired after a night of probably no sleep in the barren, hard cell, with dark shadows hollowing the underside of his eyes, and the grizzle of fresh stubble on his chin.

He'd secured a translator, a young man waiting on the telephone in the interview room. Ward waited as Miroslav sat on the chair opposite him before he too sat, with one of the constables from custody filing in to sit next to him.

'Do you want a hot drink?' Ward asked first.

Miroslav looked up in surprise, frowned, then nodded hesitantly. 'Please. Yes.'

'Tea? Coffee?' It didn't hurt to be kind. Ward had no doubt that whilst DS Metcalfe had been a steadying presence, DCI Kipling's first thought in his interview with Ferenc had been answers, not compassion.

'Coffee, no milk. Thank you.'

'Would you mind?' he turned to the constable beside him.

'Certainly, sir. Can I get you anything?'

'Tea, milk, a sugar, please.'

He waited until the young man had left before he turned back to Ferenc. 'Mr Ferenc, I don't need to tell you, our hands are tied. You're in a lot of trouble.' He stared levelly at the man.

Ferenc nodded and rubbed his face in his hands.

'I know as well as you do, you're not the top dog in any of this. But you will take the fall unless you can help us with more information...enough to help us mitigate whatever sentence you might face. You didn't talk to my colleagues, but I'm hoping you'll talk to me. I want to help you.' Ward filled his voice with earnest honesty. He *did* want to help Ferenc. The man didn't deserve to be dragged down by Varga.

Ferenc finally looked up from the table, where he'd been staring at a dent in the metal surface. 'I need to know my family is safe.'

'I can't give you that, Miroslav, you know it. But I can keep *you* safe. If Varga doesn't believe you've talked, there's no reason for your family to get caught up in this.

Have you spoken to your wife yet?' He'd expressly instructed custody to let the man make an international call to his family.

'Yes. She's scared. Taking the kids to her parents' house.'

Ward nodded. It was probably sensible when Varga was involved. The photos slipped under his own door by one of Varga's men was proof enough of that for Ward—Varga knew where he lived, when he had no direct connection to the crime lord. Varga made sure that someone knew everything necessary to protect Varga and his operations from leaks, tampering, or the authorities.

The constable returned with the cuppas.

'Thank you,' murmured Miroslav.

'Right,' said Ward. 'Let's get started.'

A rap on the door paused him. DCI Kipling opened the door. 'I'll sit in on this. Thank you,' he said to the constable, who without a challenge, left, brew in hand. 'As you were,' he said to Ward, taking the constable's seat.

Ward nodded reassuringly at Miroslav, who shifted in his seat, unsettled at the change. Ward cleared his throat and started the interview.

'So, Mr Ferenc, we've already established that you were hired by Bratislava Logistics Solutions in permanent full-time employment to drive HGVs for them, delivering goods across Europe. And that you also engage in some additional ad hoc cash work for an organisation run by Bogdan Varga, who you claim has pressured you into such work by threatening yourself and your family with violence, and who has committed, or had committed on his behalf, acts of violence and intimidation against yourself and your family to ensure your continued coop-eration. Is that correct?'

'Yes.'

'You have also stated that you did not know the contents of your lorry, due to being a last-minute replace-ment driver for that vehicle. Is that correct?'

'Yes.' That was the best lifeline Ward could throw him, innocent until proven guilty. He was *just* a lorry driver, and not a smuggler, as far as Ward believed. Perhaps that would be enough to save him from charges resulting in a stint in prison. In the best-case scenario, the man could return home and protect his family however he needed to.

'Can you run me through the day you drove the lorry —right from the start? When and how were you employed to do so, for example?'

Miroslav coughed and looked nervously between Ward and Kipling. 'It was the night before. Two men came to the house. Varga's men, I have seen them before. They said Varga had a job—same as usual, transport to the UK. Except this time, it was urgent, because the driver had fallen sick. They needed me right then.' Miroslav crossed his arms.

'How did that make you feel?'

'Scared.' Miroslav met his eyes briefly before they returned to the dent in the table. 'After what they had already done to my boy, my family...I went with them.'

'And then?'

'They took me to a local industrial park, to a yard next to a warehouse.'

'Where? Could you show me on a map?'

'Yes.'

Ward pulled out his phone and navigated to the map application. The man gave him an address. Ward showed the man the screen. 'This is the address that the men took you to?'

'It is.'

Ward took a screenshot. This was good. They could find out what business, if any, was registered there. It could be a lead. 'And what happened there?'

Miroslav took a deep breath before he replied. 'It was a lorry yard. Lots of activity. Three lorries being loaded. I was told to get in the cab of one and wait.' He shrugged. 'So I did.'

'Did you see who was there? What was being loaded into the lorries?'

'It was dark, not very well lit. I did not see Varga, but his men were there. A few, I recognised. About a dozen men, I think. They were loading lots of boxes—the same size and shape into each lorry, on crates, with two fork-lifts. I didn't see inside the boxes. There were drivers waiting in the other vans too. I don't know them.'

'OK. And you were told to do what?'

'The same as usual. Drive them to the UK. They give us the paperwork. We don't ask questions.'

'Where do you drive to?'

'The drop-off point is in Birstall. At the industrial park there.'

Ward and Kipling shared a look. Birstall. A well-known sprawling industrial park right off the M62 motor-way. Excellent connections to anywhere in the UK from such a central location.

'Did you travel with the other lorries?'

'No.'

'Where did they go?'

'I don't know. One followed me to the port, the other two, I didn't see.'

'Do you see any of the paperwork for the other lorries?' Were there more duplicates than Miroslav?

'No, just mine.'

Annoyance niggled at Ward. They had such an infinitesimally small piece of the puzzle.

'What did those lorries look like? Do you recall any of the registration plates?'

'No. They were like my lorry. White. Most of the drivers Varga finds... they work at BLS too, or other haulage companies. It's how he finds us. He knows we can do the job, and he knows we all need a bit of extra money.'

'That's how he gets you involved.'

Miroslav Ferenc nodded unhappily.

'And then, when you're in so far...you can't get out.'

'Yes.'

'Do you know if Bogdan Varga has any connections to the firm you work for, Bratislava Logistics Solutions?'

Miroslav deliberated. 'I'm not sure.'

'He uses registration plates belonging to lorries at BSL.'

Miroslav met his eyes and frowned. 'Hmm. I suppose that could make sense. Why not? He puts pressure on us to do what he wants. Why not the boss? But you would have to ask him; I don't know the man.'

'Have you ever had direct dealings with Varga?'

'No.'

'But you know it's him?'

'Yes.'

'How?'

'Because he is everywhere,' said Miroslav quietly, and his eyes flicked to the CCTV camera above Ward's head.

'What makes you say that?'

Miroslav laughed mirthlessly. 'Because it's true. He knows everything. He has people everywhere. Why do you think the police in Slovakia cannot arrest him? He lives in a mansion. They all know where. He comes and goes as he pleases, and everyone knows what he really does, and yet, he is still a free man.'

Ward ground his teeth together. 'So you're saying that there is corruption within the authorities that allows Varga to continue his operations unchecked?

'Exactly.'

Ward nodded. It wasn't exactly unexpected. Corruption was a part of life, much as he wished it wasn't. 'Do you know if that network extends to the United Kingdom?' He looked sharply at the Slovakian for any tell, any squirming, any indication that would hint at a lie or evasion.

'I don't know,' admitted Miroslav, 'but, it wouldn't surprise me. This is the first time I've been stopped.'

Ward shared a look with Kipling—how many dozens of shipments, or perhaps more, had Varga smuggled into the country without anyone realising? Or perhaps *with*. Ward shifted uneasily in his seat.

'Do you know any names for any of Varga's associates, both in Slovakia or here?'

'No.'

'Have you ever seen Varga?'

'Yeah—sometimes he comes to the yard. I've never spoken to him.' Miroslav grimaced.

Ward could understand the man's reticence. The crime lord was unpleasant to deal with at best.

'Is there *anything* else you can tell us? Anything at all about the operation, that might lead us to be able to track down and identify any of the higher levels responsible for this?'

Miroslav hung his head and shook it. He knew what it meant for him.

Ward sighed and leaned back in his chair. 'Alright. Thank you for your cooperation, it's appreciated.' He turned to Kipling and raised an eyebrow.

Kipling nodded, pursing his lips, oozing disapproval.

'Interview terminated.'

Kipling stood and buttoned his jacket.

'I'll sort him out, sir,' Ward offered.

'A word.'

Ward slipped outside, leaving Miroslav inside, his head in his hands. 'Sir?'

'We have to do better than this.' Kipling was agitated as he glanced up and down the empty corridor. 'I have the Super on my case, and she won't let up. We have to have more than a low-level pawn driving a lorry full of knock-off t-shirts. This is the brothel raid all over again, with nothing concrete to go on.

'If he's suggesting what I think he's suggesting...this may be bigger than we thought. Forget people trafficking, brothels, drugs, smuggling—if we have corruption on our hands in the border forces, or God forbid in the force, this is going to blow up in our faces fast.'

'Aye, sir,' Ward said sombrely, glancing through the crack in the door to Miroslav. 'If he had answers, I think he'd give them, to protect his family.'

'I don't give a damn what you think, DI Ward.' Kipling's voice was dangerously quiet as he leaned in close, every syllable sharp. 'I expect you to process him like any other person. I'm satisfied we've reached the charging threshold based on the evidence we have and the disclosures he's made. And then I expect you to find more answers.'

Of course, the DCI was right. Miroslav had knowingly committed an offence, and he had to answer for that, no matter the mitigating factors and circumstances which had led him into making the repeated trips. The best he could do was permit Miroslav a phone call to his family. Perhaps the man wouldn't be remanded into custody, perhaps he'd be let out on bail, but his chances of running home to live a peaceful life free of Varga's existence were somewhere between 'none' to 'when hell froze over'.

DCI Kipling strode off straight-backed. Ward watched him go. The door at the end of the hall slammed after Kipling. Ward cursed under his breath before he returned to Miroslav.

CHAPTER TWENTY-SIX

DS Nowak's heart pounded as she rang the taxi firm. Hoping they could make a critical link. They'd managed to be lucky so far with Charlotte, in a way that they hadn't been with Amelia. Instead of dead ends and guesswork, here, they had a seemingly clear trail from Charlotte's last known contact with her family and friends. She clicked her pen on-and-off and on-and-off repeatedly as she waited for the call to connect.

'Bingley Cars,' a man answered on the second ring, his voice gritty over a slightly crackly connection.

'Hello, Detective Sergeant Emma Nowak from West Yorkshire Police. I need some details of a journey one of your cars made on Friday night as a witness. Can you help me with that?' She didn't mention that the driver might well become a suspect, depending on the answers she got.

'Sure, love, whassup?' the man answered.

'I need to know which of your vehicles and drivers

made a pick up from outside *Don't Tell Titus* in Saltaire on Friday night just after ten.'

'Right.' Nowak could hear the man sucking on his lip as he searched for the information.

He replied after a minute, 'That would be Hassan Ali, love.'

'In a Vauxhall Insignia?'

'Yeah, love. YF07 CMZ.'

'Thanks. Can you give me Mr Ali's contact number? We have a few questions to ask him.'

'He's not in trouble, is he?'

'Not at this stage, sir. Just some routine questions surrounding the disappearance of a young woman. We're tracing her last known movements, and it seems she and a friend got into that taxi, but we're not sure what happened to her next.'

'Well, our Hassan'll sort you out, love. Wasn't him, I'll tell you that for nowt. Here you go.' The man relayed a mobile number. 'Do you need anythin' else?'

'No thanks. What's your name, just for our records?'

'Mo. Mohammad Zain.'

'Cheers, Mr Zain.'

No sooner had Nowak hung up than she dialled Hassan Ali's number.

'Yeah?' a gruff voice answered.

Nowak introduced herself. 'I've been passed your phone number by Mohammad Zain to speak to you in connection with a missing person we're trying to locate. I have a couple questions about a journey you made on Friday night, if that's okay?'

A rustle on the other end. 'Yeah, ok.'

'You made a pickup about ten-ish on Friday night from *Don't Tell Titus* in Saltaire, is that right?'

'Hmm, yeah, I remember that.'

'Who did you pick up?'

'Young lad and his bird.'

'Can you describe them for me, in as much detail as you remember?' Nowak pursed her lips at how unforthcoming the man was.

'Both mid-twenties I think. She was small, brown hair, all dolled up in a right short dress and off her face.'

'Drunk, you mean?'

'Yeah, pissed.'

'And the man?'

'He were taller, 'bout five-ten-ish, brown curly hair, dressed quite smart—jacket sort of thing.'

'Was he drunk too?'

'No.' Nowak could hear the frown in the man's voice. 'He seemed sober. She were drunk and giggly, but he were really quiet. Seemed a bit weird.'

'Did you drop them off together or separately?'

'Together, in Bingley, just off the main road on Sycamore Avenue. He helped her out and I watched 'em go down the street whilst I took my next job.'

'And this was when?'

She heard the rush of air as he exhaled down the phone. 'Oh, I dunno. It's not far from Saltaire is it, so between quarter past and half past ten? You'd have to check wi' the office, they'll have the time of my next job.'

'Was that the last you saw of them?'

'Yeah. I turned round and headed to Keighley for another pickup.'

'So, to confirm, at somewhere between quarter past and half past ten on Friday night, you finished your journey with these two, dropped them at the end of Sycamore Avenue in Bingley just next to the main road, and they walked away from you continuing on Sycamore Avenue, at which point you left. Did I get that right?'

'Yeah.'

'Thanks for your help, Mr Ali.'

Nowak rang the taxi company straight back to confirm Mr Ali's next journey—the details checking out —before she paused to evaluate what they had with Kasim.

DC Shahzad checked out the address the taxi driver had given her, but the domestic street of Victorian back-to-back terraces was not covered by any CCTV. At that time of night on a Friday, the residents there would have been inside. It would be highly unlikely that anyone would have seen Charlotte Lawson and the young man accompanying her, but Nowak would canvas the street anyway. They had to try. Perhaps she'd get lucky and they could trace Charlotte a little way further with a tip from a member of the public.

'Let's put together a board with what we know so far of her movements,' Nowak suggested. Shahzad had already run off a print of Charlotte and several of the blurry CCTV images of the man with her in the restaurant.

They went to the incident room together, where Nowak started drawing a timeline, from eight that night, where Charlotte had met the mystery man at *Don't Tell*

Titus, to ten-thirty, where they had established that she had gone to a small area of Bingley with the mystery man.

At the top of the board, Emma pinned the photo of Charlotte. Next to the restaurant note, Shahzad tacked up the images of Charlotte, and most notably, her date, from different angles.

Nowak jotted what biometrics they knew—male, Caucasian, mid-twenties, curly brown hair... her pen stalled.

'What is it, Sarge?'

Nowak looked between Charlotte's board, and the one next door—Amelia's.

The coincidence was not lost on her, but now, it was as though the evidence in front of her screamed for attention.

'Don't you see?' she replied quietly. 'I think these are linked.' Emma pointed between the two boards. 'For one, look how similar they look. Strikingly so—hair colour, ethnicity, build. Entirely coincidental at face value, perhaps. But look, we found a curly brown hair on Amelia belonging to an unknown male, the only potential forensic link to a killer that we have. And the location of the murder being Harden Beck just outside Bingley. Now, look here.'

She pointed back to Charlotte's board. 'A young man, with curly brown hair. They return to an incredibly precise location in Bingley, right by Myrtle Park, which is just across the river from where Amelia Hughes was murdered. Don't you think that's way too coincidental?'

Shahzad stared gravely between the two boards. 'Yup. I think you're right, Sarge.'

'They're connected.'

'They're connected,' Shahzad agreed.

Nowak drew a line from the man's picture on Charlotte's board off the side, onto Amelia's board, linking it to the brown curly hair, and the running man, with a giant question mark.

She'd looked into known offenders in the area, released, or on licence, with no results that matched the profile of the man they were beginning to build a picture of. Another dead end.

Coldness filled the pit of her stomach. Amelia Hughes was dead and they had no idea who had done it, or why. But an uncannily similar woman had also gone missing without a trace, and the trail had led to the same precise area.

Was Charlotte Lawson still alive? Was the mystery man responsible for both Amelia's murder and Charlotte's disappearance? How on earth would they find him with nothing else to go on?

CHAPTER TWENTY-SEVEN

Ward returned from the interview with Miroslav Ferenc, every step weighed down with the damned hopelessness of it. Ferenc would be charged. His life ruined. His family without a husband and father. Bail would be unlikely. They'd probably not be able to see him until he emerged from the other side of a lengthy sentence, though Ward hoped it would be shortened in light of the information Ferenc had supplied them with.

Ward wondered whether Varga would provide for Ferenc's family in compensation for his loss, soften the blow. He doubted it. Ferenc had served a purpose, and nothing more. Another cog in the machine of Varga's operation. Besides, if Varga found out Ferenc had talked, he'd probably execute the lot of them for spite.

Yet again, Ward questioned it all—right and wrong, the letter of the law. Ferenc had committed a crime, and possibly knowingly, but he had done it to provide for his family, and then to protect them, shield them from Varga's cruelty. What father, man, husband, would choose differently to protect his family, against the might of Varga and his thugs?

There were all kinds of shades of grey between right and wrong, the line so far blurred Ward could hardly see it at times. But he recognised the feeling as he climbed the stairs from the custody suite to the office. *Guilt.* That he had added to Ferenc and his family's suffering, regardless of whether Ward's actions had been well within, and demanded by, the law.

'Do we have any update on Hughes?' he asked as he popped his head into the Incident Room and found Nowak and Shahzad inside.

'No, sir,' said Nowak quietly. 'But you need to see this.'

Ward entered, letting the door swing closed behind him.

'Sir, I think Charlotte Lawson and Amelia Hughes are linked,' Nowak began, her lips thinned and her tone grim. 'I think we have our suspect, and I believe Charlotte is in terrible danger, if it's not already too late for her.'

'Go on.' Ward's guilt over Miroslav Ferenc's fate faded in the face of Nowak's unsettled stance.

Nowak tapped on Charlotte's board. 'We've pieced together her last known movements. She went on a date with a young man she met on Matchmaker at *Don't Tell Titus* in Saltaire on Friday night. They were there between approximately eight and ten, and then shared a taxi to Bingley. To right here.'

Nowak pointed to the enlarged map of that part of Bingley, to the two dots on it, so uncannily close together

—the site of Amelia's body, and where the taxi had dropped the couple off. 'The man and Charlotte left together. The taxi driver reported Charlotte seeming quite inebriated and unsteady, and the man being much more sober. Oh, and he described him as, "A bit weird."'

Ward had already examined the boards—noted the blown-up CCTV from the restaurant and the line between Charlotte's and Amelia's boards. 'It's the same man?'

'That's what we believe.' Nowak's face was pale. 'If he was capable of doing that to Amelia, and Charlotte hasn't been heard from in almost two days...'

'I come to the same conclusion you do,' Ward said. He cursed under his breath. 'Did you get the social media campaign out?' he fired at Shahzad. 'Yes, sir. Already getting very good metrics, plenty of comments, reactions, shares, retweets, and so on, on all platforms.

'Any known individuals who might match the suspect?' he asked Nowak.

'No, sir. I ran through everyone, and no one matched him based on the biometric data we have.'

'You circulated this photo too, right?' Ward tapped the blurry image of the man.

'Aye, sir,' Shahzad said.

'Then we'd better hope someone recognises him before it's too late for Charlotte Lawson.'

But Ward couldn't ease the rising cold dread within him, that the girl would already be dead at the hands of the man with curly hair.

CHAPTER TWENTY-EIGHT

I t was definitely *him*.

Harry's hand shook as he looked at the image on Facebook again. He'd been scrolling through his feed—the usual mind-numbing habit—when a share had popped up in his newsfeed. A blurry photo of him, next to a crystal clear one of Charlotte Lawson, and an urgent appeal to locate the two of them.

'Fuck.'

Harry clicked on the post. Read it. Scrolled to the comments—already hundreds, even though the post was only a couple of hours old, sharing it, tagging people, dropping comments hoping she'd be found safe and well.

Electric anxious energy charged through him, filling him with apprehension and exhilaration as he danced that fine line between fear and thrill of being caught. He ran a hand through his tangle of curly hair. Now, it felt like a beacon, singling him out, unusual as it was. It marked him out. Marked him as a suspect for anyone with half a brain cell. He matched all the descriptions they had, of course, because he was guilty. He couldn't change that, but he had to get them off his back. He couldn't risk a member of the public calling in having seen him.

He had to get rid of the hair immediately.

'*Fuck fuck fuck!*' Harry jumped off the sofa, bouncing on the balls of his feet as that nervous energy sought to discharge. 'Calm down. Calm down, Harry. Nothing to be worried about. They don't know who you are or where you live. They have a grainy picture and nothing else. It's all going to be fine.' A laugh bubbled up, a nervous tick, and despite the calm tone of his words, the seething worry inside him wouldn't abate.

Harry legged it upstairs, each step creaking with the thundering of his footsteps, and into the bathroom. He leaned on the sink heavily, both hands gripping the cold porcelain, as he peered at himself in the mirror. Worry echoed back at him in the tight lines of his face. Harry forced his jaw to unclench, his furrowed brow to relax, his lips to soften.

He could overcome this.

He ran a hand over his grizzled face. Already, he hadn't shaved since Friday morning, and in the two days since, dark stubble peppered his jawline. He'd keep growing that out. Harry bent and rummaged through the under-sink cupboard until his hands landed on what he sought. Hair clippers.

The wire tangled in the contents of the cupboard, and Harry wrenched it out, bottles and toiletries bombarding the floor as the cord tugged them all out too. Harry swore and kicked a bottle aside, storming out of the bathroom and into his bedroom where there was a plug socket and extension lead. Forcing his hands not to shake, Harry connected the extension and dragged it into the bathroom before plugging in the clippers.

Sweeping the spilled contents of the cupboard aside, he stood before the mirror. Now, he felt calmer, more resolute. Harry fitted the longest setting onto the clipper, a number four that would leave his hair roughly half an inch long, and switched it on. The buzzing was a welcome numbing sound that washed over his anxiety.

Starting at the back, he shaved up, the efforts of his clipping hidden from view. Slowly, he swept the clipper over his head, grunting as some hair caught in it and pulled. A few minutes later, and a different face seemed to stare back at him in the mirror. His curls were gone, replaced with a generic all-over cut. Somehow, his cheekbones stood out more now, his jawline more prominent, grazed with that dark stubble.

To a passer-by, he would be a completely different man from the clean-shaven, curly-haired man in the picture.

Harry smiled to himself, and switched the clippers back on, now humming along to their buzz as he tidied up around his ears, with the clumps of his former identity littering the vinyl flooring under his feet.

———

After Harry had finished and disposed of the shorn hair down the toilet, he ventured downstairs again to check on her. Charlotte was in the cellar. As with Amelia, he had kept her phone—switched off in his bedside drawer—but taken her clothes and any other trace of her to the cold underground room, wrapped in his spare bedsheet.

It had been a right job hauling her downstairs without falling down the steep, narrow staircase himself, the dumb, heavy weight of her body cumbersome to manoeuvre in the aged, cramped confines of the back-to-back terrace.

Now, he took both their phones and the Pandora bracelet he'd taken from Amelia's body downstairs, to hide in the old toolbox. He'd not leave it to chance if anyone happened to come to his house to poke around. He'd placed Charlotte's body in the nook behind the underside of the stairs, so only her legs poked out, wrapped in that pale sheet, so at a cursory glance down the stairs, the cellar would appear empty. He didn't need to answer questions about why he had multiple mobile phones, At the very least, someone would think he was a drug dealer... but with a more thorough search, the darker truth would quickly emerge.

As he opened the cellar door though, he could already smell her. Harry wrinkled his nose in disgust. He'd hoped with the time of year—autumn settling in— and the frigid nature of the cellar, that she'd remain cold and un-decaying. Like a morgue, he supposed. But death, it seemed, had already found its cloying way into the air, the pungency of it growing heavier with each step he descended.

He'd have to find a way to get rid of her. The house just wasn't big enough, and there was no way for him to get a body out without being caught. Harry chastised himself for being so careless as he tramped back up the stairs. He'd managed well enough with Amelia, it seemed, for no one had come knocking. Maybe he'd been foolish to bring Charlotte to his home. Maybe he ought to have done the job at hers. But it was too late now. He'd have to find a solution—one where he wasn't caught.

Clack. Harry shut the cellar door firmly behind him, eyeing it before he moved through to the kitchen, taking gulps of the much fresher air—but unable to get that reek out of his nose. He grabbed a can of Coke from the fridge and went to crash on the couch again, running his free hand over the soft crop of hair he now bore, and the sand-paper stubble on his jaw.

His anxiety had abated, though he still had to figure out how to get rid of Charlotte. That part of him warred with the hungry one that sought the thrill of it all again. He'd already been warming up a girl on the Matchmaker app, one who looked much like Amelia and Charlotte, but she was taking far too long to say yes.

At least he'd got a date with her the following day—unusual for a Monday, alright, but he'd take it, none-theless. The urge strengthened in him already. He loved the feeling of power, holding them in his hands and watching the life fade from them. Already, he wondered how he would kill the girl.

He *needed* to kill again. Both to assuage that...and to flaunt his mystery and power over the investigations into Amelia's death and Charlotte's disappearance, That they hadn't even managed to identify him yet, even with the CCTV footage.

Harry chuckled to himself darkly, revelling in that

power coursing through him as he relived the murders again, admonishing himself for being weak enough to be scared that they would catch him.

Harry had a short while before he was due at work. Time enough to figure out, with a little help from Google, how best to get rid of a body.

CHAPTER TWENTY-NINE

A t that moment, DC Patterson clattered into the silent Incident Room as the implications of Charlotte Lawson's disappearance and Amelia Hughes' murder being connected sunk in. 'Kasim, I think the social media appeal's pulled something in. Sir, Sarge,' he greeted Ward and Nowak before continuing.

'A woman's rung in. Sara Pearson. She had a date with a man matching the description and the CCTV image a few days earlier. Thursday evening, in fact.' The night of the day Amelia had been murdered.

Ward, Nowak, and Shahzad turned to Patterson as one, their attention laser-focused on him.

'They—er, her and the man, James Denton—met on Matchmaker that day and mutually agreed to have a one-off hook-up that night. Sara attended his home address, around Sycamore Avenue—she can't remember the exact address as he met her on the street and brought her back to his—where they had intercourse, after which she left.'

Ward and Nowak shared a heavy look. The net

closed in on that one location, near Myrtle Park. And James Denton.

'Anything else?' Ward asked.

'James Denton's profile picture, the one she's sent through, is a strong match for the man on CCTV. Here.' Patterson handed him a colour printout of a blown-up photograph—a screenshot taken from the Matchmaker app interface of James Denton's name and picture. A young man in his mid-twenties with a distinct spring of curly brown hair, a slightly beaky nose, and a thin jawline.

'She's also sent through their messages, at my request. Some of them are more, er...of a saucy nature, shall we say?' Young DC Patterson coloured slightly. 'But enough to show that they arranged to meet at the end of Sycamore Avenue that night for her to walk back to his house with him. She thinks it was right down the other end of the road, near the park, but one of the streets parallel to Sycamore.'

'This cannot be a coincidence. The man's using Matchmaker,' Ward said, turning back to the board and slapping James Denton's face in the middle of the two boards. 'Amelia had a stalker who catfished her into a date on Matchmaker. Charlotte arranged her date on Matchmaker. Sara Pearson had a date with this man, who she met on Matchmaker.'

'We need to find him,' murmured Nowak.

'I've checked on the PNC,' Patterson offered, 'but I can't find anyone matching the names James Denton.'

'Thanks, Patterson,' Ward said. 'Nowak, will you please check in with Sacha Lavigne? I want all the details she has gone over to see that we have absolutely everything. If we can find a way to track this scumbag down, we need to find it now. Charlotte Lawson is in potential danger. Sara Pearson was incredibly lucky if this is the man that killed Amelia Hughes the morning of their hook-up.'

DC Shahzad cleared his throat. 'Want me to get in touch with Matchmaker, see if they'll release the user data?'

Ward laughed entirely mirthlessly. 'Try for nothing, son, aye. They won't do squat without a warrant, and I doubt we have grounds for one yet, with the lack of hard evidence. Can you search for users on there?'

'No, sir, the app prides itself on privacy. You can contact someone if you both approve of each other with a mutual heart by the looks of it, but you can't look someone up by name.'

'Damn.'

'Yeah.'

'OK. Get on it anyway, please. If you can, I want data on who James Denton is, plus anyone else he's contacted who might be at risk. What else do we have?' Ward sucked the inside of his cheek as Shahzad left with Patterson in tow.

'He has a type?' Nowak suggested. 'Both slim women, brunette, Caucasian, twenties?'

Ward sighed. 'We can't narrow down enough on that. You know what, leave Sacha to me. Get a warrant put together for Matchmaker anyway; we have to try. There's enough here that we have reasonable grounds to suspect this man to be involved with Amelia Hughes' death,

Charlotte Lawson's disappearance, and the only thing tying him to either of them is this bloody app.'

'I'll push as hard as I can, sir.'

'Thanks. We might not have much time.' Ward fixed on Charlotte's smiling face. Where was she? Was she safe? Or were they already too late?

He sighed and returned to his desk to ring Sacha. She picked up on the second ring.

'*Oui?*' the French woman greeted.

'Sacha Lavigne? It's Detective Inspector Ward. Do you have a minute?'

She replied after a hesitation, subdued. 'Of course.'

'I need to run over what you know of the man who tricked Amelia into a date. We think this could be a significant lead. I really could do with any small detail you might have, no matter how insignificant you think it is.'

'*Mais oui.* I've been trying to remember, and I went back over all our recent messages, trying to figure out if she said or did something that might give me a clue as to what happened to her.' Sacha sighed down the phone.

'Did you find anything?'

'I'm not sure. She mentioned the week before she died about finding this great guy on Matchmaker. A marketing exec who worked in Leeds. Dead fit, she said, and the total opposite to Darren—you know, her ex? Really charming, interesting, thoughtful...she knew it was quick, but she agreed to go out on a date with him on the Saturday before she died. I think she was trying to put Darren behind her, because she was still really upset that it hadn't worked out. She thought this guy might at least distract her, you know? We texted just before she went out—she was really excited, sent me a snap of herself all dolled up.'

As she spoke, Ward typed up a transcript of their conversation as fast as he could, his fingers stumbling over some of the keys.

'The next thing I know, later that evening, she rings me in a fit of tears, and she was *furious*, but I could tell she was also a bit freaked out. She said that she'd gone to meet her date, but that it hadn't been the guy she was supposed to meet at all. Instead, it was this creep who'd bothered her on her way home a few times. She thought she'd brushed him off, but he'd gone one step further to find her on the app and catfish her there. I mean it is creepy, isn't it?'

'Aye...' agreed Ward, still typing away.

'No means *no*, you know! She wasn't interested in this weird stranger that had asked her out. I'm sure she said his name was Harry, but that he'd used a different name and photo on the app.'

'Does the name James Denton mean anything to you?'

'I'm sorry, no. Maybe Denton sounds familiar? I'm not sure. Is that the guy from the app? She didn't tell me who she was meeting from Matchmaker, said she wanted to keep it private for the moment, until she knew it was going to work out, and when she called me after the date, I think she was too angry and upset to mention his name. I don't remember a James Denton anyway, I'm sorry. But I'm *pretty* sure she said the guy who'd been harassing her was called Harry, and that it was on her way home from work that he bothered her.'

Ward finished typing. 'Right. Great. That's very helpful, thank you.'

'There's one more thing I forgot... Harry knew where she lived.' Sacha sounded even more troubled.

'What makes you say that?'

'I didn't think of this until after we'd spoken, and honestly, I didn't know whether I was clutching at nothing. I keep coming back to Darren, if I'm honest. His anger, and what he'd be capable of if he lost control.

'But...after the date gone wrong...the next day, I think, Amelia had a knock at the door. When she answered it, there was no one there, but there was a small package on the doorstep. It was a bottle of her favourite perfume. She thought it was from Darren at first, because he was the only one who knew that perfume was the one she loved, but there was a note with it, and the note was from this man, Harry. Apologising. Wanting another chance.'

'This is a few days before she was attacked, correct?' Ward interjected.

'Yeah. She messaged him on WhatsApp using the number he'd written on the note and told him to back off, never to contact her again, and then she blocked him. She brushed it off a bit, but the more I think about it, the more I think she was *really* scared by that. This man had gone so far as to bother her on her way home, then trick her into a date, and somehow find out where she lived... that's beyond disturbing.'

Ward listened, grim-faced. 'It is indeed. She didn't

happen to pass on this man's number, or any details of what he looked like, did she?'

'No, only that he was really odd, not her type at all.'

Ward wrapped up the call with Sacha with a heavy heart. More and more, it looked as though the man—Harry, James, or whatever the hell he was called—used Matchmaker to connect with and catfish potential victims, and that it had facilitated his extreme stalking of Amelia Hughes in part, which, Ward was convinced, had led to her death.

The frenzy of the attack upon Amelia, perhaps now made sense. It was a crime of passion, as the pathologist had suggested, and perhaps Ward could now understand why—because Amelia had rejected Harry in all forms, physically in person, and virtually where he had attempted to present a more pleasing character. If he was that determined to have Amelia, Ward reckoned it would be one small step to mete out such an act of brutal revenge for that rejection.

He relayed Sacha's message to the team briefly, and his own thoughts, to which they agreed.

'It looks like he's our man, sir, but how do we find him?' Nowak said, troubled.

'I don't know,' Ward admitted, looking around at them all. 'We're only human. I wish we had the answers, for Amelia, for Charlotte, for anyone else who might be in danger from this bastard. We *need* those answers. Before someone else gets hurt. How's the warrant coming?'

Nowak answered, 'Just about to submit it, sir, and praying to all the gods that they see fit to grant it.'

'Good. We can only hope. Patterson, Shahzad, how are you getting on with Matchmaker?'

'I've signed up as a user, sir,' said Patterson. 'Currently looking through all the available women in the area on the app to see if, using the profile of Amelia and Charlotte, I can narrow down any potential victims. It's a long shot, I know, but...'

'No, it's good. It might be something, and we have to hope. Keep at it. Kasim?'

Shahzad straightened. 'I've just spoken to Matchmaker HQ over in York. They will need a warrant to release specific user data, otherwise, they're in breach of data protection. That being said, they can confirm a man by the name of James Denton is registered on their database, and as soon as we can provide a warrant, they can let us know what details they hold on him and who he's been making connections with.'

'Damn it.' Ward scowled. He understood the company's predicament, but didn't they understand? A woman had been *murdered* and another had been missing for over forty-eight hours and the only thing connecting the two was their app and the profile of James Denton.

'Looks like Patterson might be the only way we can identify anyone else at risk right now,' murmured Nowak.

'Needle in a haystack, Emma. That's what worries me. We're stabbing in the dark on this one, and it's not good enough. Get that warrant in, *now*. Mark a threat to life, whatever you have to do, to get it done. We need to find Charlotte Lawson.'

CHAPTER THIRTY

The grainy black and white printout greeted Harry on his way into work. Already pinned to the automatic door of the Sainsbury's Local, word had gotten around fast.

Harry stroked his chin self-consciously as he looked at the image showing himself in *Don't Tell Titus* on Friday night with Charlotte Lawson. He hadn't realised that when it had first popped up on his phone. He'd been so spooked to even see his picture, he hadn't twigged where they had gotten it from.

Despite the drastic changes he'd made to his appearance, it still set him on edge. He was still the man in the photo after all—still had the same nose, chin, profile, build...he couldn't change any of that.

'Alright, Hazza? Local brought it in, asked if they could stick it up,' said Jamal. 'Thought it was your mop at first.' He laughed, pointing to the man's head in the picture.

'Ain't me,' said Harry with a shrug, running his hand across his head.

'Yeah, I can see that. When did ya cut your hair?'

'Thursday night after work,' Harry lied. Jamal hadn't been on shift with him on Friday to know any different. 'Already growing out. Fancied a change.'

Jamal chuckled, but his eyes slid back to the picture all the same.

'I'm gay, anyway. I wouldn't be out dating a lass.'

'Are you?' Jamal's head whipped round to Harry, his eyes wide. 'No way. I'd never have pinned you for well...*that.*'

Gullible idiot. Harry shrugged. 'None of anyone's business really, is it?' Harry knew Jamal came from an ultra-conservative household where homosexuality was frowned upon, he definitely wouldn't want to dwell on the subject.

Jamal laughed nervously and folded his arms, crinkling his Sainsbury's shirt across his chest. 'Guess not. Better get back to stocking up the freezers, anyway. By the way, the boss is after you.'

Harry gritted his teeth. He wasn't in the mood to hear it. Before Jamal could move, the stockroom door clattered open.

'Just the chap I want to see,' said Janice grimly as she strolled out of the backroom, her straight blonde bob as severe as her attitude towards him. She looked up at him with a glare, her small stature not diminishing her fearsome presence.

'Sorry, I've been ill.'

'Not good enough,' Janice snapped. 'I shouldn't have

to work the close last minute because some arsehole doesn't turn up for his shift. You make up the hours or I dock your pay, and you're on a final written warning for this. Three times in a week, I'm not having it.'

'I was *ill*! You can't fire me for being ill.'

'I can and I will when you don't follow procedure. Call in sick like the rest of us so I can at least try to get cover.' Janice narrowed her eyes at him. 'You're ten minutes late as it is. Get cracking. I expect to see you make up the difference at the end of your shift today on your timesheet. Pull your finger out if you want to keep your job. I have plenty of people waiting in line who'll do a far better job.'

Before he could reply, Janice swept away back into the stock room, where Harry could see a massive stack of paperwork. A stock count. No wonder Jamal was twitchy —he was the biggest filcher there when it came to sneaking a pack of this or that out of the cigarette stock.

He cursed her under his breath and stomped to the till to dump his jacket on the shelf underneath the counter. One day he'd tell her to shove the fucking job.

Now there's an idea.

Maybe he ought to look to move. Perhaps a fresh start in a new area, one with a greater population for him to hide amongst, would give him the scope to continue his new pastime.

It wasn't like he had ties to Bingley. It'd be good to start afresh somewhere else. Anywhere else. The possibilities, the opportunities, were glorious when he considered it.

'Are you just gonna stand there all day?' Jamal said.

'Eh?'

'You're staring into space, Haz.'

'Just considering where to tell Jan to shove her stupid bloody job,' Harry muttered.

Jamal crowed with laughter. 'Right on, man. One day, eh?' He looked at the door with longing—and the crisp, sunny Autumn day outside—before he trundled over to the freezers to continue his work.

Harry stood behind the till, hands in his pockets, dreaming of his next kill.

CHAPTER THIRTY-ONE

Half a dozen of them were on door-to-doors that Monday afternoon—Ward, Nowak, Shahzad, and three police constables they'd managed to borrow from the local area.

Ward had left DC Norris to keep digging on the Varga investigation, on the multiple documents submitted on the same import reference. It was a decoy, he was sure of it now. Varga was reusing the same reference numbers for a reason. What else was coming into the country that Varga didn't want them to know about?

Counterfeit clothing was a nice little money-spinner, but it wasn't the most lucrative business the crime lord ran by far. The only way they could help people like Miroslav Ferenc, caught in Varga's net, was to take out the fat spider sitting in the middle, spinning his web.

But Ward had no time to pay it any thought. Now, Charlotte Lawson, Amelia Hughes, and the man whose name they couldn't pin down consumed him.

Up and down the area of Sycamore Avenue they

combed, including the surrounding streets, going from door to door of each of the terraced houses with pictures of Charlotte Lawson and the man with curly hair.

It drove Ward now, the urgency of it. Finding Charlotte Lawson was no longer just a matter for the young woman's own safety, it was the best chance he had of finding Amelia Hughes' killer, who had otherwise gone to ground without a trace.

Ward had already scoured the corner where the taxi had dropped off for any hint of forensic evidence, perhaps a handbag, or something dropped from a pocket, but the pavement was bare—save for a pile of hardened dog shit. It had been a long shot. What had he expected? For Charlotte Lawson to be waiting for him? Ward gritted his teeth. Desperation was making him sloppy.

The long, straight street stretched away from him, ending in trees at Myrtle Park's boundary. A row of age and smoke-blackened Victorian terraced houses, each with a walled front garden the size of a postage stamp, but all well-kept and well to do, lined the road on either side.

Ward sighed and approached the next house. It was the middle of the day on a Monday, everyone was out at work. Hardly any of their searches had yielded a resident, much less anyone who could help. On Friday night, they had all been at home with the curtains drawn—or out themselves—and thus hadn't seen a thing. None of the residents of Sycamore Avenue recognised a young man with curly hair. The vague description—a man of average height, average build, mid-twenties—could have been anyone.

Going by the triangulation of Charlotte's phone, and Amelia's when it was switched on after her death, the signal had come from the same area. This area, if Ward had to put money on it. They just didn't know which house, out of the hundreds in that small area. That was the problem. He turned away from yet another unanswered door, turning onto Sycamore Back Avenue next. At the end of the road, that was little more than a wide alley, rather than a proper street, a Yorkshire Water van chugged away, purging one of the drains.

A few houses down, an old lady finally answered, squinting up at him through milky eyes.

Blind or visually impaired. Of course.

Not helpful for a visual identification, but he hoped she had heard something. Ward introduced himself and explained who he was looking for.

'Well of course I haven't seen nowt,' the woman snapped back at him. 'Cataracts. Been waiting months to get these seen to, you know. State of the NHS right now! An absolute disgrace!'

'Yes, well—'

But the lady wasn't done. 'And as if I don't have enough right now with my rheumatoid arthritis acting up wi' the cold, the *smell* of it, those drains. Called 'em out, I did. Wasn't putting up with it anymore.' She waggled a hand in the direction of the end of the street where the monotone rumble of the pump's generator droned.

It was true enough that the aged sewage system couldn't handle modern waste. The volume of it caused constant blockages with baby wipes and all sorts that got flushed down. Fatbergs, he thought he'd heard mentioned on TV too. Ward shuddered at the thought. Not a job he'd fancy doing.

'I'm not having it this year, I said to them! Not the first time we've been flooded when the sewers have broke, and I won't be doing it again,' she said darkly, still ranting on.

Ward tentatively sniffed the air. Sure, he could smell something waste-like, but that was hardly a nuisance, more the norm in built-up urban areas. He glanced down the road and could see a couple of overflowing rubbish bins. 'Er, yes. I hope they'll sort that out for you. I need to ask, have you heard anything unusual in the area? Any shouting or anything amongst the neighbours?'

'No, I haven't.' She turned her head and tapped her hearing aid. 'I take this off at night. I don't want to hear them! The birds are bad enough as it is, tweeting away at the crack of dawn.' She glared down the street at the leafy trees lining the park at the end. Ward couldn't help with policing *that*.

'Well, if you haven't seen anything, I'll not bother you any further, ma'am.'

Ward managed to extract himself, though the woman called after him, muttering about the disturbance of the pump's generator and how it was too noisy. Ward heard her door slam behind her as she shut it.

On to the next house he dutifully went, until the afternoon had gone, and having finished his shift, Ward headed home, resentment and frustration dogging his steps at the lack of any results from their door-to-door enquiries.

CHAPTER THIRTY-TWO

Harry eyed the Yorkshire Water van now at the end of Sycamore Avenue, pumping up the contents of the drains with a rumbling drone that drowned out the traffic noise from the main road nearby. He slipped past the vehicle, down his back street, and into the house with his bag of shopping.

That day, Monday, he'd had to lay low at work again. Janice was still on the warpath and their shifts had clashed, so he'd put up with her for a solid eight hours, almost unbearable. Only thoughts of one day moving away and leaving the place behind had kept him going through the drudgery. That, and the fact that at lunchtime Poppy had *finally* arranged a time to meet him that evening up the valley in Keighley.

He wasn't sure whether he'd take her home. He would if there was no other choice, he supposed, but it was possibly compromised, if his paranoia was anything to go by, and the *smell*. It assaulted him when he entered the house, but perhaps he was being overly paranoid.

Damn it. Tomorrow, before work, he'd nip to the hardware store to get the strongest acid he could. He wasn't relishing that part of affairs—the fun was in the killing, not the aftermath—but if Harry wanted to remain a free man, unknown to anyone, he would have to do the dirty work too.

Lesson learned, at least, he thought. Perhaps he'd not do it at home again unless he had to. Harry pulled out a can of air freshener from the shopping bag and sprayed it generously—until he choked on the fumes of it—in the hallway. It was better than the alternative, anyway.

It was a quick turnaround, so he didn't waste any time showering. He changed into his best clothes and headed on foot to the train station, a ten-minute walk away. The street was quiet now, the echoing of the York-shire Water van gone, and the stillness of the street eerie.

Stop it, you wuss, he berated himself. It was the picture on the door at work, he reasoned, that was still shaking him—that Jamal had made the comment likening his appearance to the man. No one else would realise now, with his changed appearance, but it unsettled him all the same.

Paranoia crept around the edges of his self-control, and Harry didn't like it.

That sensation, as though, over his shoulder and out of sight, someone or something was *watching*. That he'd been too cocky, taken it too far, too close to home, and that they *knew*.

Fuck off, he told the thoughts.

He caught the seven o'clock train, riding into the darkening valley as the sun set. When he alighted in

Keighley, the valley was well-dimmed already, yawning shadows stretching between the tall buildings as he walked up Cavendish Street. With that growing darkness, his nerves calmed. The darkness felt like home, shrouding him in safety, hiding his dark deeds away from scrutiny.

Poppy Nichols awaited him by the bar at *The Livery Rooms* on North Street, which was surprisingly raucous for a Monday night, though with the cheap beer and food, perhaps *not* so unexpected. It was a Wetherspoons after all. Poppy worked in Keighley at one of the banks on North Street, hence why they'd ended up meeting there. She'd had to work late with their new extended opening hours.

Poppy stood, prim and proper in her work suit jacket and pencil skirt, shiny black stilettos adding to her slender height so that when he greeted her, she turned, meeting him eye to eye. Several years younger than him, just twenty, Harry could see her nervous inexperience in her awkward posture and her slight, deer-in-the-headlights gaze.

How he already wanted to be the one to break her.

Harry raised a hand in a half wave and crossed to her. 'So great to meet you, Poppy.'

'Hi, James.' She smiled and they embraced.

'What can I get you?' Harry asked, his tone easy and casual, jerking his thumb towards the bar. Poppy held her coat looped over her clasped hands. 'Oh, erm, a glass of chardonnay would be great, thanks.'

'Coming right up. Let's sit here.' He guided her, hand

glancing on her lower back, to a high stool at one end of the bar, in a corner out of the way.

He stood next to her, shielding her from the rest of the bar with his body as the bartender served them and he paid.

'It's so great to finally meet you,' he said, smiling warmly at her. 'How was work?'

It was always the way. Ask about them, draw them out, get them talking...it was the way to disarm them so that he could strike when they least expected it.

CHAPTER THIRTY-THREE

'My name's Jamal.'

'And you have some information for us, I hear?' DS Nowak answered, her pen at the ready to record anything. The man had left his name and number with the helpline set up to locate Charlotte Lawson.

'Yeah,' replied the man, sounding troubled. 'Look, I dunno if it's something or nothin', but...When I saw the photo from that CCTV of the bloke with that missing girl... I thought it was him straight away. I mean, I don't think it is, but then it might be, and if it is, well I can't keep that—'

'Jamal,' DS Nowak cut him off. 'Please. Even if you don't think it's relevant, let us be the judge of that. Anything, no matter how small or insignificant it might seem, might be something.'

Jamal breathed down the phone for a few seconds. 'Ok. The man in the CCTV, the one with dark curly hair.'

'Yes?' the DS said encouragingly.

'I think I work with him.'

Nowak's lips parted. *What?* 'Tell me more,' she said more calmly than she felt, nerves tingling through her at the admission. Perhaps this could be the breakthrough they needed.

'Promise me that I won't get in trouble if I'm wrong.'

'Of course not,' she said to ease his distress. 'They'll never know that you've spoken to us. We can check an awful lot of details here without needing to speak to them, if we can rule them out on that basis, well, they'll never know at all.'

'Ok. Good.' He still sounded hesitant. 'He's called Harry. I don't know his surname. We work at the Sainsbury's Local in Bingley town centre.'

Harry. *Harry.* The background chatter of the office around her seemed to melt away. Amelia Hughes' friend Sacha had said that was the name of Amelia's stalker. Could they be one and the same? Another alias for this man who perhaps also called himself James? And if he worked in Bingley town centre...it placed him conveniently close to the two incidents.

'Can you tell me any more details?'

'No, I don't know anything else about him.'

'OK, well what made you connect your colleague with the man in the photo?'

'Well, he's a dead ringer. They look exactly the same —or, did look. Harry had the same thick curly hair, and it looked like him, same sorta shape, build.'

'*Had?*'

'He shaved it all off over the weekend, and he's started growing a beard. As long as I've known him, he's always had that curly hair, and he's always been clean-shaven.'

Nowak could hardly keep her voice calm and measured as she replied. Her gut instinct was screaming that this might be important. Her hand clenched around her pen. 'And how long have you known him?'

'We've worked together for about six months now.'

'And is he the type of person you think might want to hurt someone else, like the lady that's missing?'

'Well, I'd hope not, but I honestly don't know him.' Jamal sounded troubled. 'We're not friends, we just work together. Mostly, he's quiet and keeps himself to himself.'

'OK. Thank you for the information, it's appreciated. Do you have a line manager at work I could speak to?' She needed to check out Harry's background information and make a few enquiries before she could find him. She took down the phone number and name Jamal gave her. 'Thanks so much, Jamal, I appreciate your time.'

She dialled the manager's number. 'Hi, is that Janice? Hi, I'm Detective Sergeant Emma Nowak. I have a question about one of your employees. Mmhmm. Do you have a young man working for you at the Bingley shop who goes by the name Harry?'

'Yes.' The woman sounded positively disapproving. 'Not for much longer though, with his current conduct.'

'We can chat about that in a moment, it may be pertinent to my enquiries. I'm after his full name and contact details, please, as a witness in an ongoing investigation.'

'Let me check.' There was a pregnant pause. 'Hmm. That's weird. He's called Harry around the store. I never realised, his legal name on the payroll is Henry. Henry

James Denton.' She read out a mobile number. 'His address is... Forty-six Back Sycamore Avenue, Bingley.'

Nowak was reeling. 'Is he working today?' She tried to keep her voice calm.

'Sorry. He's already left. Finished at six.'

'OK. You mentioned his current conduct—what did you mean by that?'

Janice snorted with disgust. 'He's been absent without leave in the past week, skipping shifts without giving us notice. I won't have it in my store.'

'Is that typical for him?'

'No,' she admitted after a moment, 'but he's already skating on thin ice. He's not exactly a model employee—rude, late, and now this. I'm fed up of it.'

'I can imagine. I won't keep you any longer. Thank you for your help. Bye,' Nowak said, and hung up, before ringing DI Ward with shaking hands.

Denton. Like James Denton, the name used on Matchmaker. Back Sycamore Avenue. Right next to Sycamore Avenue where the taxi dropped off Charlotte the last time she was seen. This was their guy. Henry 'Harry' Denton.

CHAPTER THIRTY-FOUR

They had him. They had Henry 'Harry' James Denton at last, by name, but they didn't know where he was, or what he was capable of. Ward had authorised a BOLO—Be On the Look Out—for Denton with West Yorkshire Police, but it was far too much like a needle in a haystack. They had to get to his address and *fast*, before harm came to Charlotte, or anyone else.

DC Shahzad was still in the office and was frantically trying to find any mobile numbers associated with the man so they could attempt to track him.

Nowak had rung Jamal back straight away, but the man had only been able to confirm that Harry had finished work already and said he was going out that evening, with no further information as to where, and no, he didn't have Harry's number. Now, it was a race to Henry Denton's address for Nowak, Patterson, and Ward, to see if they could find him there, or any trace of Charlotte Lawson.

DI Daniel Ward was awaiting any further information as he sped towards Bingley, but it was the last person he wanted to speak to that was calling him.

Wicked Witch.

His ringtone silenced the radio, booming over the Bluetooth.

He glanced at the clock.

It was past time–three minutes past seven. His dear and hopefully soon-to-be divorced wife Katherine had given him all of three minutes leeway to bring the dog back. Not that he was. He was, in fact, heading in the opposite direction, not about to turn up to Baildon, but charging north-west up the Aire Valley towards Bingley.

He answered.

What other choice did he have, really?

'Where are you?' Her words fired like bullets through the sound system.

At her voice, Olly set to barking on the backseat, baying so loud he tuned her out.

Daniel suppressed a smirk—it was more pleasant to be deafened by the dog, after all.

'I'll be late.'

'I know that.' He could hear how her teeth were gritted, spitting every word out. 'We said seven. It's past seven.'

'I know you said seven,' he pointed out. 'I'd happily keep him. I got waylaid.'

'When will you be here?'

'Er...' He glanced at the clock, and slowed for another set of red lights ahead, watching as the car ahead blatantly shot through them well in excess of the speed limit. The corner of Lister Park—where, in the absence of any other dinner options, he'd just stopped to grab a Greggs pasty for him and a sausage roll that the dog had claimed—before Nowak's call had landed and his plans had changed. The dog was currently showering the back-seat with flakes of golden pastry. He'd probably regret that, but Olly was happy at least.

It wasn't too far to Bingley, but he admonished himself silently. He should have gone up and over the backs, it would have been quicker and filled with fewer morons who didn't know what a traffic light was.

'Daniel!' Katherine snapped.

'Don't know, sorry. Might not be today.'

'What? Do I have to—'

'Katherine,' Daniel barked. 'For God's sake! The whole world doesn't revolve around you, alright? It's my day off and I just got called in. I'm dealing with a murdered woman, a missing one, and a third in imminent danger—this might be the work of a serial killer. So for one damned minute, will you get your head out of your arse and cut me some slack? Not everything I do is to piss you off, alright? I'll let you know when I'm on my way, but it won't be any time soon, and you'll have to deal with that.'

He hung up before he could say anything else he would regret later, and clenched his shaking hands on the steering wheel, trying to still his thundering heart, slow his breathing. At last, the lights flipped green after the last pedestrian had crossed, and he floored it.

———

Nowak, with Patterson, pulled up just behind Ward at the end of Sycamore Back Avenue. The Yorkshire Water van was gone. A marked car arrived too, with the blessed *'big red key'* Ward had requested so they could gain entry to Denton's place, which DCI Kipling had authorised in light of the potential danger to life for Charlotte Lawson.

'Number forty-six,' Ward instructed the PC, who lugged the heavy battering ram to the house, and after a moment to plant his weight, smashed the PVC door in with one giant *crash*. He'd knocked on this very damned door this afternoon and no one had answered. Of course, *now* they knew that Henry Denton had been at work.

Ward rushed past him, with Nowak and Patterson on his heels. 'Police! Show yourself, anyone inside!' As he breathed in, he gagged and stopped dead.

Death.

The stench of death clogged the place, overpowering the faded scent of air fresheners, empty cans of which littered the bare, reclaimed floorboards beneath their feet. The neighbour next door-but-one, the old lady Ward had spoken to, had mentioned a smell and a clogged drain, but maybe she was wrong, maybe the drain had never been clogged. Maybe the stench had made its way through the cellars, under the floorboards, or perhaps through the degraded Victorian brickwork between neighbouring loft spaces...

'Charlotte? Charlotte Lawson, are you in here?' Ward called with a sinking desperation spurring him on. Patterson thundered up the stairs with Nowak. Ward glanced into the living room, and the tiny kitchen at the back. Empty. But that stench was unmistakable...

'All clear up here, sir,' Patterson called from upstairs. 'Just jimmying open the loft hatch, but doesn't look like it's been used in a while seeing as it's painted shut.'

Ward turned away from the kitchen. And halted at the sight of the door under the stairs. It seemed to regard him with baleful malevolence. The tatty, faded, and partly peeling white paint. The scuffed, round, brass handle. Just a door. It was just a door, and yet... Ward feared what he would find behind it. The source of that smell.

Ward stepped forward, steeling himself, and wrenched it open.

A dark maw called him into the bowels of the earth. No light came from below, just the darkness, blacker than night and shrouding his worst fears. Ward switched on the hallway light, it would have to do. The smell strengthened, wafting from the cellar unchecked.

'Sarge, Jake, I need you down here now.'

The tone in his voice had them thundering down the stairs even as he placed his foot onto the first stone step that led down into the cellar. With the light of his phone torch to guide him—and theirs as they descended behind him into the cramped and bare cellar—it illuminated a rickety old shelf unit with a flaking red metal toolbox on the bottom shelf, the thick dust and mould around which had been recently disturbed. 'Nowak, check that.'

Ward swung round at the bottom of the stairs. The cellar was not huge—the footprint of the small house above it. The flagstones beneath his feet were filthy, clearly showing a giant scuff mark leading from the bottom of the stairs into the corner behind and under them.

A white-shrouded bundle lay half out of the shadows as he raised his light.

On the floor, elegantly limp, emerging from that sheet, was a single, female hand.

CHAPTER THIRTY-FIVE

'Is it Charlotte?' asked Nowak, covering her mouth with an arm.

'Check the toolbox and around the room,' Ward said, though he didn't expect there would be anything else to find. The place was empty. 'I'll take a look. Patterson, get pathology here and CSI, and secure the house as a scene.'

'Sir.' Patterson thundered up the stairs.

Ward strode over to the body before his nerve deserted him. He bloody hated this part of the job. The hand was already beginning to bloat. Ward peeled back the bedsheet at the top end, reaching as far as he could so as to not have to lean in too close.

A woman's face greeted him. Charlotte Lawson. Her face was swelling like the rest of her body, her bulging eyes clouded and devoid of life, and her skin starting to loosen. She'd been dead for days. They'd been *days* too late. Baker would confirm, but Ward realised with a sinking heart that she had probably died sometime shortly after the taxi driver had dropped her and Henry Denton off on Sycamore Avenue.

He had no doubt that Charlotte had come to harm at Denton's hands. An otherwise perfectly healthy woman didn't simply drop dead, and after Amelia Hughes...

'Sir. There's a bloodied knife here. Some jewellery. And two mobile phones.' Nowak's voice broke through his train of thought.

He turned. 'They'll probably be Amelia's and Charlotte's,' he said quietly. 'A knife, you say?'

'Aye.' Nowak carefully pointed into the toolbox. She'd selectively removed a few items from the top, but dug no further, upon seeing the ill-fitting items inside. 'Massive... looks like the one Baker described. I don't want to touch them without forensics seeing them in situ first.'

'Good job. I think the body's Charlotte. We were days too late. Come on. There'll be nothing down here now. CSI can have the scene.' Ward tramped upstairs almost in a daze, stopping dead in the hallway, the dead woman's agony-filled bloated face right before him still, so fresh and haunting was she in his mind's eye.

'Are you alright, sir?'

'No,' Ward admitted, hanging his head, and dragging a hand through his hair. '*Damn it!*' We were too late, by a long mile.' Emotion surged through him. Disappointment, regret, shame, sadness, *guilt*, that they had not been able to help the young woman in time. On Friday night, they hadn't even known about Henry Denton. They'd been busy chasing Darren Winston. And Bogdan Varga.

'I feel it too, sir,' Emma said quietly. 'We couldn't have done anything differently. Come on. Let's get out of here, get some fresh air.'

Nowak was right, the stink of death wasn't helping. He followed the DS outside to the quiet road, where a uniformed PC stood next to DC Patterson, who was busy on the phone to DCI Kipling by the sounds of it.

With the fresh air clearing that clogging taste from his nose and mouth, Ward looked back at the innocuous terrace. 'We need to catch this bastard.' Two bodies were laid at Denton's feet, and who knows how many more if they didn't stop him. Was Amelia his first? Or just another in a string? Would Charlotte be his last? Ward shivered as a cold breeze brushed at him, slipping cold tendrils down the back of his neck.

'Nowak, didn't you say the work colleague mentioned Denton was out tonight?' Ward said.

'Aye,' said Nowak, turning to regard him with worry. 'His next victim, perhaps.'

'My thoughts exactly.' If someone else was in danger... there was no excuse, not now. They knew who Henry Denton was, what he had done, where he lived. They couldn't let him slip the net once more.

Ward dialled Shahzad.

'Yes, sir?'

'I need you to obtain and circulate an image from the CCTV of the Sainsbury's Local where Henry Denton was on shift today showing his new haircut and facial hair. We've just found what we believe to be Charlotte Lawson's body in his cellar, and we have reason to believe he's out on the prowl again tonight.'

'Blimey,' Shahzad said down the phone. 'Of course, sir. I was just about to ring. I have an update. The DCI pulled some strings. Warrant's come through for Matchmaker, and I've managed to obtain some information, though the detailed messaging history and login data and whatnot won't be available until tomorrow morning. Basic profile data shows that the man using the alias James Denton has been interacting today and yesterday with a young woman named Poppy Nichols, located in Keighley. I have her contact number, but she's not answering.'

'Damn it.'

'I've also used the mobile number they have on file for James Denton to triangulate his location. His phone is switched off, sir, last location around Bingley train station, but Poppy Nichols' is active. It's in Keighley right now, sir. Somewhere in the town centre, at the top by the looks of it, in the North Street area, but the triangulation isn't exact, sir, there could be some echoing.'

'Keighley. We have to go now,' Ward said to Nowak, still on the line to Shahzad. 'Patterson, stay here, do not leave this scene, and be on the lookout for Denton. If he returns apprehend him at once. We have reasonable grounds to suspect him for the murders of two women now. Nowak, with me.' He legged it through the gate and down the street to his car with Nowak behind him.

'Shahzad, keep a trace open on that phone. Nowak and I are heading to Keighley now. Do whatever you can to get ahold of Poppy Nichols. If she's meeting Denton right now, then she's in grave danger. Address, next of kin, her boss, use whatever means you have to track her down.'

'Yessir. I'll see what I can find through social media.'

Ward sprinted around the corner to his car and slid inside, Olly greeting him with a cold nose to the neck. Nowak joined him in the passenger seat, and he switched on the engine, the throaty roar of the Golf R as eager as him to hunt Denton.

———

DC Shahzad had what seemed like a million windows open in his browser—every social network site, and various police databases—as he searched for Poppy Nichols, narrowing her down.

Her Instagram was private. *Damn it.*

Her Facebook had her employer's details on—but they were closed when he rang.

She held a provisional driver's licence. *Bingo.* Shahzad texted the address to Ward and Nowak, before he checked on the cell triangulation again.

Gone.

Shahzad blinked a few times, and refreshed the feed. Nothing. He checked both Denton's and Nichols' numbers. Gone. He checked the last ping—it had moved, along North Street, towards the church. Possibly towards her home address, which was up the hill in that direction. Had she and Denton shared a taxi back to hers? Or perhaps moved on to another bar?

Shahzad's eyes flicked to the corner of his screen—to the time. It was creeping past eight. *Would they be going* out-*out on a Monday night?* Shahzad chewed the inside of his cheek and dialled Ward. The DI would make the call whether to hedge his bets that they were still *somewhere* in Keighley, or heading back to Nichols' house.

Would Denton be heading to either—or neither?

CHAPTER THIRTY-SIX

Poppy laughed. 'You're so funny, James!'

'I don't mind you laughing at my expense, you have a beautiful laugh.' Henry James Denton chuckled too, his eyes warm. He leaned in and winked, sliding a hand on her knee. The ladies always loved the wet dog story. 'But you have to promise not to tell anyone else. I was well embarrassed.'

'I suppose not,' she said colouring and leaning into his attention. They'd foregone food at the Wetherspoons and moved onto *The Lord Rodney* by the church green.

Poppy's phone vibrated on the table again. *Unknown number*. 'Again? Ugh!' she exclaimed, exasperated. 'Sorry. You know what, I'm just going to switch the stupid thing off. It's just one of those nuisance calls.'

'No worries,' grinned Henry. 'I already switched mine off. I don't need a phone when I have an evening with you.'

'I'd better head back soon,' Poppy said with a sigh. 'Work in the morning and all.'

'Yeah, same.' Henry winced. 'The joys, eh? I'd much rather spend it with you...We could always head back to yours for a nightcap? Then it wouldn't be too wild or late?' His hand stroked up her thigh.

Poppy bit her lip. 'I'm not sure...I live with my mum, and she doesn't like me taking anyone home that she doesn't know.'

Henry affected a sad expression, nodding, his head drooping. Inside, he was a whirl of cunning. *I can't do it at hers if there's someone else there. It needs to be mine. Private. I'll dump her in the river before dawn.*

'I understand. Just, if I'm honest, I think we have a great connection. I *really* like you, Poppy. Can you forgive a guy if he doesn't want to say goodbye yet?' He grinned and held his hands up.

Poppy looked coyly at him, and he could tell, although shy, his flattery was working.

'You could always come back to mine?' he suggested lightly. 'We can chill, and then I'll make sure you get home safely?'

'Just chill?' she glanced up at him, and he could see the worry in her eyes.

'*Just* chill,' he affirmed. 'No pressure from me, ok?' *Not yet. That would come later.* 'We can do anything you like at your pace. I just meant to hang out.' He smiled encouragingly. 'I have a little place in Bingley—cosy, we can snuggle up on the couch and put something on telly for a bit, or have a drink in the kitchen, whatever you like.'

He'd been careful not to drink as much as her, but even so, the alcohol had given him a buzz of confidence, and with his new stubble and haircut, he felt like a different man. No longer did that paranoia dog his steps —he'd gotten away with Amelia, gotten away with Charlotte, and he'd get away with Poppy too.

'Alright, then,' she said with a shy smile. 'Let's do that.'

'Great. You drink up. Let me call a cab from the bar.' He stood from the barstool and leaned in close. 'May I?' he murmured.

She nodded.

He placed a gentle kiss on her lips, sliding his hand around her waist. 'I'll be back in a mo.'

As Henry Denton turned away, his stomach flipped with excitement. Sure, he had to play a slowly, slowly catchy monkey kind of game with this one, but he'd get there. She was shy, inexperienced, scared. He'd coax her out of her shell—the alcohol would help, and the little something he'd slipped into her last drink. He'd enjoy this conquest even more, the achievement of getting her to yield to him one way or another.

Henry Denton was going to *very much* enjoy taking control of her before he broke her. He still wished he'd gotten that chance with Amelia. He'd watched her and her ex screwing through the window of her house enough times to imagine it vividly. Alas. The chance of that was long passed now, but he had Poppy. And whoever came next.

———

Shortly after, Henry and Poppy slid into a taxi back to his.

'Sycamore Ave, Bingley, mate,' Denton said to the driver up front, tucking Poppy under his arm, just as he had done with Charlotte a few days before. Poppy was bonier, taller, he noticed.

'She overage?' the taxi driver asked. His stare lingered between the two of them.

Poppy flushed, the red on her cheeks quickly hidden as the internal light automatically switched off a few seconds after Denton had shut the door.

'Yeah, twenty.'

The driver nodded slowly. 'Right. Ok then. Just gotta make sure. I have a daughter of my own—I worry about her now she's going out too.' He turned to his steering wheel and set off.

Harry grinned. *You should be worried, with monsters like me around.*

The taxi driver's eyes lingered on him in the rearview mirror for a few seconds before they flicked back to the road, and he took the turning for Bingley.

CHAPTER THIRTY-SEVEN

'Sir, I have an update,' Shahzad said as soon as Ward picked up from the Bluetooth in his car, as he and Nowak raced towards Poppy Nichols' residence in Long Lee up the hill from Keighley.

'Fire away.'

'They're going back to Henry Denton's, sir.'

'What?' Ward barked, pulling over immediately.

'Aye, sir. A call's just come in; taxi firm. One of their drivers has pushed a silent alarm in his car.' Most taxis were fitted with them in case of emergency. 'He's managed to send a text too. *Wanted man in car. Call police.*'

'How do you know it's Denton?' Ward's fingers drummed on the steering wheel, as beside him, Nowak held her breath, listening, waiting. Which direction should he head in? He was so close to Long Lee. Ward couldn't risk the chance of saving Poppy Nichols slipping away.

'Because the destination address in the driver's satnav

is streamed back to their central office. It's Sycamore Avenue in Bingley, sir.'

'Shite!' Ward cursed, and immediately pulled out, spinning the car around and flooring it back down the hill. He had to get to Bingley at once.

'Aye, I'll put out an alert to say he's in the area at once, all local units will attend, and I'll let Patterson know as well.'

CHAPTER THIRTY-EIGHT

The taxi driver jammed the silent alarm button a few more times for good measure. He knew it'd go through, that the extra presses wouldn't make a damn bit of difference, but it made him feel slightly less on edge. He hoped his text message had got through to Jimmy at the office—that he'd be picking up his texts, and not too busy pissing around on *Call of Duty* on his phone, as usual.

He knew something had been off about the lad the moment they'd set foot in the cab. He was quiet, standoff-ish, just... *weird*. And when the light had caught his face... the taxi driver knew he recognised him.

Taxi drivers kept up with the latest police alerts. It was in their best interests to know who's who, for they were at a high risk of being attacked in the job they did.

He was sticking to under the speed limit tonight, no racing around for this chap and the pretty young thing he was groping on the backseat. Still, it wasn't far. He was less than ten minutes out from Bingley now. He glanced in the rearview mirror again—the chap in the backseat was wholly focused on the young lady and didn't notice his glance.

Anger seethed in the man's belly. What he'd do to any scrote who dared feel up *his* lass like that. Twenty-one or not, she'd be his baby forever and he'd protect her. God forbid she ever found someone, but he knew the day would come.

A marked police car drove past him in the opposite direction, and his heart stuttered with fear that he couldn't stop the police car, and hail them. He didn't know what this man was capable of, only that he was wanted in connection with the disappearance of another young lady a few days before... and that the police had updated their appeal to note his changed appearance. That didn't feel like an innocent man to him.

CHAPTER THIRTY-NINE

Ward drove like a mad man, throwing the car around the Toby Carvery roundabout at the bottom of Keighley, and flooring it on the bypass, no idea how far behind the taxi he might be. Denton might not have been going home and once he set foot outside that taxi, they'd have lost him.

Where's Poppy?

Ward didn't know whether they'd be together or not. Had they parted ways? Had he already harmed her? They had no way to know until they managed to trace her, or find her with Denton. He hoped and prayed that she would be alright, that he wouldn't be too late like with Charlotte. All the while, Nowak clung on for dear life beside him in the passenger seat and Olly-dog panted in the back.

CHAPTER FORTY

Heart hammering, the driver accepted the fare from the young man in the backseat. No sign of any blues and twos yet. Sycamore Avenue was silent and dark, pools of streetlight casting an amber glow over the cold, empty street. He fumbled with the change as he passed it back.

'Let me open the door for you, lass.' He slid out of the car and opened it for her, scanning the street around him. 'Are you alright?' He frowned as he helped her out, she was bleary-eyed, but he was certain she'd seemed *fairly* sober when the two had entered the taxi.

'I've got her, she's fine,' the young man snapped at him, glaring as he hoisted Poppy away from the driver. The young man pulled her away, supporting her around the waist with a strong arm.

The driver watched her stagger away with his help, dithering. He knew what his gut instinct called him to do —stop them. Help her. But what if he was wrong?

They passed under the first streetlight, and turned away, onto Sycamore Back Avenue.

I'm sure it's him. The short-cropped hair, the stubble... the man was *the* spitting image. Too much to be a coincidence.

He hovered, agonising.

'Damn it!' If it was his daughter at risk, he'd want someone to help her in the same situation. The driver locked his car and legged it after them.

CHAPTER FORTY-ONE

The house was lit up behind Patterson—CSI inside, a white forensics tent shielding the small front garden, and cordon tape stretching like spider's web everywhere. He'd been guarding the scene just like the DI had asked, but if ever there was a time to abandon that duty, it was *now*.

Patterson sprinted up the back avenue, away from the floodlit scene, his phone still in his hand as Shahzad hung up on him. He'd seen a figure at the end of the road—two people, he realised, and as he drew closer, he picked out the staggering woman and the strong, assured man holding her up. He was instantly recognisable from the Matchmaker app profile picture, despite the lack of curly hair, as he passed into the glow of an outside light affixed to one of the terraces.

'Police! Henry James Denton, you're under arrest!' Patterson roared, his legs and arms pumping double-time as he sprinted towards the pair.

Henry stopped dead. No doubt, he could see the

harsh illumination of the forensics light behind Patterson, realising where the source emanated from. His own house. Busted. He dropped Poppy, wheeled, and legged it in the opposite direction. Poppy toppled with the sudden loss of support, crashing to the ground with a cry.

'Stop!' yelled a silhouetted figure at the end of the alleyway.

Henry bowled into him, knocking him aside, and dodged past.

'Watch the lass!' Patterson passed the man, who surged towards the fallen young woman behind him.

Henry had disappeared around the corner at the end of the alley. Patterson slowed for a moment until he spied the figure ahead, legging it to the main road.

Headlights raked the street as a white Golf R turned into it. They lit up Henry Denton like a beacon.

Henry, in the middle of the road, slowed as the car screamed to a halt across the street, cutting him off. He changed direction, darting back.

Patterson collided with him with an almighty *crack* and they both went down.

Denton grappled with Patterson, trying to make off, but Patterson hung on doggedly. He wasn't that far out of his beat days as a PC and it wasn't his first rodeo by a long mile.

Patterson rolled Denton over on the pavement, where the stench of dog shit burnt his nose, cutting through the plume of Denton's alcohol-laced breath. Denton bucked him, serving Patterson with a knee to the groin and nutting his chin with a vicious headbutt.

Pain blinded Patterson as his bollocks felt like they

were going to explode and his teeth jarred together. He fell. Denton slipped from his grasp—booze or not, desperation gave him an edge. It gave Patterson one too.

Patterson lunged—catching him by the ankle.

Down went Denton, crashing onto the tarmac.

Patterson launched himself onto Denton's back, crushing him into the rough surface with a knee on his back, two hands on Denton's shoulders.

'Fuck you! Pigs! Fucking pigs, fuck you all!' Denton screeched, the sound driving into Patterson's pounding skull.

Nowak joined him then, her cuffs already out as she wrenched Denton's arms behind him, and cuffed him—he still shouted and screamed, spewing profanities, and bucked on the ground underneath Patterson, but with Nowak's weight, they had him.

Panting heavily, and with the jagged spikes of pain from his groin still surging through him, Patterson groaned, and hung his head.

'Nice one, Jake!' Nowak clapped him on the shoulder.

'Patterson, good job,' Ward said, striding over from his car, which still blocked the street, with Oliver the dog bounding after him.

'The woman. She's on the back alley,' Patterson forced out, his lungs aching from the sprint. 'Might be hurt.'

'On it.' Ward raced off with Olly, just as two marked cars entered Sycamore Ave, halting before Ward's car. Patterson flagged them down with a wave.

'Fucking hell, he got me a blinder,' Jake groaned.

Leaving Denton on the ground, pressed into the pile of dog shit, Nowak helped Patterson stand, but he bent double, hands on his thighs. 'Come on then, do the honours.'

Patterson stood, glaring at Denton. He bent with Nowak and they hauled him, an arm apiece, to his feet. His cheek was grazed where he'd hit the ground, and muck and shite smeared the front of his formerly suave jacket.

Patterson stepped smartly back out of the trajectory of the globule of spit Denton launched at him. 'Henry Denton, you're under arrest for the murders of Amelia Hughes and Charlotte Lawson, and resisting lawful arrest, assaulting a police officer, perverting the course of justice, preventing the lawful burial of a body, and conspiracy to murder.'

Boy, did that feel good.

He read the police caution as Denton's profanities spewed forth again.

'Get him back to the station, will you, lads?' Patterson said to the two PCs approaching from one of the marked cars which lit the street up with blue flashes. 'Needs a night in the cell to take the edge off that attitude.'

The PCs guffawed and took Denton away, forcing him into the back of their car, the tirade of screeching silenced as the door slammed behind him.

'Bloody hell. What a twat,' Patterson said.

Nowak clapped him on the back. 'You said it. Come on.'

Patterson and Nowak followed Ward onto the back street where he already sat with a sobbing young woman, and an older man hovering about. Ward looked up as they approached.

'Sir, Denton's in custody. Heading back to the cells.'

'Top work, DC Patterson.' Ward gave him a grim smile.

A rush of pride filled Jake Patterson. The DI had been hard on him since he'd started with HMET a few months ago. He knew he was too much of a joker, that the DI thought he was a waste of a good place on the team. Now, perhaps, he was beginning to earn that place after all. Showing the DI just what he was capable of. 'Cheers, sir.'

'Right.' Ward blew out a large breath. 'This is Poppy Nichols. We made it in time. Thank God. I have an ambulance en-route to check her over. Nowak, can you take over here and make sure we get in contact with a next of kin, mum or dad, see if they can come and comfort her. We'll need a statement though, Miss Nichols, before we can let you go, I'm afraid. And this here is Dilip, the taxi driver who called it in. Patterson, can you take a statement from him, please? I'll see how CSI is getting along at the house.'

For one moment, before they parted ways to attend their duties, the three detectives shared a glance and a tired smile. They'd done it. They'd found Henry Denton before he'd struck again, and Poppy Nichols was safe.

CHAPTER FORTY-TWO

It had been a long and late night. CSI eventually finished up at Denton's house, and Charlotte's body had been removed to the hospital morgue to await a post-mortem and formal identification by Mark Baker. Then, they would be able to pass on the heartrending news of Charlotte's murder to her desperate loved ones. There would be a while yet before the full circumstances could be confirmed, so that Amelia's and Charlotte's families could be informed as to how and why they had met their ends.

An upset Poppy Nichols had given a brief statement at the scene, and been taken away by her equally shaken mother, with the promise that they'd attend the station the next day to give a full witness interview.

Likewise, Dilip the taxi driver had given a full account to DC Patterson of what had happened, with his phone number in case they needed anything else from him.

The person they really needed to talk to, however,

was Henry Denton. To determine why on earth he'd done any of it, and whether he was fit to stand trial. Ward could never understand it, what drove a person so far as to commit such acts, where grounds for diminished responsibility didn't apply.

Gods, the young woman, Poppy, that they'd picked up, had been terrified to learn she'd been in the company of a man most likely planning to kill her, as he had with two other women in the past week.

Ward's eyes burned as he drove back to the station, Olly dozing on the backseat. It was closing in on midnight, and there'd be a long night ahead interviewing Denton and gathering evidence to make their case for charging watertight, whether or not he admitted to anything.

Will we get him?

That was Ward's next big fear. Would they have enough to put him away for good so that he couldn't harm anyone else?

Back at the office, Nowak, Patterson, and Shahzad were busy as they mucked in to pull the evidence together. All the while, Olly snored under the desk, totally oblivious to the thrum of coiled anxiety within the office as they prepared to interview Henry James Denton, the murderous catfish they had at last unmasked.

———

Ward made it home for a couple hours' sleep before the case dragged him back to the office again. Denton had given them nothing in his interviews, but it was alright.

By the end of the day, they had enough to be going on and then some.

The blood on the knife found in Denton's cellar matched Amelia Hughes'. The phones located there proved to belong to Amelia Hughes and Charlotte Lawson.

Charlotte's post-mortem confirmed she had died late on Friday night or in the early hours of Saturday by strangulation, and her identity was confirmed by dental records. She was naked in the sheet and had had intercourse just before death. Her clothes were bundled in the sheeting with her, and a used condom with Denton's sperm inside, and some forensic evidence linking it to Charlotte was located in the kitchen bin.

A search of Denton's phone, found on him at the time of his arrest, yielded a bounty. All his Matchmaker contacts and messaging history, backed up with disclosures from Matchmaker that morning—Amelia, Sara, Charlotte, Poppy. WhatsApp showed the message Amelia had sent him to back off, and the many attempts he'd made to contact her in the aftermath. Not to mention the less than savoury search history. Denton had actively tried to hone his murder techniques, cover his tracks, and planned to dispose of Charlotte's body.

Ward returned from the final interview, where a stony-faced Denton hadn't given any comment when presented with the evidence before him, nor any explanation when Ward had asked *why*. Ward had charged him all the same with a list of offences enough to see Denton serve a life sentence without parole, and remanded him into custody until he could appear in court. It would be for a judge and jury to hear any excuses he had to try and wriggle out of it.

Forensics was a fine art and open to interpretation, but in this case, it was overwhelming. Ward knew with total certainty that they'd found the culprit behind Amelia Hughes' murder, Charlotte Lawson's disappearance—and now death—and that catching him had foiled at least one more murder.

Ward could at least walk away knowing that Denton would serve life—but he still carried the sour guilt of Denton's victims' deaths, all the same. Much like the victims of Bogdan Varga, they would dog him until justice was served to the letter of the law. Even then, it wouldn't be enough. It could never bring them back and erase what had been done.

CHAPTER FORTY-THREE

A s Ward returned upstairs to the office that Monday afternoon, fresh from the cells, DC David Norris collared him.

'Have you got a minute, sir? I have an update on the Varga case.'

Ward didn't like the strange tone in his voice.

'What is it?' Ward crossed to David's desk. He examined the man's computer screen. 'Is that what I think it is?' Anger surged in him, ragged and tired after days of surging adrenaline.

'Yes, sir.' David's reply was quiet—almost apologetic.

The DC's screen showed two CMR notes accepted by the port authority in Liverpool. Two *identical* references for two different cargos. Both had entered mainland England at the port on Saturday.

The first was the lorry they had stopped early on Saturday morning with the help of Liverpool's Major Crime Team. The second, with the *same* references, was an unaccompanied container on the afternoon ferry that day.

Norris showed Ward how the second container—the one they hadn't seized—had been loaded onto a lorry. That had subsequently hit several ANPR cameras heading east on the M56 and then the M62, before all trace of it had vanished heading out of Manchester, over the Pennines to Yorkshire. No doubt, the plates had been changed before it crossed the border, because it hadn't hit any of the ANPRs this side of the hills—or any others for that matter.

'The one we got was a decoy?'

'Aye, sir, possibly. They might know not to use that CMR again, surely. To assume we *won't* have realised by now is arrogant at best.'

'But what was he transporting...?'

'That, we won't ever know, now.'

Ward could guess. Unaccompanied freight container, less likely to be checked out by port authorities... he reckoned there was something more precious than counterfeit clothing inside.

'No one thought to flag the duplicate CMR? I mean that's how we found out about it in the first place, right?'

'No sir.'

'That's unbelievable.' Quite literally. That CMR would have been burned into everyone in the port's brains that day, *everyone* would have known it was coming. Everyone would have recognised the duplicate, if they had half a brain. It hadn't even been flagged, let alone stopped—and that meant something far worse than Varga's shipments coming into the country unchecked.

It meant complicity. Beyond a reasonable doubt. As if Varga's unchecked smuggling operations weren't bad enough. Ward cursed and ran a hand across his beard. 'This is bigger than we thought. Someone's on the take.'

Varga had people on the inside helping his smuggling operations. People at the ports, in the border forces, possibly in the police itself.

It wasn't the news he wanted to bring to the DCI... but Ward had no choice. Varga's shadow empire didn't just extend throughout the criminal underworld...he'd bought his way into the authorities too, like a cancer, insidiously spreading its reach.

Ward didn't know what he'd hoped, maybe that finding the lorry would leave a trail of breadcrumbs back to Varga. But it was clear, it wasn't over. Not by a long shot.

CHAPTER FORTY-FOUR

I t was the next day, Tuesday, that Ward finally made it back to Katherine's with Oliver, after his shift. He had treated the dog to a feast that morning of the finest butcher's meat and the biggest bone he could get, and on the way over, a last walk out through the fields. He didn't want to lose his canine companion again.

He was bone achingly tired, after naff-all sleep. But he would see the investigation through to the end, and the next one, and the next one. It was his calling, but it would be a distraction too, from losing Olly again.

'You're a good boy, Olly,' he murmured, reaching a hand across to the passenger seat to pat Olly, who lay there, his tongue lolling out quite contentedly. 'I won't give up. Maybe one day, she'll let me have you.'

He'd texted ahead—he couldn't bear to speak to her on the phone. After the last few days, he had no energy left, let alone enough to deal with her. He had enough fight in him to say what needed to be said, and then the chips would fall where they may.

She was waiting for him as usual, the voile twitching, as he pulled across the drive. The door was open before he'd even gotten out of the car. She stood there, her arms folded, as Oliver bounded towards her excitedly, happy to see his mistress. The hard lines around her eyes softened as she bent to pat him on the head. Daniel knew she didn't truly have a heart of ice. She was just bitter. Both of them were.

'Katherine.'

At his quiet tone, she looked up from Oliver, rose, regarded him in silence, her face closed, but without the usual hostility.

'I'm sorry,' he said, his voice level. 'For everything. Neither of us have been perfect, but... I'm sorry for not being there. I'm sorry for not fighting harder when we started to drift apart. I'm sorry for not being there for you when we had the miscarriages—for walling up and shutting off when you needed someone most. I'm sorry for burying myself in work, letting it consume me, because I couldn't deal with our lives outside my cases.'

Her lips parted, her sternness falling away with surprise, and for a moment, he caught a glimpse in those eyes of softness, of the woman he'd once loved, of the goodness still in there.

'I can't take any of it back, and for that, I have so many regrets, because you deserved more... but more than anything, I'm sorry. I hope you can forgive me one day.'

She wavered before him, and he could have sworn he saw a sheen of tears shining in her eyes. For a moment, he truly saw her as she had been—his wife, the light of his life. Beautiful, fiery, passionate, caring, vivacious. She had lost her laughing eyes and her easy smile over the years, and he blamed himself for it. He was sorry for that too. It had been his fault, as much as it was hers.

Katherine swallowed, folding her arms again. 'I only kept the dog to torture you,' she admitted quietly. 'He was always your baby. The one thing I could take from you—hurt you with—after you'd hurt me so much, but it never made me feel any better, for any of it. He's always been a reminder of what we had, and what we've lost.'

She looked away, and pain flashed across her face, before she smoothed out her expression through sheer force of will. 'I—If you want him, you can have him.'

'What?' Daniel's eyebrows rose. 'Are you serious?'

Katherine nodded, staring at the tarmac drive. 'I'll get his things.' She disappeared inside, and a few minutes later appeared with some Bags for Life filled to the brim with dog bowls, chew toys, a blanket, and a dog bed under her arm. 'Go on. I'll put them in the boot. Open up.'

Hardly daring to believe his luck, Ward flipped the boot open, and relieved her of the bags, packing them in the car with the giant dog bed on top.

When he turned, Katherine crouched on the drive-way, with Oliver trying to lick her face—she'd always hated that—his tail swishing from side to side with happiness. She murmured at the dog, words Daniel couldn't hear, and stroked his face with both hands, scratching behind his ears just the way he liked, before she stood. 'Bye, Olly-dog,' she said softly, and with a glance at Daniel, she retreated. 'Bye.'

He opened his mouth to reply, but she had turned back.

'Oh! I forgot to mention. I put the house on the market. The estate agent is coming to value and photograph it tomorrow, a board will go up on Wednesday, and it'll all be live by Thursday at the latest. I'll... keep you informed.'

Daniel nodded. 'Thanks.' The thought made him feel surprisingly empty. Grief, he recognised, that he was shutting away with the rest of it, another chapter closing on their life together. One painful end at a time. 'Look... if you need anything, just let me know, alright? I might... We're not, I know, but...' He couldn't get the words out. He might not have loved her that way anymore, but she would always be his first wife, the love of his life, no matter how much had gone sour between them. He would always care for her.

She seemed to understand what he was trying to say. 'Thank you.' It was the most sincere thing he'd heard her say in months. The first time she had spoken to him really without bitterness, resentment, or anger. 'Bye, Dan. Take care.'

And as Daniel Ward turned away, for the first time, the cold autumn air that brushed his cheeks no longer seemed to be a cold reminder of his aching loneliness and the pain between them, but a cleansing touch that swept that chapter of heartache behind him.

There was just one more thing he had to do before he went home for the night.

———

A short while later he pulled up outside a small shop in the village of Wilsden, just over the hill from his apartment in Thornton. *Griffith's Fine Art and Framing*. It was almost closing, but he hoped it wouldn't take long.

It was dark outside, but the shop was illuminated with golden light, the framed artworks in the front window brightly lit, showing everything from dogs sleeping to a meadow of grass before rolling hills in the summer.

'Right. Wait here, Olly. I'll be back in a few.'

Daniel grabbed the rolled-up paintings he'd put in the boot and entered the shop. An old-fashioned brass bell tinkled over his head as it caught the door. As the door closed behind him, the road noise outside muted. It was quiet, calm, expectant, with the smell of artist's paint on the air—a smell so weirdly familiar it almost threw him back into memories of sitting with his mother as she painted so many years ago.

'Hello?' he called. The small room was empty, the counter standing alone before an ajar door.

'Just a moment,' came a muffled reply from the back.

A moment later, the proprietor emerged, wiping her paint-stained hands on a rag. 'How can I help you?' she asked, meeting Ward's gaze and smiling. In her mid-thirties, she was a tad younger than Ward, her style eclectic—paint-stained, figure-hugging jeans and a floral blouse hidden behind a short beige apron covered in speckles, splashes, and smears of paint in all hues.

For a moment, he could do nothing but bask in the genuine spark of delight in her eyes at whatever she'd just been engrossed in—such a breath of fresh air against the gritty determination he faced most days.

'Er, these. I'm wondering if it's possible to frame these?' he recovered, holding up the bin-bag-covered roll.

The lady cocked her head, and tucked a stray lock of mousy-brown hair that had escaped from her long plait behind an ear. Ward noticed she had a faint smudge of turquoise paint on her cheek. 'Sure, pop them up on the counter here, let's take a look.'

Ward extracted them from the wrapping and unrolled them carefully on the glass display case, inside which, were samples of frames. 'They're a bit damaged,' he muttered by way of apology.

'Not to worry,' she said. 'I've seen far worse.' She flicked through them carefully. 'I can definitely frame these for you. What sort of thing were you thinking?'

'I'm not sure. Not really my area of expertise,' Ward said with a smile that was half a grimace.

She laughed, a melodic tinkle that set him at ease. 'That's not a problem either. What sort of style do you like? Grand and traditional, modern and minimalist?' She pointed to a couple of opposing samples in the case.

'Modern and minimalist.' Christ, the traditional gilded frames were bloody awful to him. More suited to manor houses, not a boxy apartment.

'OK, wood, white, metal effect?'

'Wood?'

'Are you sure about that?' She glanced up, kind mirth dancing in her eyes.

'Let's say yes.'

She chuckled. 'Well, I can frame them for you, not a

problem. If you're happy to trust me, I'll select something that complements your artwork.'

'Oh, it's not mine. They were my mother's.'

'I see.' She looked over them appreciatively. 'I'm a watercolour gal myself. They're lovely. The Bolton Abbey one really captures the grandeur of the landscape.'

'She painted that after we went there one summer in the middle of a heatwave.' He and Sam had spent all day doing the stepping stones across the river—falling in, and pushing each other.

The lady grinned. 'Aye. It's a lovely place to go as a kid. We ventured up that way too—and Burnsall, of course. Great playing in the river.'

'It is.' Ward smiled warmly. This woman set him at ease, her steady presence reassuring. For some reason, he felt he could trust her with his most precious items.

'Do you have a budget in mind?'

'It doesn't matter.'

'Alright.' She reached beneath the counter and placed a form on the glass top. 'Fill in your details here—sorry, I didn't catch your name?'

'Daniel. Daniel Ward.'

She smiled again, that captivating open warmth lighting her up. 'Daniel. Nice to meet you. I'm Eve Griffiths.' Although he'd surmised as much, now he knew the shop was hers.

Daniel filled in the form with his contact details and number of articles. Eve took the form from him and added some description in a handwriting so ornate it looked as though it was from a Victorian letter.

'Right. We're all good. I should have them back to

you within a couple of weeks—I'll ring when they're ready, alright?'

'Sure. Thank you.' Ward's hand grazed the painting on the top—Filey Brig.

'They're in safe hands,' Eve said, as though she could sense his attachment to them.

'Thank you. These are really important to me. They're all I have left of her.' It wasn't like him to open up to anyone about that sort of thing. Hell, he hadn't even told Metcalfe and they'd been friends for donkey's years.

'And soon, they'll be adorned in beautiful frames and hanging on your walls to bring back all those happy memories.' Eve carefully rolled them up again, holding them in the crook of her arm.

Ward nodded with a faint smile. There were unhappy memories there too, but he'd do his best to only remember the good ones of his mother when he looked at those paintings. It was what she deserved. 'I'd best go, anyway, I've left the dog in the car. Do you need anything else?'

'Nope, we're all good. I'll let you know as soon as they're ready.'

'Thanks, Eve. See you soon.'

'Nice to meet you, Daniel.'

He met her eyes, smiled, and left that quiet haven of paint and serenity—back to the bonkers dog in the Golf who let out a great volley of barks loud enough to wake the dead as Ward approached, Olly jumping from the front seat to rear seat and back again.

Ward sat for a moment in the driver's seat as Olly trampled him and fussed for attention.

He'd not even considered anyone else, ever. Katherine had consumed most of his adult life. And he knew he shouldn't, but Eve Griffiths had just blindsided him.

There was no chance, none at all. He didn't even *know* Eve. He'd see her again to pick up his mother's paintings, and that would be that. It was the spark in her soul that had called to him so powerfully, and for the first time, Daniel Ward felt like perhaps there might be a life after Katherine, and maybe he didn't have to spend it all alone and unhappy. Maybe one day, he could believe that he *deserved* not to be lonely and unhappy.

Eve Griffith's smile and her laughing eyes followed him all the way over the hill and home to his empty apartment. Ward climbed the stairs, hushing Olly who thundered up and down them in his excitement, circling Ward's feet like a sheepdog.

Ward didn't notice the bundle shoved in his letterbox until his key was already half-turned in the door, so dazed was he by the encounter with Eve.

'What the...?' he murmured. Daniel pulled out the lumpy item—black fabric. Clothing. He unravelled it.

HUGO BOSS was emblazoned across the chest of the t-shirt. But the label didn't match, nondescript and written in...Slovakian, he realised.

Olly sat beside him now, tail thumping on the floor, looking up at him expectantly.

Ward peered down the stairs.

Up the stairs.

Silent and empty.

The garment was soft in his now-shaking hand, but he wanted to drop it as though it had burned him.

Another message from Varga. A specific one. Varga *knew* Ward hadn't stopped digging. Varga knew Ward was involved with seizing the lorry filled with counterfeit goods on Saturday morning in Liverpool. And Varga wanted Ward to know that he knew.

Stop looking, the unspoken message said. *Stop looking. Or I'll start punishing.* And Ward could only guess what Varga was capable of. Murder, extortion, coercion, bribery...corruption.

Ward opened his apartment door, Olly shooting in first, and closed, locked, and bolted the door behind him. Only then did Daniel throw the garment violently to the floor at his feet, where it lay, a malignant reminder of the crime lord's web of influence.

Ward checked the apartment first—empty, and no signs of entry—before he leaned heavily on the kitchen counter, ignoring the Beagle nipping around his heels.

Ward wasn't done with Varga. And that meant Varga wasn't done with Ward, either.

THE END

A NOTE FROM THE AUTHOR

Hello! I don't know quite what to say, but I will start with a warm and heartfelt 'thank you' for reading the second DI Daniel Ward book. I'm so grateful and encouraged by your lovely reviews, messages of support, and that you buy and read my books – it's humbling and I appreciate it hugely. It allows me to write stories for you full time, which is, quite honestly, my dream career. I truly hope you enjoy joining Daniel and his team on their adventures through West Yorkshire and will continue to return!

This book is set in Bingley, a lovely little town in the Aire Valley just a couple of hills over from where I live and write all my books. It was a true pleasure to journey into Saltaire for a little while. It's a World Heritage Site, but more than that, it's a place on my doorstep that I love very much.

If you get the chance to visit, please do. Salt's Mill, and the village as a whole, is the most lovely, quaint place, filled with incredible Victorian architecture, steeped in history, and rich with culture. Salt's Mill is one of my favourite places to go – from the art gallery featuring the great David Hockney's work, to the *Salt's Diner* café (Excellent cake...need I say more?), to the independent book store, and the stationary store downstairs (like magpies are to treasure, authors are to notebooks and pens!).

Not to mention, *Don't Tell Titus* is quite real. It's a very lovely place to visit for lunch, dinner, or drinks. Do look up the history of the name, which is quirky and somewhat tongue in cheek regarding Saltaire's origins with Titus Salt himself!

I also have a little nod to Keighley in this tale. It's a place where I spent a lot of time passing through to the Dales or back, or to visit family, as a child, and where I obtained my first 'proper job' as a trainee accountant, fresh out of school and absolutely certain that I couldn't do what I really wanted for a career – write stories. Happily, I was wrong, and here we are!

I'm excited to take you to more wonderful Yorkshire places in the *DI Ward Yorkshire Crime Thriller Series*, and I hope you will enjoy the forthcoming adventures with Daniel and his team! If you enjoyed this one, I'd really appreciate if you could leave a review on Amazon or Goodreads. :-)

So, for now, '*si thee later*' as we say here in Yorkshire. DI Ward returns next in *The Mistakes We Deny,* for an adventure encompassing Skipton, the beautiful Yorkshire Dales, and Harrogate.

Warmly yours,
Meg Jolly

ABOUT THE AUTHOR

Meg is a USA Today Bestselling Author and illustrator living amongst the wild and windswept moors of Yorkshire, England with her husband and two cats. Now, she spends most of her days writing or illustrating in her studio, whilst serenaded by snoring cats.

Want to stay in touch?

If you want to reach out, Meg loves hearing from readers. You can follow her on Amazon, Bookbub, or sign up to her newsletter. You can also say hi via Facebook (author page and reader group) or Instagram (@megjollyauthor).

You can find links to all the above on Meg's website at:
www.megjolly.com

Printed in Great Britain
by Amazon